Nothing Human is Alien to Me

Aijaz Ahmad
in conversation with
Vijay Prashad

First published in October 2020

LeftWord Books
2254/2A Shadi Khampur
New Ranjit Nagar
New Delhi 110008
INDIA

LeftWord Books is the publishing division of
Naya Rasta Publishers Pvt. Ltd.

'The Lessons of Aijaz Ahmad' © Vijay Prashad, 2020
Interview © LeftWord Books, 2020

leftword.com

ISBN   978-81-947287-1-9 paperback
         978-81-947287-0-2 ebook

Printed and bound by Chaman Enterprises, Delhi

To Aruna
For Times Yet to Come

Contents

Vijay Prashad

The Lessons of Aijaz Ahmad

Kuchh nahin to kam se kam khwab-e sahar dekha to hai
Jis taraf dekha na tha ab tak, udhar dekha to hai
                    Asrar-ul Haq Majaz ('Khwab-e Sahar', 1936)

It is impossible for me to think without thinking alongside the
work of Aijaz Ahmad. I first encountered his ideas in two journals—
Economic & Political Weekly (Mumbai) and *Social Scientist* (New
Delhi). The essays ranged from such topics as the emergence of the
far right in India to the novels of Salman Rushdie to Edward Said's
Orientalism. It was not just the breath of the topics that impressed me
but the way in which Aijaz Ahmad was able to marshal to his analysis
entire traditions of thought, with Marxism as the centre, and entire
worlds of knowledge about history and sociology. Those who typically
wrote about India's far right, for instance, had a narrow analytical
horizon that stayed within India's boundaries, or at the most imported
the concepts that came out of the debate around European fascism;
Aijaz brought to bear the full literature of fascism and the far right,
both the theoretical work and the empirical work on its European
history, and he mobilized the depth of Indian historiography, but he
went further, outwards to the role of the far right in South America
and in the Arab world, in other parts of the world whose stories
seemed essential for a full grasp of what were not parochial but global

developments. More than anything else, Aijaz challenged us to think of the Indian reality from a wider perspective, a perspective that—for him—is the very normal protocol of Marxism.

Those Marxists of my generation in India who read Aijaz in the immediate aftermath of the destruction of the Babri Masjid at Ayodhya in 1992 will know exactly what I mean when I say that he shaped our thinking. He oriented us to understand that attack in a context much wider than the rise of the forces of Hindutva; by putting that atrocious attack in the chain of a series of disasters—the fall of the USSR and the communist state system, the emergence of liberalization, the enduring atrocities of social hierarchy in India, the surrender of social democracy, the weakness of the Left—he prevented us from seeing that act as one of mere horror. We were horrified surely, but we were also being given the armour to build a theoretical assessment of our times—rooted in Marxism—not only to fight against the howl of the far right, but to understand the depletion of the reservoir of the freedom movement; we learned that no easy answers exist for our predicament, that the struggle against the torrents of the far right and the complicities of liberalism will require revolutionary discipline and patience. The road before us was going to be long, and we were going to have to learn how to think deeply as much as we had to learn how to struggle with persistence and clarity. Those are the lessons of Aijaz Ahmad.

~

Aijaz Ahmad's classic book—*In Theory: Classes, Nations, Literatures*—came out in 1992. The Soviet Union had just collapsed and the Eastern European communist states began to fall one by one; India abandoned its formal commitment to secularism and dismantled its state capitalist system for a neoliberal or liberalized one; globalization had begun to set in, with the countries of the Third

World delivering their citizens to the cruelties of wage arbitrage along the global supply chain; and the United States appeared as if it would be paramount for the next period. This was a time of great disillusionment. All the older certainties began to dissipate, and the prefix 'post' appeared before many of the important ideas, such as *post*-modernism, *post*-structuralism, *post*-colonialism, and *post*-Marxism. New certainties rushed in, except they seemed to offer no proper theory for an analysis of the reconfiguration of the world order. Many of them seemed frivolous, exercises in mental gymnastics rather than serious attempts to understand the shift in the social tectonic plates. It was in this context that Aijaz's book appeared with a powerful blurb from the Marxist literary theorist Terry Eagleton on the back cover of the first Verso edition:

> Some radical critics may have forgotten about Marxism; but Marxism, in the shape of Ahmad's devastating, courageously unfashionable critique, has not forgotten about them.

Two points immediately make themselves clear. First, that those who had been 'radical critics' had abandoned any commitment to Marxism, and their departure and the arrival of new ideas had made such a position 'unfashionable'. Second, that Aijaz came out of a tradition—Marxism—and he held fast to that tradition through this period of the 'posts'. It would be an error to assume that Aijaz was stubborn and—in the face of fast-moving changes—refused to come to terms with them and held on to an anachronistic theory. This is precisely the attitude that met Marxism in the immediate years after the fall of the USSR, a period of outrageously flamboyant American exceptionalism. In fact, what was remarkable about the introduction to *In Theory* is that it offered a history of the present based on two features of thought that define the lessons of Aijaz Ahmad: first, his evident wide reading about the history and sociology of the world which allowed him to provide the necessary global context for his study and for our new times that remained tied to the contradictions of a longer history, and second, his grip on Marxism, a living Marxism, a Marxism that had absorbed both the streams of Western Marxism and of national liberation Marxism. Just this introduction to *In Theory* affirmed Lenin's important statement that 'the very gist, the living soul of Marxism [is] a concrete analysis of a concrete situation.'*

India, unlike many countries in the world, did not see the attrition of our Marxist traditions for at least two reasons. First, there was a deep seam of Marxism that had rooted itself in our universities and in our intellectual culture during the freedom movement and had become an essential part of contemporary Indian thought. Second, communist parties around the world found themselves deeply in crisis after the fall of the USSR, but this was not the case in India, largely because the communist movement had already begun to settle accounts with the Soviet Union decades before and because the communist movement had become essential to the ongoing struggles of a range of social forces in India, from agricultural workers to industrial workers to proletarianized white-collar workers.† There were, of course, limitations of all kinds—both in the universities and in party practice—but that is not the point; Aijaz Ahmad was writing from a location in this period where the entire traditions of Marxism and communism had not been set aside.

Before the publication of *In Theory*, Aijaz had built a significant set of texts about Pakistan and about under-development, just as he would write essential texts after 1992 about India and about the rise of the far right. That book was merely one—indeed a classic—step in a long career. Throughout the texts by Aijaz one finds Marxism as

---

* Lenin, *Collected Works*, vol. 31, Moscow: Progress Publishers, 1974, p. 166.
† *Contemporary World Situation and Validity of Marxism: Proceedings of International Seminar of Communist Parties Marking the 175th Birth Anniversary of Karl Marx*, New Delhi: CPI(M) Publications, 1993.

the orientation, but a Marxism that emerges out of the anti-colonial, anti-imperialist, and national liberation movements. 'We are anti-imperialists because we are Marxists, because we are revolutionaries, because we oppose capitalism with socialism, believing them to be antagonistic systems and that socialism must follow upon capitalism,' said the Peruvian Communist José Carlos Mariátegui at the First Latin American Communist Conference in June 1929.* This was the lineage of anti-colonial Marxism and communism out of which Aijaz's work emerges, a Marxism that had to come to terms with the backwardness of our social development, the ugly old hierarchies conscripted by capitalism to do its work, a Marxism that needed to understand how to grapple with revolutionary processes in a context where the Russian Revolution could not be easily repeated, a Marxism that had to engage with nationalism in a critical way, deeply aware of the inadequacies of bourgeois nationalism but driven by a proletarian nationalism that was both internationalist in its outlook and nationalist in its programmatic defence of sovereignty. This Marxism, as opposed to what is called Western Marxism, does not stray far from praxis because the world of this tradition does not easily allow theory to drift away from the imperatives of action.

Since Lenin, it has become familiar to say that Marx unified German philosophy, French socialism, and English political economy.† The key word here is unified, for Marx drew various traditions into a conversation at the structural level; his struggles to do so are evident in his many manuscripts and even in his finished texts. There is a false divide between Marx's political writings (such as his texts on France) and his economic writings (*Capital*); Marx's various plans for *Capital* always included texts on international trade and on the state, elements

---

* José Carlos Mariátegui, 'The Anti-Imperialist Perspective', *New Left Review*, no. 70 (November–December 1971), p. 72.

† Lenin, *Collected Works*, vol. 19, Moscow: Progress Publishers, 1977, pp. 23–24.

that would have enabled him to show the integration of these various strands of his thought.* As Marxism entered the academy, however, it could not always resist the pressures of specialization; the unified tradition began to dissipate as Marxists became more or less experts in economics or philosophy or politics, with few Marxists well-versed enough to keep these various strands of the Marxist method together.

In Aijaz's work, a careful reader can see the various strands of Marxism integrated: there is certainly a clear-sighted awareness of the development—not always in a positive direction—of productive forces; there are both the structural elements of imperialism, in the way capital accumulation operates and the political dimension of militarism; there is the zigzag whiplash of class conflict that sometimes manifests itself in national liberation and socialist movements, or at other times appears in a gnarled and inchoate form as rebellions that could feed into toxic movements of the far right, or even as the surrender of entire populations before the onslaught in time by the pressures of social reproduction, the manipulations of inherited social hierarchies to numb the possibilities of social transformation. There is a fealty to the *totality* that is at the heart of the Marxist method: not to understand this or that aspect of human life, but to grasp it all, and not to understand it for itself, but to take hold of it to understand its gradually decipherable journey, 'the *real* movement which abolishes the present state of things'.†

There is a good reason why this book of interviews is called *Nothing Human is Alien to Me*, a line that Marx used in his *Confessions* written for his children in 1865. A focus on productive forces is necessary, but they will not reveal the entire predicament; in an 1853 report on India, Marx warned that 'human progress' with colonialism as a fundamental

---

* Vijay Prashad, 'Writing Capital', in *Marx's Capital: An Introductory Reader*, New Delhi: LeftWord Books, 2011.
† Karl Marx and Frederick Engels, *The German Ideology*, Moscow: Progress Publishers, 1964, p. 47.

part of the bourgeois epoch 'resemble[s] that hideous pagan idol, who would not drink the nectar but from the skulls of the slain'.* Advances in production, the utilization of science by capitalism, and the immense productivity occasioned did not necessarily move history along; weaknesses of the working class in the class struggle, for a variety of reasons that had to do with ideology and culture and with the lack of organization, prevented humanity to advance its general interest. Everything that helped explain why the class struggle did not sharpen into a class conflict that could move history in a progressive direction had to be studied. The vast sweep of history, in the work of Aijaz Ahmad, has to be understood as the totality of human potentialities, with social individuals at the centre of it all since it is these people who suffer from the consequences of the social order and who struggle—in one way or another—to go beyond it.

The headquote to this introduction is from Majaz. He sings, 'If nothing else, we have at least dared to dream of the dawn / That which we have only glanced at, towards that our eyes drift'. It is a poem written against the chains of religious thought; but it works as well against all thought that prevents an engagement with the chains of the social order, chains that can only be broken by the conscious activity of human beings.

∼

In 2019, Sudhanva Deshpande, Moloyashree Hashmi, and I travelled to see Aijaz Ahmad for a few days. We spent all day of each of the days with him, conducting this long interview about his life and work, listening to him reflect on the essays and books he has

---

* Karl Marx, 'The Future Results of the British Rule in India', in *Marx and Engels on the National and Colonial Questions. Selected Writings*, ed. Aijaz Ahmad, New Delhi: LeftWord Books, 2001, p. 75.

written over the years. He was generous with his time and his wisdom, filling our minds and hearts with his ideas about the past and of the contradictions that will drive history forward. This book collects that long interview, edited down certainly. The interview was transcribed by Shreyoshee Bandhyopadhyay with care and dedication. The cover design is by Greta Acosta Reyes from Cuba; her work perfectly captures the expansive, internationalist spirit of the theory of Aijaz Ahmad.

It was a magical few days. We hope that some of the magic is captured in this text.

Interview

Vijay Prashad (VP): Tell us a little bit about the books you read in your youth.

Aijaz Ahmad (AA): The books that I read? Well, that's an interesting question. I grew up in a village that had no school and no electricity. So I was tutored at home and went to school late, just for three years before matriculating at a very young age. I came from what you might call village gentry, a class fraction whose members had enough land to have very considerable leisure but not enough to be wealthy. You know, Albert Hourani, in his famous book *Arab Thought in the Liberal Age* says that in late nineteenth-century Egypt the most creative class was the class of the rural gentry, by which he means a social stratum of small-scale landed property, above the peasantry as such but also far lower than the owners of feudal property. They were traditional and secure in their cultural grounding but were not invested in defending the old order and were therefore receptive to new ideas. For Hourani, those 'new ideas' were ideas of religious, social, judicial and educational reform, represented my men like Muhammad ʿAbduh, the great Egyptian jurist and reformer—but represented even more by the following that reformers like ʿAbduh developed among the educated sections of that social stratum. In the India of UP Muslims among whom I was born, the rough equivalent of ʿAbduh would be Syed

Ahmad Khan. By the 1940s, though, those 'new ideas' also included anti-colonialism, anti-feudalism, communism, etc. Nehru in politics, Premchand in literature were household words.

I was born just before Independence in a kind of milieu where no women in my family had ever gone to school and no man had ever attended college but the house was full of books. A passenger bus would arrive every afternoon from Muzaffarnagar, the district headquarters, which would also bring the mail, including the newspapers, journals and books that had been ordered. In this milieu, then, I grew up reading very widely in Urdu literature which included great quantities of progressive fiction and poetry. And this was a very interesting phenomenon, where the girls were in *purdah* and had not gone to school but there was no ban on their reading Ismat Chughtai, Manto, and so on who were all supposed to be, you know, pornographers, and there were vigorous discussions of their writings. This is what I meant by a milieu that was comfortable in its traditional ways of life but was also very much responsive to 'new ideas' that served as a window on the larger world.

At some point my father discovered that I was reading too many works of fiction. Most of that fiction, he thought, was a waste of time. He called me in and handed me four books. One was *Company ki Hukoomat* ['Company Rule'] by Bari Alig, an old communist.[*] The other was *Farangi ka Jaal* ['White Man's Trap']—I don't remember who wrote it. And then, an Urdu translation of M.N. Roy's *The Historical Role of Islam*, and a short biography of Lenin. So, I grew up in that sort of world, from Manto to Lenin. I had a very rich education in Urdu literature and progressive writing of various kinds, non-fiction also, but primarily in Urdu. When I went to school I became a very good student of English so far as the reading and writing in it went but I did not learn to speak English with any degree of fluency until I was in my

---

[*] Bari Alig, *Company ki Hukoomat*, Lahore: National Book Foundation, 1976 (reprint).

twenties. Meanwhile, I was preparing myself to become a writer in the Urdu language. I don't think my experience in this regard is all that atypical. Many progressive writers and communist militants in UP, especially among UP Muslims, came from that social background of petty landownership. I am thinking here of the generation immediately preceding mine, the ones who influenced and inspired me. Even those who did not grow up in villages often had their roots in that social world, at a remove of not much more than a generation.

VP: Why is that so? Why is that small, landowning class the one that produces the creativity that Hourani mentions and why is it so that, in UP, this is proved correct by so many of them becoming communists.

AA: Well, one interesting fact is that the ones who became communist writers, poets and activists were, to my knowledge, the ones who discovered communism in college. My father never went to college but from his reading and furtive sort of involvement in local politics, he had become a very recognizable sort of left-Nehruvian. K.M. Ashraf, the famous communist and an important historian who had worked with Nehru, especially on the Muslim Mass Contact Campaign—Ashraf was a distant relative whom my father greatly admired. His origins were also in what I am calling the rural gentry. Many such people went to the colleges and universities in Allahabad and Lucknow, and also Aligarh. Many went into the Congress, many, especially from Aligarh, into the Muslim League, but a remarkably large number became communists and made lasting contributions to progressive literature. This is an interesting phenomenon. These are people who have the means to encounter modern ideas and to make life-decisions accordingly while they also incline towards a social radicalism produced by a certain attachment to the soil and a rebellious contempt for the feudal grip on the larger society in which they had their moorings. And, in the generation of writers I was reading in my adolescence there was an excruciating sense of being crushed by foreign rule. The same thing happens in other parts of the larger Asian world, actually, wherever there are major agrarian societies, including in Iraq and Syria, and so on. The petty landowners produce a very frustrated youth that feels suffocated by the existing order of power and become anti-colonial and anti-feudal almost instinctively. Many turn to the right, to the Ikhwan-al-Muslimun in Egypt or the Ba'ath party in Iraq for instance, but an extraordinary number move left.

I must add, though, that this is not some permanent feature of a sub-class or class fraction. This happens conjuncturally, when societies are in transition, the old world is under stress and a new, more modern world is getting glimpsed in the shape of social reform movements, anti-colonial movements, communism. The young born to petty property have the means to get educated, move into various kinds of opposition and give literary form to their anger, frustration and hopes for a better world.

You know, we underestimate the impact that progressive literature had. I'll give you one example from a different period of my life when I was in Karachi doing study circles and trade unions work and so on. Most of the proletariat in Karachi came from the North-West Frontier Province [NWFP]. They were Pathans. I would ask them how they gravitated towards the Left. Each of them, without fail, talked about having read progressive literature—mostly fiction. They read Manto, Rajinder Singh Bedi, Krishan Chander. The same kind of stuff I read as a child. And I had also read the Russian and Soviet writers—Gorky and Turgenev, Chekhov, etc. They were translated into Urdu and published by Progress Publishers. Many progressive writers from India and Pakistan went to Moscow as full-time translators. For the workers among whom I was working in Karachi, the combination was the same, a broader range of Realism together with progressive literature produced at home in Urdu.

VP: You used an interesting word; you used the word 'frustrated' and you had said that you had anticipated you would become a writer in the world of Urdu literature. What kinds of things would you have written about or did you want to write about when you were reading these books by Bari or, for instance, M.N. Roy on Islam? What kind of things were you interested in writing about—out of that frustration, perhaps?

AA: I read Bari, M.N. Roy and others when I was not even ten. I was not thinking of becoming a writer at that time. As a child and then right into my adolescence I felt no frustration of the kind I was talking about: young men and women feeling 'frustrated' at the power structure controlling their society. That is an adult emotion, so to speak. Mine was culturally a very secure childhood. I was still a small child at the time of Independence. That day, 15 August 1947, is one of my two earliest memories, and I remember it as a day of jubilation with my father's uncle hoisting the Indian flag in the village. It was the fact of Partition that began creating anxieties but in ways that were vague to me and became vivid only gradually. The real jolt and then mounting frustration came to me when in the mid-fifties my father decided to migrate to Pakistan. I said earlier that he was a left-Nehruvian, almost pink in his convictions. So, he did not really want to migrate. He tried to continue his life where he was but he felt more and more hemmed in by the atmosphere of rising Hindu communal aggressivity around him and that was now seeping into much of the UP Congress at the local level. That migration wrecked my family, including my father himself. Had I been younger when we migrated, the experience might not have been so traumatic and I might have adjusted to my new country more easily. But by the time we migrated I was in my teens, having spent all my childhood in India in what was for me personally a very secure emotional zone. As I entered college in that new country I was inwardly very unsettled.

So, responding to your question: by the time I began to prepare myself to become a writer I had been fully cut off from the milieu in which I had grown up. Writing about it was no longer an existential necessity for me and would have been an exercise in nostalgia if I were to now try to write about it. On the other hand, the recent experience of having been dislocated and thrown into a different social world was too new, too raw, too shapeless for me to want to start writing about it. I think I was quite unhinged for some time and escaped into learning about literature as a *craft*. The self that had gone through the trauma of dislocation was much too wounded, and I needed to go through a period of healing. That's what I think retrospectively. So, I did not allow myself to develop a strong sense of what I wanted to write *about*; I concentrated on teaching myself *how* to write. So far as intellectual conviction is concerned, I was left of centre. By the time I was finishing my high school—which I had attended for just three years, still in India, in my early teens—I had become very close to the son of a friend of my father who was a young communist (his father, my father's friend, was in the Congress). With him I would go to various kinds of political and cultural events and would participate in whatever needed to get done. So, I was active on the margins of those kinds of activity without thinking of myself consciously as a communist. But in that world of the very early '50s communism was very much a fact of the world one inhabited. I think I wanted to emulate the progressive writers without any conscious intent to do so. That is just what literature meant to me at that time.

VP: And what were some of the first things you did write that you remember?

AA: The very first thing actually was a school play. A juvenile pastiche of things picked up from Dilip Kumar's movies and Balraj Sahni's *Do Bigha Zamin*, about the wretched conditions of the peasantry. By the time I went to college, I was writing quite seriously. I started publishing short stories and translations when I was still an undergraduate. Poems and critical essays came later.

VP: And where were you in college and what did you study?

AA: I finished school in India when I was not even fifteen, closer to thirteen perhaps. I don't really know my date of birth. We then migrated to Pakistan. I went to college in Lahore, to Forman Christian College. I studied literature and social sciences. When I was in my third year of college, I started to publish my work. I did my MA in English. But my main activity was writing and spending time in tea and coffee houses, with much older Urdu writers such as Intizar Hussain, Nasir Kazmi, Ahmad Mushtaq and others.

VP: And did they take well to young people coming around and bothering them with questions?

AA: In Lahore those days, there was a cafe culture of a type you don't have in Delhi. Maybe in Calcutta but certainly not in Delhi. There were norms and protocols. Everyone knew when to disturb whom. Novices who broke the protocols were disciplined more or less politely. On the whole, the established writers welcomed talented youth.

VP: What were the main books that you read at this time?

AA: The whole range of Urdu literature. The whole range. From the old classical and earliest poetry to my own contemporaries. I studied some Persian. If you really know Urdu it is easy to pick up some Farsi, which I did. I of course did a Masters in English Literature, which I read voraciously, but I read a great deal from many other literatures through translation. I didn't have a specific set of books that I read. My interests were shifting very fast. Those days, the undergraduate degree used to be divided in two parts. After the first two years you sat for a university-level exam and you were given an Intermediate certificate. Two years later, you again sat for a university-level exam and were then awarded a BA. In the two years of Intermediate I was steeped in Economics, a subject I had just discovered because there had been no Economics while I was in high school. I had a perfectly good Economics professor but in the two successive years of the Intermediate I had two magnificent History professors. So, during the two years of BA, I was absorbed in History. By the end, my primary academic interest had shifted again and I registered for Masters in English. You might call that eclecticism but this breadth of interest would stay with me through all later life, to the point where I came to believe that the sharp line of demarcation between Humanities and the Social Sciences is intrinsically false and an older kind of unity between what we might call Poetics and Pragmatics—conceptual knowledges and practical knowledges—needs to be restored.

That is how I wandered through different academic disciplines. But there was also something else that aided me greatly. I wanted to read what was important, not caring whether it was from one academic discipline or another. If someone told me there was someone important called Freud, I would go to the Forman Christian College library—a limited but very good library—and say, *I want to read Freud. What should I read?* That was a great habit I developed without really knowing how good it was: to read the original authors, before reading anything about them. That is how I read Marx, Lenin, Freud, Sartre, etc. Or Plato for that matter. It did not matter how much I understood. I just wrestled with the text. At that point in my life it never occurred to me that I should first read commentaries.

VP: Do you remember the decision to study English for your MA?

AA: If you were doing literature—even Urdu literature—then the degree you worked for was English Literature. Urdu was an established language in Pakistan (I mean 'West Pakistan' of that time, where I was, and which became Pakistan after the separation from Bangladesh) and it became quite genuinely a *lingua franca* through other processes. One could pursue professional degrees in Urdu at the Oriental College but that was a hotbed of literary as well as social conservatism. So, I studied English literature. I was perfectly happy to be trained academically. I had to read all the important books in English literature, the *canonical* literature. I actually did not mind that. I still believe that a solid grounding in a literary *ouvre* is a good thing. But if one wanted to read that literature from a progressive point of view, one was on one's own. Among the faculty was a young British couple who were Leavisite in literary pedagogy and modernist in literary tastes—T.S. Eliot, Pound, Lawrence, that sort of thing. They were in conflict with the Americans who drew from New Criticism which had its roots in the agrarian conservatism of the US South, a kind of conservatism that you can trace back to the slave-owning times. American New Criticism—not I.A. Richards; the more successful *American* version—is not just a technique of reading; it is also a sort of phenomenology of the world. Students were given to understand that the difference between these two stances, Leavisite and New Criticism, mattered.

During this period, I lived in two different worlds. There was the MA English world, where I read the canonical. Then there was the intellectual world of the writers, where I read chaotically in world literature strictly from the standpoint of my own tastes and intellectual needs.

VP: Tell us a little bit about the forms of reading; the ways of reading in this other world. I mean, in *In Theory*, you have a very precise analysis of the literary critical history in Britain, of the New Criticism movement in the West, of the emergence of McCarthyism, and of how young people in the anti-war movement negotiated these traditions. You came from a different context. Could you tell a bit more about the forms of reading from the tea house tradition, where you learnt to read?

AA: That was a world of writers, not a world of critics, professional critics. Those same writers might have written some criticism but theirs was a world of writers, of both fiction and poetry. Different writers had different interests, although all were steeped in literary texts. Some were interested in French literature, so you were persuaded to read Saint-John Perse, Baudelaire, the whole range. One very important preference was for reading what would be useful for your own writing, *as writing*. I wanted to learn how to write Urdu prose. Reading Proust posed a great problem for me. He was writing after Einstein and after Freud. And he was obsessed with time, with how time is experienced subjectively, with multiplicity of perceptions within a single fraction of time, with relativity of points of view, about the same object but at different points in time, etc. So, grappling with those sorts of philosophical issues, many of his sentences ran to five, ten, fifteen, even twenty clauses. In Urdu, we only have a full stop, no commas, no semicolons, no colons. We could not truly write a compound sentence that can express a multi-dimensional perception within a single grammatical construction. Proust was not alone in this. Virginia Woolf and Joyce grappled with a similar problem. So, one read in order to pose problems of that kind for one's own writing. But there were other registers of reading. Because of my friendship with Intizar Hussain I read an enormous amount of traditional Urdu fiction, the whole *Dastan* tradition for instance. I wanted also to write Urdu verse, but *modern* Urdu verse, more unscannable than what was available in extant Urdu poetry. This had ironical consequences for me. I felt that I had to truly study the whole evolution of Urdu poetics before I could genuinely break free from its more conventionalized protocols. Friendship with poets like Nasir Kazmi certainly helped me negotiate that terrain of creativity and scholarship, not because I wanted to write like him—no, he wanted to write like Mir Taqi Mir—but because I wanted to know what it is that I wanted to be free of, and Nasir had a very subtle, extensive understanding of Urdu poetics. That was the crux of that other kind of tradition of reading—what you called 'the tea house tradition'. It was critical reading but not a critic's reading;

rather, it was the writers' reading of previous writings for the sake of writings yet to come. For me, certainly, it was largely an apprenticeship in the craft of writing itself.

EARLY POLITICS

VP: Tell us a little bit about where your active political life began.

AA: I think my first political act was in response to the Anglo-French-Israeli invasion of Egypt's Suez Canal zone. This was in 1956, during my first year in college. I joined the huge student demonstration against the invasion. That came from the anti-British, anti-colonial conviction—the bloody Brits are doing this all over again in Egypt! I joined that demonstration and then—as I now look back with some humour—jumped onto the veranda of the residence of an official in the British Consulate, picked up a chair, and smashed it.

Some of that conviction I had brought with me from my childhood in India: my father's pinkish convictions, my readings in progressive literature, my brush with communist student politics while still in high school. By the time I came to college in Lahore, my parents had lost everything and were struggling to make ends meet while they were also sending me to a very upper-class college (because it was a missionary college the fees were very low). There were some very wealthy students all around me and I had social resentments of that kind. Raymond Williams and Terry Eagleton have both written very perceptively about being working-class boys in the Oxbridge world and never quite belonging there even after each became a famous Don in his own right. When Williams writes of his Welsh working-class background with such warmth and vivid affection and then, elsewhere, describes Cambridge as one of the coldest corners on this earth, I know exactly what he means. Bourdieu, the legendary French sociologist and himself the son of a provincial postman, writes again and again in a similar vein of the fact that a first generation intellectual who arrives at the apex of the institutional ladder always lives with a sense of non-belonging, of being an outsider, possibly an interloper. Whenever I come upon those analyses, I recall my days at Forman Christian College.

That was one kind of difficulty. I also resented the conservatism, the lack of political spine in that institution. I was in college when the Ayub Khan coup came in 1958. The college was told that two ministers wanted to come and address the students. The principal was to assemble all the students. I was the vice president of the Students' Union and we said, 'No way. What do two martial law ministers have to do here?' We felt that the military dictatorship had no right to enter our campus. The principal said, 'Times have changed. I don't have a choice.' So, we said, 'Well, we are not going to welcome these ministers.' In short, we all resigned. That kind of resentment against the administration was of course there.

VP: These were heady times for Pakistan. The country was by then eleven years old, with the military starting to exert itself much more forcefully. What was your sense of the country at that time?

AA: You see I was very young. I was taught at home and went straight into eighth class. I must have finished my high school when I was thirteen or fourteen; something like that. I took my MA before I was twenty. On the other hand, we had migrated to Pakistan but were not true Muslim Leaguers. We were not religious at all. I was forbidden to do any kind of religious ritual when I was a child. We went to Pakistan in a panic and were ruined. So, my resentment of Pakistan was also very personal. I ended up in Lahore where I was Urdu-speaking in a Punjabi-speaking city. I'm very glad that I didn't end up in Karachi, which is a pure ghetto—a refugee ghetto. But there was this sense of great dislocation. Pakistan represented for me that dislocation, a loss of home. India was always the country that you compared yourself to. Most people were caught up in a strange kind of doublethink. In official ideology, that was also widely internalized: India was the enemy, the very name of a whole historical past that you had rejected, but united India was also that unrecoverable past that was once your larger home. Stuff of a veritable intellectual and moral vertigo, I would say.

VP: At the emotional plane.

AA: At the emotional plane. And socially. So that, for example, in the whole span of Urdu literature, you do not find a single piece of fiction of any merit—that anywhere you would recognize as literary merit—which celebrates the creation of Pakistan. It's always a tragedy. And this is Pakistani literature; Urdu literature in Pakistan. There is no such thing as the 'creation of the Great National Homeland'. Not a single piece of writing of any worth on this theme. I had written about it for a long lecture called 'In the Mirror of Urdu.' There is no writing in Urdu in India either that celebrates the birth of the country because the Partition overshadows the Independence. Urdu literature right up to the 1965 India–Pakistan war is completely traumatized by Partition. In Pakistani literature as well, the creation of Pakistan is completely secondary; in fact, it is not there in the literature as something good. The comparison with Bengal would be useful. A lot of the Calcutta intelligentsia celebrated the Partition and Independence. It would be valuable to do a study if this is the case across the various languages. In Pakistani literary imagination, the creation of a whole new bloody country was not looked at as some kind of liberation or some kind of achievement.

VP: In this period, while you were studying and the military comes out of the barracks, did the communists—few as they were—come across your path?

---

* Aijaz Ahmad, *In the Mirror of Urdu: Recompositions of nation and community, 1947–65*, Shimla: Indian Institute of Advanced Study, 1993.

AA: Pakistani communists were politically suppressed and socially ostracized. Total repression against communists came in early '50s, as Pakistan moved close to the US and reached its zenith with the Rawalpindi Conspiracy Case; this was before the coup. So, by the time the military dictatorship came, the suppression of the communists was already an established fact. The big thing, the most prominent thing that the military did was to take over the communist-oriented press, such as *Pakistan Times*. After Partition, Mian Iftikharuddin—who had been a left-Congressman—made money out of a connection with the Soviet Union when he was awarded a permit to import coal. Some of that money funded the Communist Party in the early days after Partition. He also established *Pakistan Times Private Limited* whose English newspaper was edited by Mazhar Ali Khan, Tariq Ali's father and a lifelong communist. Faiz Ahmad Faiz was the chief editor of all the newspapers in the group. So, you had communists who were running these mass circulation newspapers and other periodicals. The government took over all of them and threw them out in the coup of 1958. Faiz went to prison. Mazhar Ali Khan probably did not.

Did I interact with the communists? Yes and no. The party was banned and then dissolved itself, though one set of the old party re-grouped and established an underground party. Then that underground party also split, mirroring the split in the Indian party. So, what remained of the Communist Party of Pakistan [CPP] was very small and consisted mostly of splinters. No communist could identify himself publicly as such. In some cases one knew, in other cases one suspected but did not try to verify. In the older generation, I of course knew quite a few because they had been known as such before the ban. There was Faiz of course, much too well known since his early communist days, or Sibte Hassan who was one of those sent by the Calcutta Congress of Communist Party of India [CPI] to organize a party in Pakistan. Sibte Saheb was the one who gave me my first methodical education in communist texts.

I knew Habib Jalib, of course. He was much more plebeian, not proletarian but plebeian; he was very poor. He was very closely associated with the CPP, which was an underground connection. Some of us knew this, but most of us actually surmised that this is what must have been. He was therefore very close to the National Awami Party of Wali Khan, which is where most communists did their mass work. The difference in class background between Faiz and Jalib was very great, which was reflected also in their literary culture and style. Jalib was much more a poet of mass mobilizations.

VP: One of the themes that becomes important in your work is what we can—in shorthand—call Dependency Theory, or how to understand our part of the world in the context of global capitalism. In Pakistan, the name that comes up in this tradition is Hamza Alavi. How did this sort of thinking enter your own work?

AA: Hamza was slightly—a decade or more—older than me. He had been part of the Indian financial services at the time of Independence. When Pakistan came into being, they had neither a bureaucracy nor a technocracy nor a managerial elite. People who had been in fairly low-level positions were given very high positions. Hamza joined the Reserve Bank of Pakistan in a fairly high position, came to dislike what he was doing and eventually resigned. He first went to East Africa, then to England, and remade himself into a social scientist. His own research was on the Punjab peasantry but he was a man of very wide intellectual culture. He was influenced by Dependency Theory for a while but not for long. By the time of the Bangladesh crisis he was doing very different kind of work. But Hamza was an exception. Social sciences were not very well developed in Pakistan for a whole generation.

If you look back at India, you'd be struck by the fact that there was an enormous growth and development—qualitatively—in scholarship in India after Independence. You know, all the most influential historians

and economists that we think of—D.D. Kosambi, Irfan Habib et al.—
they all come after Independence. After that, scholarship in India took
a great leap forward in terms of quantity and quality and the *quantity
of that quality.*

Now, Pakistan came into being in what were essentially peripheral
areas of the subcontinent in intellectual terms. Lahore was a big cultural
centre but even in Lahore a substantial part of the intelligentsia had
been Sikh and Hindu. The intellectual centre of Bengal was Calcutta;
Dhaka University was provincial by comparison. The ruling party in
Pakistan had no anti-colonial ethos, communists were successfully
disorganized and the new middle class was politically much more
quiescent, keen to get absorbed in civil and military bureaucracies or
in the new but rapidly growing private sector. People like Hamza, Eqbal
Ahmad, and myself were exceptions, and for one reason or another
ended up outside the country.

You asked me how we gained our understanding of the place of our
countries in the world capitalist order. The only Pakistani intellectual
with whom I had a productive and fairly extensive encounter was
Hamza, though that was mostly in one-to-one exchanges, not in
writing. For the rest, one looked to scholarship in India, to some Soviet
writers and the Marxism that came to me through British or American
publication. *Monthly Review* was a major and lasting influence for me
with not only the work of Baran, Sweezy, Magdoff and others among
their colleagues but also what their Press would publish from—and
about—the tricontinent. Looking back, you will find that the archive
of such publications, in the journal and from the Press, was quite
extraordinary. As for Dependency Theory, I took from it what I found
useful but never accepted the total framework as such. By the mid-
seventies certainly my theoretical engagements with Marxism had
become far too deep for me to work with that kind of framework.

EQBAL, FEROZ, AND AIJAZ

VP: When did you start writing about politics, or Pakistani politics more specifically?

AA: I was politically active, and I had a very active literary life when I was in Pakistan. But I was neither writing nor thinking in a conceptual way about politics. My conceptual world—my intellectual world—was actually literary. My political activism was framed by my opposition to militarism, my engagement with student activism, my connection with the Left, most of which was underground at the time. It is when I arrived in America—partly as an exile, both political and personal—that I immediately became, virtually within a week, a part of the anti-war movement—the anti-war movement of the Vietnam days—and soon enough, part of the Black Liberation movement. And I had very intense identifications with both. That is where I learnt my politics, you know, learnt to think politically about the larger world as such. I started to meet people who were thinking politically in a very mature way; they were experienced and thoughtful activists. And that meant not only people who were active in US politics but also people from Latin America, the Arab world, even Cuba or Vietnam, communists from South Africa and Yemen and so on.

In New York City, I became part of one of the two major coalitions of the anti-war movement—the Coalition for Peace and Justice. The Coalition would, every two or three months, elect a coordinating committee—of forty members if I recall correctly. At some point and very briefly, I got elected to that committee. At one of the meetings, while a boring speech was going on, I started looking around to see who the others were. I can't remember exactly but the numbers ran something like this: there were five or seven pacifists, people who came from one church tradition or another; there were, maybe, ten from the New Left, as it was called; and then ten or so members of the

Communist Party and an equal number of former Communist Party members. In other words, roughly half were either in the Communist Party or were former members.

Through the years I interacted with a whole range of people. For a period of some months I worked fairly closely with Dave Dellinger, the pacifist socialist, and with Eqbal Ahmad for some years.

VP: Did you know Eqbal Ahmad before New York?

AA: Yes and no. I came to know of Eqbal soon after I came to the US and, as it turned out, he too had known of me but we had never met. When we finally met, after he got arrested on the false charge of conspiracy to kidnap Henry Kissinger, I discovered he had actually been my History professor in my first year of college. He told me that he had read a piece I had published in *The Nation** and had been looking for me ever since.

VP: Were you studying at this time for a PhD?

AA: I never did. I went to Columbia University for about six months and quickly realized that this was a waste of time for me. Must have been around 1970 or 1971. I was involved in very interesting things, political things, and a PhD just didn't make any sense.

One of those interesting things was my involvement in the Black nationalist movement, the college struggles and the campus takeovers. I was fairly prominent in one such takeover in New York and got blacklisted for employment in institutions of the New York state university system. That's how I ended up teaching across the river at Rutgers in New Jersey because I could not get a job in New York state.

VP: What were you reading in this period, as you were involved in these struggles?

* Aijaz Ahmad, 'Law and Order in Pakistan', *The Nation*, 14 April 1969, pp. 455–58.

AA: Well, mountains of books. It is hard to recall all that. I do remember reading a great deal about Vietnam because of the war and the anti-war movement, about US imperialism which has remained a major preoccupation through the decades, and about Black history and Black literature and especially what is now called the Black radical tradition. This latter was particularly pressing because I wanted to teach all this to my Black students at Rutgers.

VP: One of the things we haven't yet entered into is when you started to read Marx.

AA: Furtively I had started to read Marx when I was in Pakistan. The usual texts: *Communist Manifesto, German Ideology*, things like that. The *Manifesto* I read when in college. Also sections of *Civil War in France, Eighteenth Brumaire*, but not yet *Class Struggle in France*. These texts were not easy to find in Lahore at that time. I read *Capital* much later. I didn't have the capacity to read *Capital*; I wouldn't have known how to read it. The *Manifesto* was the bible. I was teaching the *Manifesto* in my graduate seminar just a few weeks ago, and I could still find new things in it. It's a remarkable text. I was very much taken certainly by its prose; the compactness of its prose. I was surprised yet again by the whole range of things that such a short text actually covers; the brevity, the elegance of the writing, and by writing, I mean the elegance of the formulations. It has a prophetic quality. When it was republished from LeftWord—in fact, the first book that LeftWord published, in 1999—the text came alongside a set of essays from some of us.* In that book, I remember writing that Marx is writing of his time but writing in such a way that every succeeding generation has seen its own time in the book. What is remarkable for me is that, looking back, there is a quality of *Capital* that it tells you what capitalism is going to become rather than merely what capitalism is at the time when the

---

* *A World to Win: Essays on* The Communist Manifesto, ed. Prakash Karat, New Delhi: LeftWord Books, 1999.

book is being written, because Marx read correctly the dynamic of what was happening in his time. That's pure logic.

VP: Out of logic comes prophecy, not out of mysticism.

AA: Absolutely! Absolute logic. That is why Lenin said that those who have not read Hegel's *Logic* cannot fully understand *Capital*. It is such pure logic. The text will always be a central text for the analysis of capitalism as long as the capitalist mode of production exists. Marx captures the logic of it.

VP: Let us return to your essay in *The Nation* that Eqbal had read. Tell us a little bit about what you had written and how you saw that uprising, because maybe some of the writings that come later hinge on that.

AA: Four features came to structure how that uprising was represented in contemporary and subsequent writings: that Lahore and Rawalpindi were the focal points, that it was largely student-led, that Zulfikar Ali Bhutto turned out to be the main beneficiary, and that, in transferring power from General Ayub to General Yahya the uprising ended with the Army still in charge, perhaps more so, until this new dispensation also collapsed with the Bangladesh War, paving the way for Bhutto to rise to power in the much smaller Pakistan that emerged out of that war. Each of those emphases is only partially true. Lahore was certainly the epicentre but all the main cities exploded fairly quickly and the uprising spread to all regions of Pakistan, East and West, even into smaller towns and parts of the countryside. Students were certainly the most prominent, particularly in the early phases, but that was greatly exaggerated by the mediatic and academic representations. Trade unions and the working class in general, the underground communists, leftists of various persuasions, popular masses of various kinds, even the religious groupings, all such social forces participated and the movement soon became very much larger than just 'students' or the all-purpose category of 'youth'. Bhutto and his Peoples Party [Pakistan Peoples Party, PPP] were certainly the beneficiary in Sindh and Punjab but Mujib and his Awami League were equally the beneficiary in East Pakistan (later Bangladesh); and Bhutto was *not* the beneficiary in the other two provinces of West Pakistan, namely NWFP (today's Pakhtunkhwa) and Balochistan where the secular National Awami Party [NAP] and the God-intoxicated Jamiat Ulema-e-Islam [JUI] emerged as the two equally prominent parties that were to form coalition governments in both those provinces after the Bangladesh War. And, the idea that transfer of power from General Ayub to General Yahya was just a simple re-alignment of Army rule is equally misleading. The basic fact is that the elections of 1970 that gave Mujib's Awami League a clear majority *in Pakistan as a whole* were the only completely free and fair elections in the history of Pakistan and the only ones since 1958 in which the Army remained strictly neutral, even though all this happened on General Yahya's watch. He was perhaps more keen on whisky than on affairs of state. In any case, he seems to have thought of himself as a caretaker head of state and his dispensation included rather interesting figures like the Naval Chief Ahsan. The fact that Yahya ended up invading and then losing half of his own country, with Bhutto pushing him onwards, was perhaps an instance of what Hegel called 'the Cunning of History'.

What is interesting about that uprising is not just the short period between the first demonstrations and the Yahya takeover but what happened in its aftermath, over the next two years and beyond. Pakistan's political society had been very successfully repressed during the Ayub dictatorship. The uprising took the lid off and the Yahya government was never able to put the lid back on. Out of what had been repressed new forces emerged. The political parties I have just mentioned got consolidated very greatly by those two forces. Bangladeshi nationalism grew greatly and became irreversible. The labour militancy that enveloped Pakistan, Karachi in particular, especially during the first year of the Bhutto government; the mass peasant movement among the Pashtuns in the '70s; the Baloch insurgency of those same years! ... [The years] 1968 to 1971, following the uprising, were the years of gestation and growth for all those forces.

Much of that became clear to me only later, as I participated in some of that, first from my exile in New York and then from within Pakistan when I was able to return during the 1970s. And much of that wisdom came to me through sustained, careful reflection as I matured politically and began to grasp Marxist analytic procedures more firmly.

Zulfikar Ali Bhutto had played an important part in this uprising. Initially, I had misread him and had high hopes of him. Bhutto presented himself as a leftist and as a very thorough anti-imperialist, in the Nehruvian mould but the Nehru of the famous Red Years. My own naïve understanding of the man was reflected in the article you mentioned earlier. The truth of Bhutto came to me only when I witnessed his monstrous cynicism during the Bangladesh crisis. When I lost my illusions about Bhutto I also lost illusions about much else— Mujibur Rahman, for instance, and the whole sorry lot that led the Awami League. Discussions with Eqbal were certainly very helpful. He had been in Tunis during the Algerian revolution and had a much more shrewd understanding of political postures and personal ambitions. I did not think of the break-up of Pakistan as a tragedy as Eqbal did but he and I shared a rather similar position on Bangladesh. Both of us supported the logic of independence for Bangladesh fully and openly but primarily because of the genocidal actions of the Pakistan Army and the enthusiastic support for it among much of the West Pakistani political elite. Neither of us had much use for Mujib and the Awami League high brass. Nor did we admire that kind of nationalism— not even a Bengali nationalism, since it excluded West Bengal, but a nationalism exclusively of the Bengalis who had become citizens of Pakistan.

VP: You were in New York by 1970. In the months ahead, you were following the events on both flanks of Pakistan. You were engaged in the question of East Pakistan—Bangladesh by 1971—but also Balochistan.

AA: I was politicized very intensely by the anti-war movement and the Black nationalist movement, and I was reading episodically but quite extensively in Marxism and anti-imperialist archives of various hues. Those three or four years of my life moved very fast, both intellectually and practically. Then came Bangladesh—right at that time. The apprenticeship that I acquired through the anti-war movement and the Black nationalist movement and more abstractly through my readings then got concentrated on the events in Pakistan. I was shocked by the scale of the genocide in East Pakistan.

VP: It was at this time that you began small magazines to produce a Left analysis of what was happening in Pakistan.

AA: There were two successive magazines. The first was *Pakistan Forum*. I knew Eqbal already. He knew Feroz Ahmed, whom I did not yet know. Feroz had actually started *Pakistan Forum* earlier as a tribune for left-wing or at least secular and anti-military Pakistani students in North America. He lived in Sault Sainte Marie in Canada. Eqbal asked him to come over and the three of us—and Eqbal's younger brother Saghir Ahmad (who actually published a book with Monthly Review Press*)—met in my flat in New York and the new version of *Pakistan Forum* came to be. The editorial board consisted of Feroz, Eqbal and me. Feroz did most of the work, I must confess. This went on for roughly two years until Bhutto took over. Then it became possible for Feroz and I to move back to Pakistan.

---

* Saghir Ahmad, *Class and Power in a Punjabi Village*, with an introduction by Kathleen Gough, New York: Monthly Review Press, 1977. Saghir Ahmad died in 1971.

VP: In 1975, Feroz Ahmed produced a book called *Focus on Baluchistan and the Pashtun Question*. You had two essays in that book, both essays about Balochistan.* Tell us a little about the title, which links Balochistan and the North-West Frontier Province. Why is that so?

AA: Feroz was very unhappy with my Balochistan articles. He was in a rage. They had appeared in a journal of which he was the main editor, namely *Pakistan Forum*. After Bangladesh, two things had happened and then were beginning to converge. The success of Bangladeshi nationalism had greatly encouraged separatist tendencies in all three (West) Pakistani provinces outside Punjab, namely Balochistan, Sindh and NWFP. And, while Bhutto's PPP had formed governments at the national level as well as in Punjab and Sindh, non-PPP governments had emerged in NWFP and Balochistan, with an armed insurgency re-surfacing in the latter. Bhutto had unleashed naked repression there, including military repression, with three distinct purposes: to overthrow the non-PPP government, to suppress the armed insurgency and to restore to the Pakistan Army the 'honour' it had lost in East Pakistan. I was deeply and openly opposed to that repression, had met some of the Baloch leaders, was quite familiar with the involvement of the left wing and outright communist elements in the armed insurgency. They had all my sympathies but I was deeply sceptical about the whole rhetoric of the Baloch 'national question', 'right of secession', etc., on theoretical as well as practical grounds. I need not rehearse that argument. It is all there in those articles you have referred to. I no longer agree with all that I wrote there but the main thrust, I think, was correct. As I said, Feroz was enraged. He always was a passionate Sindhi nationalist and became more so over the years. In my view, he never took quite seriously Lenin's comment that

---

* Aijaz Ahmad, 'The National Question in Baluchistan' and 'Baluchistan's Agrarian Question', *Focus on Baluchistan and the Pashtun Question*, ed. Feroz Ahmed, Lahore: People's Publishing House, 1975.

supporting the right to divorce does not mean that all marriages must be dissolved. For Feroz, national right was absolute and that right was nothing if it did not include the right of secession. He wanted to rebut my argument conceptually by framing the Pashtun question as he saw it, which would be an implicit critique of my approach to Balochistan. So, that was one reason why the book was on Balochistan and the Pashtun question together. But the other was because the Pashtun question was becoming more central in Sarhad [NWFP]. Wali Khan's National Awami Party, one of the two governing parties in the province, always had a strong streak of Pashtun ethno-nationalism. But there was more and more unrest and revolutionary militancy in parts of the province, which was the main battleground for the Mazdoor Kisan Party [MKP] in the Pashtun world. Hashtnagar particularly was the centre of it, but this unrest spilled over into Charsadda and Swat as well. The Pashtun leaders of that all-Pakistan party did not preach secession but were not altogether immune to ethno-nationalism. Meanwhile, there were increasing and serious communications between the Peshawar-based leaders of the MKP and the Khalq and Parcham factions of the People's Democratic Party of Afghanistan (the PDPA), which would then form a government in August 1978. There were already connections with the people around Nur Muhammad Taraki, with Afghan party's literature getting published in Peshawar and then smuggled across the border, not to speak of militants coming and going across the border. A question was often discussed in this Pashtun section of the MKP: if there is a successful revolution in Afghanistan, should the Pashtun-dominated regions not break away from Pakistan and unite with revolutionary Afghanistan?

Well, actually, there is something euphemistic about talking of just the MKP. That was the open political front of an underground communist formation, the Mazdoor Party. I was fairly prominently active on both levels, working closely with the central leadership of the underground level. The idea of a larger revolutionary homeland straddling the Durand Line was quite attractive to Pashtun comrades and I had no difficulty with that. On this, my thinking was simple: there is nothing sacrosanct about national boundaries as inherited from the colonial period. I don't like ethnic nationalism, but if you want to break up the existing national boundaries to make a revolution, that's fine. So, that was my view—a view obviously regarding a hypothetical possibility. I don't think that was on Feroz's mind. He had a much more enthusiastic identification with ethnic nationalisms and with the right of secession for Pakistan's minority nationalities, though it was hard to say so categorically if you wanted your book to circulate legally in Pakistan.

The Pashtun question has been hanging like a sword over the region for over a hundred years, unresolved. But it cannot be resolved simply by making a little statelet of the Pashtuns inside the territory of Pakistan without handing it over to the *mullahs*—and this I believed already in the '70s, well before the rise of militant Islam in that region. In the early years of the Soviet Union, Lenin had refused to hand over those so-called 'Islamic republics' to the *mullahs* in the name of national rights. That's exactly what he said: if self-determination means that you hand it over to the *mullahs*, then no; now that these are part of a revolutionary state, I'm not going to hand these areas over to the *mullahs*. So that has been my position on these things—that handing over a statelet to the wealthy classes of the ethnic nationalities is not my understanding of self-determination. Self-determination, in both Lenin and Luxemburg, has class limits. In the context of Pakistan in the 1970s, this was not a theoretical question. I've always held that the colonial question is quite different from the nationalities question in a state that is itself a post-colonial sovereign state. Although the way these things get printed—Lenin's texts—they are usually presented as if the national and colonial questions are identical but these are two different questions.

VP: Can you say a little more to specify the difference?

AA: Okay. One is that pre-revolutionary Russia was a very strange conglomeration. It was an empire which had its colonies within the geographical boundaries of the empire itself. So, they were colonies as well as provinces all at once. In Russian Marxist analyses, those colonial provinces were regarded as homelands of distinct intertwining nationalities with distinct cultures, often with some similarities with each other but all of them very distinct from the colonizing Russians of the Tsarist imperial state. So only in Tsarist Russia were the colonial and national questions mixed up in that way and if you read Lenin and Luxemburg without understanding this context you may miss the distinction as it applied to other situations. Luxemburg's argument, for example, was that the respective bourgeoisies of Russia and the Russian part of Poland had become so deeply integrated that it was no longer possible to speak of a national bourgeoisie that was distinctly Polish or a distinct Polish economy of a colonial kind. She argued in favour of a Polish cultural identity and cultural rights but not for secession. (It was different in Marx's days. Poland was much more of an agrarian society and Marx thought that Poland needed to be independent in order to make an industrial transition.) I think Lenin was interested in the colonial question for three different reasons. One, after the Revolution fails in Europe—country after country, from Germany to Hungary—Lenin starts to look towards the East as the possible weak link in the chain of international capital. Hence great emphasis on the absolute right of independence for the colonies; 'Backward Europe, Advanced Asia'—from the standpoint of world *revolution*, not technological advance. Second, very basic and quite old in Lenin's thinking is precisely the question of the colonies *within* the empire, and this is where the colonial question and the national question get very closely aligned—the colonized regions of the empire, homelands of the oppressed nations within the empire, have all rights of national self-determination, including the right to secede. Secession in that case is simply independence from the colonizing empire! However, once the Revolution comes, and this is the third point, Lenin modifies his position and says that the context has changed utterly, the former colonies have been liberated by the revolution as much as Russia itself, and nationalities that were colonies can now become autonomous republics in a revolutionary state and can pursue further national consolidation for themselves. Moreover, to break away from this Union of Soviet Socialist Republics would spell a counter-revolutionary takeover by the *mullahs*. That is a class point of view and that is a way of framing the question of rights within the dynamics of revolutionary politics. In all this, I think, Lenin and Luxemburg are very much closer than people generally believe. And that is a very important way in which I look at national questions in our region. That is how I looked at the Balochistan question in the past and that is how I look at the Kashmir question in India and Pakistan today. Reactionaries can and often do take hold of the national question. This one must not forget.

VP: Because it can end up becoming merely a statelet for some petty ruler.

AA: Absolutely! . . . And it usually does. Not only that, now, at this moment in history, it is likely to be truly dominated by real religious reactionaries.

VP: In an earlier period, about ten years before this debate in Pakistan, the very opposite happens in Katanga, the province in the Congo that was then governed by a revolutionary government led by Patrice Lumumba, which declared its independence so that it could deliver its copper to the multinational corporations. This secession came to deliver resources to the multinational corporations and to drive a socially reactionary agenda.

AA: That's right. That is what is going on today in Balochistan itself, decades after that more or less non-debate between Feroz and myself. Here, the Americans want to destabilize Iran and they want to sabotage Chinese involvement in the Pakistani economy. Baloch nationalists now say that they are going to fight in Gilgit to stop the Chinese from coming into Balochistan. A large part of the Baloch armed movement has now become increasingly a US front against Iran and against China, on both sides of the Pakistan–Iran border. Why should I support it on the basis of some abstract, ahistorical notion of national self-determination?

VP: This issue is not to be settled at the level of abstraction. There it has a moral resonance which can become meaningless. The position has to have concrete meaning.

1975–79: A TIME OF POLITICAL CRISIS

VP: ... We are now in the 1970s. It looked like history could go in any direction. You are in New York City, writing about Pakistan, meeting Iranian students, following events in Afghanistan. Pakistan has a counter-revolution in 1977, with the arrival of the military dictatorship of Zia-ul-Haq. Two major revolutions take place at the close of the decade: the Saur Revolution in August 1978 in Afghanistan and the Iranian Revolution the next year. How were you looking at all of that? What were you thinking at that time?

AA: By then, I was not looking at Pakistan by itself. To me, between 1975 and 1979, there was a political crisis—but I myself was in a political crisis, and I needed to understand the world that I lived in. Between the declaration of Emergency in India in 1975 and the military takeover in Pakistan in 1977, then the communist coup in Afghanistan in 1978 and the Islamic revolution in Iran in 1979, the world had changed very rapidly and in very contradictory ways. The largest proletarian uprising in the history of the greater Middle East

leads to the creation of an Islamic Republic that unleashes the most
horrific repression against communists and all other left tendencies in
the country. So I had to look very seriously at all that. I immersed myself
in very voracious readings about Iran, about histories of communism
and the anti-imperialist movements across the region, in histories of
insurgent as well as Quietist Shi'ism, the Ikhwan in their many avatars,
not to speak of the very considerable impact that European Fascism
had had on a wide spectrum of forces in the Middle East that ranged all
the way from the Lebanese Phalange to Ba'athists in diverse countries
to charismatic figures such as Ali Shariati and Jalal Al-e-Ahmad in
Iran (the latter had once been a communist and Shariati was actually
a paradoxical character). By then I had spent much of the 1970s in
Pakistan but also travelling frequently to places like Cairo, Beirut and
Damascus, and I was publishing some pieces in publications like *Rose
al-Yousef* in Cairo and *As-Safir* in Beirut. I had also come to India soon
after the Emergency but did not know much about the intricacies of
Indian politics and therefore swallowed whole the very un-nuanced
anti-Emergency rhetoric that was rampant among circles that also
ranged from the RSS [Rashtriya Swayamsevak Sangh] to the Maoists
and their admirers in the Indian diaspora.

But Iran was for a while very much at the centre of my thinking.
It was then that I lost my romance with the category of 'the people'
and it was Iran that provoked my passionate and abiding interest
in understanding fascism in all its variants. I came quite soon to
characterize the Khomeini regime as clerical-fascist. Clerical obviously
because it propelled the clergy as the nucleus of the new ruling class.
And 'fascist' for a variety of reasons. First, because it came to power
at the head of a real mass movement that was propelled by the largest
popular uprising in the history of West Asia; it was not a Bonapartist
coup, nor a military dictatorship of a kind so common in that region.
And it was fascist in its two-faced class character. On the one hand, it
was determined from the beginning to suppress the workers' movement

and all varieties of communists. On the other hand, it successfully put itself at the head of anti-monarchical revolution which sought to dismantle all aspects of the existing ruling order. It got rid of not only the King but also the class fraction which [Ervand] Abrahamian calls, quite appropriately, the 'monarcho-bourgeoisie', in other words, the two hundred or so families that dominated the Irani economy and were the lynchpin of monarchic stability. This revolution of the Right did have its own side of class radicalism. One now forgets that the Nazis also included a very powerful left tendency which got suppressed only when Hitler and his close associates decided to align themselves fully with finance capital. The left wing of the Khomeini regime itself was similarly suppressed gradually as the regime consolidated itself. But that class radicalism has never disappeared entirely, which can be seen in the contradiction that the neoliberal policies that favour the new Islamist bourgeoisie and its foreign friends is combined with extensive state controls and numerous measures that favour the working class and the poor ('*mustazafin*', in Arabo-Farsi). A combination of such measures and the naked aggression that the whole of the Irani society faces from imperialism keeps the great majority of the populace attached to the regime. Like all fascisms, this one also has an ethno-nationalist ideology at its core, and religion plays the same role in it as race did in Nazi ideology or religion does in RSS ideology in India. In the case of Iran, however, this religious element has two distinct layers. Irani clergy sees itself at the core of the Shia sectarian world and seeks alignments particularly in that world. However, Iran also has much broader 'Islamic' claim, so that it is aligned with Hamas in Palestine and has had a very complex relationship with the Taliban in Afghanistan even though many among the Taliban are deeply anti-Shia. The crux of Iran's opposition to Saudi Arabia is not that it is Sunni but that it is monarchical and it is a stooge of the Americans. We have to remember that the political roots of Islamic revolution in Iran were anti-monarchical and it created not a Shia *rashtra* but an

Islamic *republic*. Buttressing that ethno-religious nationalism is also a layer of a very familiar kind of romantic nationalism with its pride in a great imperial past, great cultural traditions of literature, architecture and the other arts that have had profound influence far beyond the boundaries of modern-day Iran. Like the Chinese but unlike the Indian ruling class, the Irani elite remembers all the wounds that the West has inflicted and continues to inflict on their country. The US detests Iran for the same reason that it detests China; both these states wish to be treated as sovereign entities. It is on such grounds that this regime is in contradiction with the US. The fact that they are clerical fascists does not necessarily resolve their contradiction with imperialism, just as the fascist character of the Nazis did not resolve their contradictions with British and US capital. I must confess that when I started writing about India, communalism, RSS, etc., what I had learned during my extensive work on Iran and the larger West Asia was very much a part of my intellectual baggage.

VP: What was your view at that time of the rapid developments in Pakistan?

AA: Hamza Alavi wrote a very interesting piece in the early 1970s on the potentials for Islamization in Pakistan.* He acknowledged that Islamist political parties had little influence in Pakistani society but he also argued that the Pakistan Army, once a pillar of secular power in the country was changing radically, with its soldiery as well as rising sections of the officers' corps becoming far more socially conservative and religiously oriented. The crux of his argument, which proved to be true, was that if Pakistan ever undergoes an Islamist takeover the initiative for it will have come not from within civil society but from the Armed Forces. That perception had come from two very different sources. On the one hand, Hamza had many connections with a

---

* Hamza Alavi, 'Rural Bases of Political Power in South Asia', *Journal of Contemporary Asia*, vol. 4, no. 4 (1974), pp. 413–22.

section of the Pakistani establishment simply because of his previous work at the Reserve Bank and thanks to his family background. So, he could develop a good grasp of tendential possibilities growing within the existing state organisms. On the other hand, he had spent studying economic and social changes in Central Punjab.

When Pakistan came into being, the top half a dozen or so Muslim officers in the Indian Army became the core of the leadership of Pakistan's army. They were whiskey-drinking officers who had been trained in Sandhurst and who therefore brought into the Pakistani military brass the ethos of the old British Indian Army. As the army expanded, the officer corps expanded. The first generation came from either the relatively upper crust of Urdu-speaking migrants of UP and Bihar or from the professional classes of Lahore and its environs, with a sprinkling of Pashtun officers from old military families. But the third generation came from among the kulaks of Central Punjab, many of whom had migrated at the time of the Partition from eastern Punjab and still carried within their psychic structures the wounds of that time, [and] some other officers but specially large chunks of the soldiery came from arid zones of the Pothohar Plateau or from other socially conservative regions such as the Bahawalpur and Multan divisions. Many of the younger officers in the Pakistan Army that went to war in 1971, the lieutenants and the captains, came from distinctly reactionary and Islamist backgrounds, resented their English-speaking, whiskey-drinking seniors and now carried the wounds of defeat as well. By the late '70s, they were the new brigadiers and the young generals, many of whom had also served in Pakistani military contingents in Saudi Arabia and other Gulf countries. Petro-Islam of those countries now entered the already lethal brew. Hamza projected that this Pakistani army was going to be the main conduit of political Islam. He didn't predict beyond that, but he made this insightful observation. I remember it so vividly. That is what stuck in my mind, this really solid explanation for Zia-ul-Haq and his supporters in the

Army. Zia was a semi-literate progeny of a kulak background who had become a non-commissioned officer in the British Indian Army, and if I remember correctly, got his commission after the creation of Pakistan. He was the right man to lead this new, socially backward, Islamized, puritanical, war-wounded officer corps who also despised, among others, Zulfikar Ali Bhutto with his upper-class manners, leftist pretensions and fame for love of the bottle. That was the social base for the coup by the Islamist wing of the Army in 1977.

At another level, though, the separation of Bangladesh in 1971 produced in the remainder of Pakistan a deep crisis of what is generally called identity. I had written about this then.* Before 1971, Pakistan was the homeland of the majority of the Muslims of British India. After that, it had fewer Muslims than even those who lived in India. Before 1971, Pakistan competed with Indonesia in the claim to be the largest Muslim country in the world, with half of it on the borders of India and West Asia and the other on the borders of India and Southeast Asia. Now, after 1971, it lost its eastern half and majority of its population, becoming the third largest Muslim country in the subcontinent itself— with a smaller Muslim population than Bangladesh or even India. Why did it exist? The war with East Pakistan—then Bangladesh— bankrupted and disrupted the economy of the western half. Between the economic crisis and the identity crisis, Bhutto moved to become a vassal of Saudi Arabia. So, petro-Islam entered Pakistan to resolve this crisis. Henceforth, the *raison d'être* of the country was not that it was the homeland of the majority of the Muslims of British colonial India but that it was now the homeland of the truly pious. Bhutto does not Islamize Pakistan, but he reorients it from South Asia to Desert Islam. Then comes this military Islamic wave which has very narrow and shallow bases in the larger society. How then to build a widespread mass acceptance for political Islam? Some of those dilemmas began

---

* Aijaz Ahmad, 'Democracy and Dictatorship in Pakistan', *Journal of Contemporary Asia*, vol. 8, no. 4 (1978), pp. 477–512.

to be settled only after the US war begins in Afghanistan. In Salman Rushdie's novel *Shame*, when Zia hears of the Soviets entering Afghanistan, he brings out his prayer mat and does his *namaz* along with his three aides. This was 'the greatest gift' that Allah had given him, Zia would say; now the dollars and the weapons will be showered on him and his Army to launch the *jihad*.

VP: In this period your children were born, and you were busy with them. But you were also reading ferociously. A three-part essay follows from this reading between 1982 and 1985 that is called 'Political Islam: A Critique.'* What were you reading at that time to help you get your bearings?

AA: Most of what I wrote during the 1970s and early 1980s, before I returned to India, was actually in Urdu, and much of it had to do with politics and political economy, and with figures ranging from Lenin to Cabral and Lê Duẩn. But the question you asked me was about what I read and you asked me that in relation specifically to my three-part essay on Political Islam. Well, among other things, quite literally hundreds of books on Islam and the Middle East. The reflection on political Islam was motivated initially by the Iranian Revolution but by then Islamism of various kinds was spreading all over the Arab world as well. I was reading from Marxist to perfectly liberal to right-wing CIA-sponsored scholarship on the Middle East. At the same time, I was also reading lots of Left writing, not necessarily on political Islam but on the region. And most of what I was doing—which is why I am re-reading Carl Schmitt these days—was to read writers of the far right and cull from them what I needed for my purposes of analysing what

---

* Aijaz Ahmad, 'Political Islam: A Critique (Part I)', *Pakistan Progressive*, vol. 4, no. 4 (Winter 1982/83), pp. 14–42; 'Political Islam: A Critique (Part II)', *Pakistan Progressive*, vol. 5, no. 2 (Summer 1983), pp. 3–33; 'Political Islam: A Critique (Part III)', *Pakistan Progressive*, vol. 7, no. 2 (Fall 1985), pp. 19–49.

actually exists. And I read a lot of history and social science. You have to have a body of empirical data for you to think your own thoughts, which then helps you to assimilate but also to transcend the analyses of those whose books you are reading.

VP: It was easier to say for the earlier period that you were involved with people like Eqbal Ahmad and Feroz Ahmed in intellectual and political projects. This was whether you agreed with them fully or not. From Zia's ascendency in 1977 into the mid-1980s, who were your interlocutors?

AA: Well, after 1973 I got involved a lot with the currents in Egypt, Palestine, Lebanon, Jordan, and Syria. I wrote extensively for *Rose al-Yousef*—the Egyptian journal that was founded in the 1920s—from about 1973 to 1979.* My interlocutors were mainly Egyptian and Palestinian. I would go to Palestinian camps in Jordan after 1971. I could see that Islam was fully present there; the camps were just full of Quranic recitations, full of Islamic cassettes of various sorts. You come back to Lebanon and you meet your comrades from the PFLP [Popular Front for the Liberation of Palestine] and the DFLP [Democratic Front for the Liberation of Palestine], and they are talking to you about Islamism in Birzeit, Islamism in the camps. I go to Turkey and take a bus from Istanbul to Konya—to see Rumi's mausoleum (the only time I've gone to somebody's mausoleum). I went through Anatolia for three weeks, stopping in small towns, and basically trying to understand

* Email from Aijaz Ahmad, 4 August 2018: 'My real regret, not so much from the standpoint of the interview you are planning but an absolute regret of my own, is that a box which contained copies of my publications in Urdu and Arabic was lost in one of my many, far too many, moves. I don't write in Arabic myself but throughout the 1970s I published many articles in *Rose al-Yousef* in Cairo and *As-Safir* in Beirut, which I would compose in English and Ibrahim Mansoor, a dear friend and a well-known Egyptian translator, would then translate into Arabic. I always threw away the English text but kept the Arabic copies, which I then lost.'

something that I had felt viscerally from some Turkish writers—that there are two Turkeys: one Europeanized and concentrated largely in Istanbul, Ankara and some other urban centres, mostly in the western parts of the country; and there was another Turkey which I had felt in the poorer districts of Istanbul itself. But when I went into the interior of Anatolia in the early 1970s, I realized that there was this new bourgeoisie that was Muslim. They had their oldest institutions— the mosque, the coffee shop, the bourse and the market—all cheek by jowl; they would take their coffee here, do their bargaining there, and then they would go to the mosque for their prayers. The entire rural, peri-urban, small-town Anatolia was still quite intact in the 1970s, except that a new, solidly Islamist bourgeoisie was rising in those small and medium-sized towns. My leftist friends in Istanbul thought that much of it was anachronistic and would be swept up into the Kemalist paradigm sooner or later. I said to them: Istanbul and Ankara may turn out to be your past, the small-town Anatolia may have the seeds of your future. I was seeing political Islam seeping through in the most surprising places. Turkey was the last place I would have expected it but it was everywhere except in the very large fashionable districts. I had seen this on the peripheries of Cairo and then I travelled into the townships of the Delta. There was a whole issue on this in *Rose al-Yousef* in which I wrote on these themes. My memory is dim now but as I recall the over-all title of the issue was 'Hukoomat al-Mashaikh' (Rule of the Sheikhs), in 1973.

VP: Sadat had already changed the Egyptian constitution in 1971, bringing in Islam as the highest arbiter.

AA: Yes, that was Sadat who had once been useful for Nasser because of his connection with the Muslim Brotherhood. Nasser then appointed Sadat to oversee the trial and sentencing of Sayyid Qutb, so that there would be a blood feud between him and his erstwhile Brotherhood comrades and he would have no choice but to remain loyal to Nasser. Yes, Sadat Islamized the Egyptian constitution but the Islamist radicals who killed him had two main charges against Sadat: his capitulation to Israel and his role in the killing of Qutb. In any case, with Sadat's rise the Nasserist and socialist pretensions were set aside very quickly. The main consequence of the Egyptian defeat by the Israelis in 1967 was the relegation of Egypt to the side and the rise of Saudi Arabia as the dominant force in the Arab world. The war that Egypt and Saudi Arabia had fought in Yemen, to settle the confrontation between monarchism and republicanism, was now settled by the Israelis. The Israelis fought the 1967 war to realize their dream of occupying the rest of Palestine. In addition, though, with so complete a defeat of Egypt, which had been the dominant power in the Arab world where monarchies were tottering, the balance of power shifted decisively. Saudi dominance grew gradually but inexorably. I thought—even at that time—that the consequence was going to be more and more Islam—political Islam, right-wing Wahhabi Islam, what I sometimes call 'Desert Islam' which has none of the civilizational grandeur and subtlety of what you might call Mediterranean Islam. The Gulf with its petro-Islam was bound to be ascendant after that. When Nasserism came to Libya in 1969, it came as a form of Islamic Nasserism. In other words, Gaddafi's treatise—*The Green Book*—was a mishmash of left-wing radicalism and political Islam.

VP: In all this, which thinkers were you in dialogue with?

AA: One of the consequences of having to change home every decade or so is that I have had the privilege of leading a life in which I have had a large number of interlocutors but mostly for short durations. To have a sustained, stable dialogue with particular people one has to have some kind of permanent residence. It happened for me in India because I lived there for thirty years. Before that, with respect to Pakistan, Hamza was an intellectual interlocutor for many years or the militants of the Left inside the country, mostly of the Mazdoor Party, people like Major Ishaq and Afzal Bangash, but also many others from other leftist shades. In Egypt, for example, I would go repeatedly and meet a lot of people again and again over five or seven years; these were are all leftists, communists, left-Nasserists, editors—half of them had been in and out of Nasser's prisons. But this was not a milieu in which I was actually rooted. The same was the case in Lebanon, where I would publish in *As-Safir* and would meet people in the various Palestinian groups (PFLP, DFLP, even the small Baʿathist faction). Or independent Marxists like Sadiq al-Azm. From them, I would get real politics and their understanding of it. I met people like Fawwaz Traboulsi later. Among Arab intellectuals, my main interlocutor in the Arab world has been Aziz al-Azmeh, a magnificent scholar of Islam and many, many other things. My book *In Theory* and his book *Islams and Modernities* were published roughly within a year of each other. He and I have had very sustained conversations since the mid-1990s. Unfortunately, the two of us have never lived in the same place and neither uses the medium of the email for intellectual interlocution.

I must say, though, that the right-wing scholars were far more alert to what was going on than much of the Left. Much of the Left was at that time far too sanguine about themselves and their own view of the world. They looked at these Islamists as anachronisms, not part of a very complex world of Islamic politics and culture. The Left was overconfident about the secular nature of Arab nationalism and the Kemalist state. A typical example of this is Fred Halliday's otherwise very useful book on Iran.* It was clearly composed and sent to press just as the Islamic revolution was taking off but had hardly anything useful to say about the clergy.

VP: What about the Palestinian Marxist Hanna Batatu?

AA: I didn't meet him, but his very admirable book on Iraq I know

* Fred Halliday, *Iran: Dictatorship and Development*, Harmondsworth: Penguin, 1979.

very well.[*] Again, for Batatu, the book traces the struggle between communists and Marxists and Ba'athists, but there is nothing on the old class, on the clergy, which is deeply connected to landlordism in Iraq. The big landlord class and the traders have an intimate relationship with the clergy in Iraq, and they formed a very important political force in the country. But there is very little on this in Batatu's very detailed and otherwise magnificent book. If you wanted to understand the historical background for what transpired in Iraq after the US invasion his book would have limited value. It is very good on a great many other things, partly because he was lucky enough to get hold of a very substantial part of the colonial government's secret archive.

VP: What about Ali Shariati, who—like the Sadrites in Iraq[†]—appeared to engage Marxism and even Frantz Fanon (Shariati translated Fanon into Farsi for a volume published in 1960, and Fanon wrote to him the following year[‡]).

AA: Yes, Fanon's own canonicity and then the evidence of Fanon writing to Shariati is currently getting deployed in authenticating Shariati's revolutionary, quasi-Marxist credentials. I don't want to get into the very complex case of Fanon, his complexities and ambivalences, his streak of romantic messianism, all the exaggerated Algerian-ness he often claimed for himself and even a defence of the veil. He contrived to occlude the significance of the fact that he was neither an Algerian nor a Muslim. And even though he had started his work for the FLN [National Liberation Front] by identifying himself with the leftist, often

* Hanna Batatu, *The Old Social Classes and the Revolutionary Movements of Iraq: A Study of Iraq's Old Landed and Commercial Classes and of Its Communists, Ba'athists and Free Officers*, Princeton: Princeton University Press, 1983.

† Vijay Prashad, 'Sadrist Stratagems', *New Left Review*, no. 53 (September–October 2008).

‡ Frantz Fanon, 'Letter to Ali Shariati', *Alienation and Freedom*, ed. Jean Khalfa and Robert J. C. Young, London: Bloomsbury, 2018, pp. 667–69.

Marxist tendency, he had eventually ended up in the more socially conservative and pious milieu of Boumedienne and the followers of Ben Bella. For the sake of keeping his position in the movement, Fanon allowed himself far too many silences, and large parts of *The Wretched of the Earth* are both an allegorical compensation for those silences as well as something of a dirge for a revolution that was already decomposing. In any case, whatever Fanon might or not have been he certainly was neither an ethno-nationalist nor a religious revivalist. That is a very thick line of demarcation between him and Shariati.

Ali Shariati, in my view, is intellectually a schizophrenic. When he was studying in Paris, he came under two different influences. One, people such as Charles Bettelheim introduced him fairly systematically to Marxism. Two, he was deeply marked by the whole intellectual legacy of French fascism and what in France is known as 'integral nationalism', a main precursor of modern fascist thought and the whole legacy that made Vichy France possible. Maurice Barrès was a direct inspiration for Shariati. There are certainly traces in his work of the Marxism he encountered in his student days but the main forms of his rhetoric are derived from lineages of European irrationalism and religious messianism which Shariati then re-structures into a specifically Shi'i discourse. I was fascinated and repelled by that discourse but I also had a great fear that this is a man who can speak to the schizophrenia of the modern middle class because modern middle classes in countries like Iran and India are themselves schizophrenic. Shariati remains influential in many circles. The organized political tendency that took Shariati's thought to heart while also espousing an Islamic Marxism at the time of the Islamic Revolution was the Mujahedin-e Khalq which first tried to cultivate Saddam Hussein and have eventually ended up as agents of the US–Israeli axis. This later fact is not a reflection of Shariati's thought but it does illustrate the kind of confusion and schizophrenia of the milieu that had once responded very practically to Shariati's thought.

GHALIB

VP: Let's go back to when you first came to the United States. Almost immediately, you seemed to have got involved with a series of poets in a project to translate Ghalib. Early versions of this work with Adrienne Rich, William Stafford, and W.S. Merwin, were published in *The Hudson Review* and *Poetry* in 1969, and then a book—*Ghazals of Ghalib*—came out from Columbia University Press in 1970. Tell us a little about this project.

AA: I had arrived in the United States with virtually no money and this is the only thing I've ever done for money. There was a celebration of the centenary of Ghalib. The Asia Society asked me to do a book of translations towards this celebration. By then I was writing and publishing a lot in Urdu, had met some American writers who had visited Pakistan and one of them suggested to the Asia Society that since I am in the country they could ask me because I have a literary capacity in both languages. So, they asked me to do this. I told them that Ghalib is untranslatable and I will therefore not attempt a strict translation of him. However, I said, I could ask some eminent American poets I had come to know either personally or through correspondence and some others who may want to get involved and provide some literary responses to Ghalib. They agreed, and I then did three or four things. One is, I did those literal translations that appear in the book. Then I prepared cassettes—those days we used cassettes—with me reciting some forty or so *ghazals* of Ghalib, and then another cassette with singers like Begum Akhtar singing Ghalib. I found quite a few *ghazals* of Ghalib sung by Begum Akhtar but there were a few other singers as well. So, I said to the prospective collaborators: here's this literal translation with some minimal glossary, and here is what it sounds like when it is recited, and here is what it sounds like when it is sung. They were then free to do whatever they wanted. Much of what they gave me was very good poetry in English that was very much grounded in Ghalib's texts at hand but they were not, strictly speaking, translations. I called them 'Versions' in the subtitle of the book. This shift from 'translation' to 'version' was, in a nutshell, a tribute to the idea that what poetry says is essential and essentially communicable across languages but good poetry is much too deeply entrenched in its own original language to be wholly translatable in the literal sense.

VP: So, you have this book done; it's a method I've never seen elsewhere. Is that true? I mean, I'm not familiar with it.

AA: I invented it. I invented it just to carry out a conviction and to resolve an impasse.

VP: Would be nice to have more like this.

AA: Well, yes and no. Yes, for a very particular historical reason. Very many of the modern masters of English verse tend to know other European languages very well and can therefore translate even Latin American poetry, from Spanish and Portuguese—or for that matter from French poetry from Africa and the Caribbean. Merwin himself is a prime example, as would be Rich and Mark Strand—three of my collaborators—or look at Eshleman's magnificent translations of Césaire. But none of them knows a language like Urdu. If we are going to have translations of true poetic merit in the English language a collaboration between an Urdu poet/scholar and the masters of English verse, from either side of the Atlantic, is essential but with the understanding that the translation is going to be only an experiment and an approximation that will not be able to render the literal equivalent of the original, in the manner of, say, A.J. Arberry's very literal but also very turgid and cliché-ridden, tin-ear translations of Hafiz. We shall have to often accept the provisionality of the 'version' as it comes through the work of Rich or Stafford with the version of Ghalib I gave them. But also, 'No'. The problem with this method is that it can fall easy prey to charlatanism and sheer self-indulgence. Anyone fancying her/himself a poet can feel free to take all kinds of liberties with the original poet. William Hunt's compositions in *Ghazals of Ghalib* are, well, not the worst example but nevertheless an example of that sort of self-indulgence. Those are his own compositions with sometimes not even a tangential connection with what he had received from me. Merwin actually said to me later that I should have done more of those literal translations and just published them as they were, and not asked any of the American poets to do anything with them.

I had no interest in doing something like that ever again. I translated a lot of poetry from other languages into Urdu. These were published in Indian and Pakistani journals. That remains my interest: how to write modern verse in the Urdu language, and how to transfer the accents and forms of very different kinds of poetry into Urdu. And of prose as well, of course. At one point I got so fed up with the turgid Urdu translations of Lenin that had come from Moscow that I sat down and re-wrote some of them in the real Urdu diction and syntax as is common among the speakers of the language. My version of *What Is To Be Done?* became a very popular text in many communist study circles in Pakistan at that time. My interest as a translator is in Urdu, not in English.

But yes, my Ghalib book itself was taught in translation programmes all over the United States. It was the method that fascinated them and the fact that famous poets like Adrienne Rich and Merwin and William Stafford were wrestling with a poet's work they had never heard of and with a poetic form, the *ghazal*, they had never encountered, with the help and mediation of someone, myself, they had never heard of—all of this published by the Columbia University Press, a prestigious and fastidious academic press. With Adrienne Rich, in particular, I worked very closely on draft after draft of her translations. She wanted to remain as close to Ghalib's original meaning while being careful not to turn the couplet form into something aphoristic but also not sacrificing the demands of excellence in composing what was after all in the English language and therefore within the range of English poetics.

I can share one anecdote with you. Merwin was living in France. He sent me his poems from there, his versions, to which I had not responded. When he came to New York a little later he called me and said, 'I am in New York. How are you?' I muttered something or the other and he then asked, 'Did you receive them?' And I said, 'Yes, yes, I want to talk to you about them. Why don't you come home?' So, he came to my flat and we were talking about France, and this and that. So, after about half an hour, he stood up and said, 'So, clearly, you didn't like my drafts. I'll be back.' He left and some twenty minutes later he reappeared with four bottles of Châteauneuf-du-Pape and put them on the table, saying loudly, 'Now let's talk. Tell me what's wrong.' So, we had a night-long conversation, and I basically said: 'Bill, you have a very unique voice in the English language. Never has anybody had this voice and probably never will. It's not there in the drafts. These are too neutral, the versions you have done. So therefore, it is neither Ghalib nor Merwin.' So, we went through two of those bottles arguing over this and that because he immediately said, now show me what you mean. We went through them and then he left. I didn't budge from my position. I told him that if he wanted me to publish those as they were I undoubtedly would because I had promised everybody that I will publish whatever they give me—but I would be disappointed in publishing them under his signature. Two weeks later I received an envelope from Merwin. 'I've done a few things,' he wrote, 'just take a look.' And all of them are in the book. Some fifteen years later, he did a volume of his selected translations and all the translations that I had not published were there in those selected translations and none of these.

VP: In this period, you were writing in Urdu about literature?

AA: Not about literature only. I was publishing a lot of poems, a lot of translations, some critical essays, one or two pieces of fiction, short stories.* Much political writing in Urdu came in the 1970s. Poetry for me has always been something very personal, largely a private pleasure. I have published my poetry extensively but I hardly ever recite it. The political inevitably seeps into the poems in great many places and I have published translations from intensely political poets but I have never wanted to write poetry for political purposes. For one thing, I'm very interested in craft. When I was in college and training myself to write, I would sit down at night—usually at night—and translate from very different writers and very different kinds of writing. Style, Whitehead had once said, is the morality of the mind. And Roberto Schwarz, the great Brazilian critic, a Marxist in very much the Frankfurt School mould but less mystificatory, writes again and again that literary forms are really condensations of social relations. That formulation is actually more Lukács than Adorno. I had that kind of interest in translation as well. To engage with literary forms but also social relations that come from worlds very different than the world that produced Urdu literature. I mentioned Proust earlier. I would do that sort of thing one day and the next day I would sit down and translate *Dubliners* of James Joyce; short, pithy sentences, hard as diamonds, impossible to cut. Can that kind of completely non-sentimental, objective prose, full of emotion but even more committed to restraint, can this be written in the Urdu language and get recognized for its social acuity and literary excellence? Can the poetry of William Carlos Williams or Forough Farrokhzad, from Farsi, etc.? So various forms of writing. I wrote a piece on Meeraji, the Urdu poet, that was

---

* Email from Aijaz Ahmad, 4 August 2019: 'For Urdu, publications were extensive, across genres—political analyses, critical essays, poems and literary criticism of my own, Urdu translations of poetry from other languages but also of much revolutionary writings (from Cabral to Lê Duẩn which appeared in five volumes)—I do have printed copies of one or two things and huge pile of handwritten versions of the poems that were published in literary journals in India as well as Pakistan—but no copies of the actual publications.'

published in two instalments in *Savera*. They had recently bought the whole paraphernalia to use type for publishing. I said, listen, now that you have this type, I'm going to sit with you and give you my prose with all the colons and semicolons in it to write a compound sentence of a kind we don't traditionally write in Urdu. So that was one of the things I introduced into Urdu, the syntax of a proper compound sentence and the appropriate typesetting for it.

More broadly, I would say that a good bit of my own personal Urdu style was carried over into my English writings. By the time I started writing in English I was already a fairly experienced Urdu writer very attuned to stylistic matters. I carried all that into my English writing but it is hard to specify what that is. Detecting that sort of thing is itself a very writerly interest.

ANTI-IMPERIALISM

VP: In 1973, the British communist Bill Warren wrote an essay in *New Left Review* which made the case that capitalism would develop in Third World countries, and that therefore imperialism was now superseded. This was an argument that was elaborated in his posthumous book *Imperialism: Pioneer of Capitalism.*[*] You wrote an extended review essay on that book, tearing it apart. Later you wrote an essay on the 'intermediate classes'. Both of these were re-printed in a volume of selected essays from Tulika, with the two essays side-by-side. Could you tell us a little about the Warren essay, and the essay on 'intermediate classes'?

AA: I was in the United States, teaching, after spending quite a bit of time back in Pakistan and West Asia. The reason why those two

---

[*] Bill Warren, 'Imperialism and Capitalist Industrialization', *New Left Review*, no. 81 (September–October 1973); Bill Warren, *Imperialism: Pioneer of Capitalism*, London: Verso, 1980.

essays have a continuity of themes—and of course appear around the same time—is that Dale Johnson, the Latin Americanist who was my friend and colleague at that time, launched what was expected to be a series of books on problems of this kind. The two essays came in the first and second volume of that projected series. The intermediate class essay was written in a volume that is on the middle classes.* The Warren essay was written for a book on dependency theory.†

I was very offended by the Warren essay. That is a very early version of what is going on now, with David Harvey in some ways but more particularly people like Hardt and Negri and others of their kind. Harvey argues that imperialism is behind us and flow of capital has been reversed, going from West to East as contrasted with the age of imperialism when the West was appropriating wealth from the East; further, that China is now the 'workshop of the world' as UK and the US had been, successively, in the past. Negri and Hardt go much further, arguing that there is now only a de-centred, de-territorialized 'Empire' of free-flowing capital and that any criticism of the US, the power that is leading the Jeffersonian democratic project globally as an imperial power is outright reactionary. Compared to these, Warren was still rather old-fashioned—but then that difference is itself a sign of changing times. Warren begins by arguing that colonialism played a progressive role in the sense that it introduced capitalism in a whole range of precapitalist societies. There are of course several stray remarks in Marx that have often been used to argue that this is a Marxist position. Three things get lost in that kind of

---

* Aijaz Ahmad, 'Class, Nation, and State: Intermediate Classes in Peripheral Societies', in *Middle Classes in Dependent Countries*, ed. Dale L. Johnson, Beverly Hills: Sage Publications, 1985. Reprinted in Aijaz Ahmad, *Lineages of the Present*, New Delhi: Tulika, 1996.

† Aijaz Ahmad, 'Imperialism and Progress', in *Theories of Development: Mode of Production or Dependency?*, eds. Ronald Chilcote and Dale L. Johnson, Beverly Hills: Sage Publications, 1983. Reprinted in *Lineages of the Present*.

argument. First, already in the early 1850s, when Marx was new to writing about colonialism, he viewed the phenomenon through the lens of a progressive/regressive dialectic, largely applying to Asia the argument he had developed about the transition from Feudalism to Capitalism, though with a far more sceptical attitude towards *colonial* forms of capitalist expansion. Second, one only has to go back to the *Manifesto* to read those immortal lines in which he denounces the history of enslavement and rapaciousness in the founding structure of capitalism, and then come forward to Marx's later writings when he lost whatever hopes he had ever had of any progress made under colonial rule. Third, neither Marx nor Engels ever wavered from their absolute support for the right of national self-determination and independence for colonized and semi-colonized countries like India and China. Even on this last count Warren misreads Marx. The theory of national self-determination for the colonies does not originate with Lenin; it originates in Marx and Engels, beginning with their writings on Ireland; Lenin gives the theory a more rounded articulation at a later stage of history.

But there are also two other contexts to Warren's essay. By the time he started writing on these issues, a great excitement was growing about what were then called 'Asian Tigers'. His essay was written partly out of excitement about South Korea, very much as Harvey builds his theory of the end of the age of imperialism on the spectacular growth in China. And, I was particularly interested in writing about it because Warren taught at SOAS [the School of Oriental and African Studies] where he taught people like Fred Halliday, and a whole generation of English students who were Marxists and internationalists. He was very influential amongst them and many of them have remained very reluctant to grant colonialism a founding role in the primary accumulation and rise of capitalism in Europe itself. So that was a major motivation for wanting to write about him.

It was not just Bill Warren. He was part of a large tendency growing out of certain kinds of Western Marxism and European communism. For instance, Étienne Balibar and some of his comrades who had been raising many dissenting issues inside the PCF (the French Communist Party), starting with their dissent from the party's ambivalent and intrinsically French-nationalist position on the question of Algeria, finally got thrown out of the party in 1981 because they had again raised the question of imperialism. The party newspaper had published a picture of the latest, most advanced aircraft from the French aeronautic industry as an achievement of French workers. Balibar and a group of his comrades wrote a joint letter saying that France, which continues to have a military presence in all its former colonies in Africa, where it is militarily involved, cannot be seen merely as a producer of technology. That new aircraft was meant essentially for a continuation of the colonial mission. They said that there was a long history in the PCF of either denying or evading the whole question of colonialism and imperialism, and that it is impossible to imagine a communist programme in a European country without raising the question of paying back retribution and damages to the colonized, whose wealth has brought up this standard of living in European countries.* They were expelled. This was another example of the denial of imperialism in the Western Left including large sections of the communist Left. Many of them just provided a Marxist wrapping to the old idea of colonialism as a civilizing mission. Writing about Warren was a way of engaging that tendency.

VP: There were some exceptions. You often point to *Monthly Review* as one exception.

AA: Paul Baran and Paul Sweezy were both extremely perceptive and major scholars of Marx, and therefore when they looked at capitalism in their time, starting in the late 1940s—when they launched *Monthly Review* in 1949—they observed the period of decolonization

_____

* *Le Nouvel Observateur*, no. 852 (9–15 March 1981), pp. 56–60.

and asked: now that these are independent states, will they have a chance to develop? They updated and rethought some of the categories of Marxism and added the very category of surplus as such—distinct from surplus value—in order to understand the political economy of growth (which was the title of Baran's 1957 book).*

Baran's book grapples with the issue of capitalism in what often gets called the periphery but I prefer to call the tricontinent. Prospects for real growth in the newly independent countries seem very bleak to him, thanks to conditions created by imperialism. A decade later, Harry Magdoff, who became the third editor of *Monthly Review*, wrote *The Age of Imperialism*, where he revisited Lenin's categories of imperialism.†

There is nothing of that kind in the *New Left Review* tradition or in the tradition of French Marxism. *NLR* and its publishing house of course publish many things on imperialism, quite a lot of them very good. But the engagement with imperialism at the level of theory itself that one found in the *MR* tradition is often missing. In that sense, what *MR* did was quite unique, and then having this tradition, they published from their publishing house an enormous amount of superb writings on China, India, and particularly on Latin America. And starting with Bukharin and Luxemburg, they also published very many theorists of imperialism. For instance, they published virtually all of Samir Amin's work in English, a practice that current editors of *MR* have continued. They were very open to publishing Marxist work on any part of the tricontinent. This included national liberation struggles, of which they did several books. Sweezy and Magdoff were in and out of Cuba. They published brilliant stuff on Cuba, Chile, on Guinea-Bissau, on Mozambique; on revolution, counter-revolution, and national liberation struggles. They were the ones who engaged with the whole

* Paul Baran, *The Political Economy of Growth*, New York: Monthly Review Press, 1957.

† Harry Magdoff, *The Age of Imperialism: The Economics of US Foreign Policy*, New York: Monthly Review Press, 1969.

range of politics and economy in the tricontinent, any region wherever they would find a good Marxist analysis. And they never compromised on the fundamentally Marxist character of the books they wanted to publish and, likewise, *Monthly Review*—the magazine—did exactly the same thing. I knew Magdoff quite well. Sweezy was responsive and affectionate but he had the manners of a New England patrician which I sometimes found hard to negotiate. I used to go often to lunches in their office where many like-minded people congregated, including Marxists and communists from around the world who happened to be visiting New York at the time. There would be Portuguese communists one time and ANC [African National Congress] militants some other time or individuals like Mészáros on some other occasion. When I was living in New York I used to drop in quite often and also published a few articles with them.* They wanted articles that were not more than five thousand words, preferably less, which did not use any jargon because the reading publics they had in mind included students, prisoners, and so on. They wanted to create a particular kind of Marxist political culture unlike any other journal.

VP: While you engaged with Bill Warren, Ronald Reagan and the United States are making their push into Central America as the military dictatorships in Latin America flourish—blatant imperialism, no?

AA: Yes, but that too is a broader and continuing tendency in which Warren participated at the time. If the occasion arose, Warren would of course denounce Reagan and CIA and Pentagon and so forth. But when it came to the theoretical argument, he and others would say that

---

* For instance, Aijaz Ahmad, 'Bangladesh: The Internationalization of Counter-Revolution; Supplemental Remarks', *Monthly Review*, vol. 26, no. 8 (January 1975); 'Imperialism and Revolution in South Asia', *Monthly Review*, vol. 26, no. 10 (March 1975); 'The Arab Stasis', *Monthly Review*, vol. 27, no. 1 (May 1975).

they were tracing the long-term logic of capital—that capital *per se* is blind to race, nationality, etc. The terms of their thought are very much like the argumentation that goes into Francis Fukuyama's notion of the 'end of history'. The victory of neoliberalism is permanent, Fukuyama will argue, but that doesn't mean that there won't be episodes and hiccups, like the little wars in Afghanistan and Iraq. Imperialism in the long run will bring capitalism, Warren and the like would say, which is better than feudalism and other forms of precapitalism, and so—says Warren—imperialism is an instrument of progress.

VP: At this time, across the tricontinent there are intellectuals building their own accounts of imperialism—I'm thinking of the ECLAC [Economic Commission for Latin America and the Caribbean] school in Chile, Walter Rodney and Issa Shivji in Tanzania, and those involved in the mode of production debate in India. All these, in different ways, are Left critics of dependency theory. Reading your critique of Warren, it seems like your voice is less the voice of somebody reading Warren and responding to it, and more the voice of someone in dialogue with those debates in the tricontinent. It seems that in your article there is an enormous amount of reading behind it—work from Latin America and India.

AA: Yes, in several ways, yes. The Marxist scholarship in India of this period is of a very high quality. I knew the transition debate here. I had read Irfan Habib admiringly and extensively, including his writing precisely on this question of whether or not a transition to capitalism was possible in India without the colonial intervention; I learnt a lot from his essay on the subject even though with one caveat. I am for the most part a bit sceptical of too much emphasis on the counterfactual; what *might* have happened *if* this did not happen. And I read a lot on Latin America, by Latin Americans, including the dependency theorists, as well as Western Latin Americanists, some of whom were my friends and even colleagues in two cases. *Monthly*

Review, the magazine and the press, was important in that regard but I also had whole files of NACLA [the North American Congress on Latin America] and *Latin American Perspectives.* Some of the members of editorial collectives of those journals were friends. I was also just besotted with left-wing Latin American cinema of that time and often used those films in my courses on the sociology of development. The Cuban Revolution had of course been a central event in my political formation. I was very much aware of all those debates and, therefore, the position of that essay is essentially, sort of, a tricontinental position against this particular brand of Western Marxism.

VP: The 'intermediate classes' essay is a cautionary tale. There's a quote from Gramsci that anchors the essay: 'In the typical peripheral countries, a broad spectrum of intermediate classes stretches between the proletariat and capitalism—classes which seek to carry on policies of their own and with ideologies which influence broad strata of the proletariat but which particularly affect the peasant masses.' I was rereading the essay and I thought this is very interesting because this refers back to the work you had already done on Pakistan and this question of intermediate classes emerging in these societies. Societies with states that were not strong enough to withstand imperialist pressure and the relationship between intermediate classes and imperialism are things one needs to think about a lot if one wants to understand the weakness of some of these newly independent countries. What were the kinds of debates that produced this essay?

AA: This essay is partly in debate with Hamza Alavi. Hamza was actually the first to write about the post-colonial state.* He asked: where does the military-bureaucratic state emerge from? He then argues that in the post-colonial situation, the landowning classes are unable to dominate that state by themselves while the indigenous bourgeoisie is

---

* For example, Hamza Alavi, 'The State in Post-Colonial Societies: Pakistan and Bangladesh', *New Left Review,* no. 74 (July–August 1972).

weak and the colonizing bourgeoisie has retreated so that the military-bureaucratic state becomes relatively autonomous of the indigenous dominant classes, which are too weak, as well as the external ruling class which can now intervene only through the agency of the formally independent post-colonial state which helps negotiate the competing interests of the various propertied classes inside and outside the country thanks to its relative independence from all those classes. My argument with Hamza is that his argument is not really anchored in class politics; that his is a structural-functionalist argument. Where do these bureaucratic, military strata come from? What is their social basis? His 'military-bureaucratic strata' is not anchored in any class. The bourgeoisie as a class is too weak but the state has to be anchored in some kind of class formation. So, what is the class situation of this relative autonomy of the state? It is here that the intermediate classes come in since these provide the social basis of the state, not as a ruling class but as what Engels called 'the governing caste' which he distinguishes sharply from the ruling class as such. Personnel drawn from the intermediate classes use their positions of power in civil and military bureaucracies for a sort of primitive accumulation through what gets called 'corruption' so as to become a distinct fraction of the propertied ruling classes. It is, in fact, a competition between the bourgeoisie—the existing, weak bourgeoisie—and the rising strata from the middle classes on its way to becoming the bourgeoisie of the future. So that was the idea, the main motivation for me. I was also reading Gramsci and trying to come to terms with many things in Gramsci, and yes, conceptually also trying to figure out how to think about Gramsci in terms of Pakistan, India, Malaysia, and so on. Gramsci has remained a major anchor of my thought ever since.

VP: Pakistan was the immediate reference for the essay, but this was a dynamic that had resonance from the Andean countries to Southeast Asia (Thailand had a coup in 1977) and then across Africa.

Ruth First's *Barrel of the Gun* engaged with the question of the coup and the military-bureaucratic state.[*]

AA: I think maybe I should read Ruth First's book again. I have no memory of it. I was thinking about Algeria—not through Fanon, but the Algerian Revolution itself—a country where the bourgeoisie of the colonial period was entirely external and where the army of the revolution—the *external army*, one must remember—became the new military-bureaucratic governing caste that has been more or less successful in occluding its accumulation of property directly through governance of the country. My absorption in studying various aspects of the Algerian revolution predates my encounter with Fanon. I had high regard for Amílcar Cabral, and I was thinking a lot about his essays which, as you know, pose this problem of the petty bourgeoisie as something of a surrogate bourgeoisie in the Portuguese colonies.[†] The Portuguese state and its own metropolitan bourgeoisie were too backward to have produced a colonial bourgeoisie even to the extent that British colonialism did in India. It had produced a petty bourgeoisie of colonial functionaries who were alienated from the people. According to Cabral, social alienation is specific to the petty bourgeoisie in such situations and accounts for even a cultural contradiction between the petty bourgeoisie and the peasantry which is not alienated from its own cultural roots. The problem of identification with the culture of the colonial masters is strictly a petty bourgeois problem, not that of the peasantry. Again, this whole line of argument in Cabral can be read as a variant of the question of the intermediate classes.

VP: This alienation can lead into nationalisms of resentment;

* Ruth First, *Barrel of a Gun: Political Power in Africa and the Coup d'Etat*, Harmondsworth: Penguin, 1972.
† Amílcar Cabral, *Return to the Source: Selected Speeches of Amilcar Cabral*, ed. Africa Information Service, New York: Monthly Review Press, 1973; and *Unity and Struggle: Speeches and Writings of Amilcar Cabral*, New York: Monthly Review Press, 1979.

very toxic, backward-looking kinds of nationalism. This is there in Gramsci's warnings about how this kind of petty-bourgeois alienation impacts the peasant masses, because it is from this petty bourgeoisie that the schoolteachers are recruited.

AA: Absolutely. The argument here is that the petty bourgeoisie *imparts* its own alienation to the peasantry through its pedagogical function as schoolteachers and even as country priests. Actually, Gramsci has a very dialectical view of the social location of the priest in the countryside and neighbourhoods of the poor in the cities. The priest carries out the project of conservatism and conformism on behalf of the upper echelons of the Church but he also identifies with the real material conditions that structures of property impose on his flock. This social functionary of religion is thus often quite capable of class radicalism. This too is part of Gramsci's highly dialectical view of the role of religion and of the Church itself in Italian society and particularly in the South. Some of this comes through in *The Southern Question*, which is about the peasant masses of Italy. A key argument here is that in the Italy of his time, where the peasant strata are the bulk of the country and where there is a great gulf between Northern and Southern regions, winning over the peasant masses—who have their own organic intellectuals, namely the priests—is critical for the proletariat to make any great advance. He also argues that classes of the capitalist mode were not fully polarized as in the advanced capitalist countries; there were layers and layers of intermediate classes, class fractions, diverse social strata, between the bourgeoisie and the proletariat, and then a destitute peasant mass beneath them, especially in the South. Gramsci himself was a Sardinian, a Southerner before he became a militant and a leader for Italy as a whole. For Gramsci, this whole complexity—even ambiguities—of class formation all along the axis, from the apex to the base, was the real thing—what he sometimes called the 'physiognomy of the country'. But I was also thinking of Algeria, precisely because the upper layers of the *colons* constituted the ruling class among the settlers; even though there were also other class layers among the *colons*, urban and rural, and some of them were very impoverished, but if you remove the *colons* all that is left in the upper levels of society are the Algerian intermediate classes without a bourgeoisie or even large landowners. The intermediate strata do not have any accumulation of their own. Some of them have adopted the French language and imbibed French manners, while the bulk remains Islamic and Arabic-speaking, and both of these, the Franco-Algerian and the Arabo-Islamic, want to evade, even suppress the Berber— the Amazigh—question. How will these contradictions among the indigenous middle classes be settled? What will be the glue of their nationhood? What will be their respective relations with imperialism? What will be the relations between the new state and the vast pools of Islamic reaction? Such questions have been on my mind for a long time.

VP: But when I was reading this essay, I was thinking of the RSS. Now obviously, the Indian story is different; a confident bourgeoisie emerged before Independence, having written the Bombay Plan in 1944, they have a vision for the country. It is a vast country and the bourgeoisie is not able to command the entirety of the country. Intermediate groups emerge. What do they have to do with the RSS and the rise of Hindutva?

AA: Well, that is a whole other can of worms. I want sometimes to draw lines of demarcation between capitalist and bourgeois. We use the term 'bourgeoisie' for Indian capitalists, and I do too because that is customary. But the Indian capitalist class as such, with few exceptions like Jamshedji Tata or some other Parsi capitalists, have never struck me as particularly bourgeois; they are more like carpetbaggers, largely *lalajis* in their mentality. Their religion is money. They have no historic or cultural mission of their own. The German capitalist classes did not oppose the Nazis out of the genuine class fear of communists and surrendered themselves to Hitler only after his power had become unassailable. The Indian capitalist class never put up any bourgeois resistance to the horrifically plebeian conduct of the Shiv Sainiks or the RSS goons. Shiv Sena was in fact largely their own creation as a gang of goons to fight communists and trade unions, before that gang got out of control and developed autonomous sources of power as spokespeople both of Maratha sub-nationalism and the Hindutva variety of religio-ethnic nationalism. After the Bombay carnage of 1992 Jamshedji is reputed to have been the only capitalist who called for the arrest of Bal Thackeray, though that too in the privacy of secret meetings between government and Business. The non-bourgeois character of this capitalist class explains their many collaborations with Shiv Sena thugs in India's financial capital itself, long after Shiv Sena had ceased to be just a gang of anti-communist goons. And it also explains why so many of them gravitated so very easily towards the RSS, just as the princely families of yore had done in the past and just as urban merchants of the *Vania* castes have financed the RSS and its fronts all along. Whatever bourgeois culture exists in India comes from distinct fractions of the middle classes. Even the chief luminaries of the Indian nationalist movement came from the middle classes and an inordinate number of them were barristers and lawyers. Nehru, a Kashmiri Pandit and son of a wealthy lawyer, came to be seen as 'aristocratic' because in his personal culture he was a proper bourgeois. Which could not be said of the Mahatma, Patel and the rest. So, this question of the middle classes in India cuts in far too many ways.

The nationalist character of the Indian bourgeoisie—of the Birlas and the Bajajs and other patrons of the Mahatma—is largely a myth. They wanted the British to leave so that they could inherit the vast machinery of exploitation. They fit perfectly the Fanonian portrait of the national bourgeoisie as a useless class. As for the Bombay Plan, it came into being because Nehru and some others of the Congress Left succeeded in getting sections of the Bombay capitalists to understand that an extensive public sector, a protectionist economy, etc., were in their own long-term class interest. Much of the inspiration that went into the Bombay Plan died bit by bit after Independence.

The question of the RSS is also very complex. I have written many essays on Indian communalism and *inter alia* also about the RSS and its fronts but never methodically of its class character. That is a great weakness of my writings on the RSS. I have been preoccupied by its political project; its character as a formation of the far right and its relations with capital and empire are taken as givens of the situation. Even when I have written about its impact on various classes and castes in India that is still not about the class character of the RSS itself. I have never budged from my position that the RSS is intrinsically fascist in character and, like the classical fascisms of yesteryear, it is not simply a creation of either the landlord class or of the bourgeoisie. The Maharashtrian Brahmins who founded it and have always played a major role in it came from various fractions of the middle classes. However, a petty bourgeois of the upper castes often has ideas of exaggerated grandeur for himself and his kind. The middle-class Maharashtrian Brahmins of the RSS fancy themselves as the inheritors of the state Shivaji built, hence of the state that opposed the Mughals and was dismembered by the British, hence the rightful rulers of India after the Mughal and the British rulers are gone. That is the ideological fabrication of their self-image which is then shared by all the top brass of the RSS whether or not they are Maharashtrians themselves. In this ideology, Hindu *rashtra* was really the very expansive version of the old Maharashtra, the last of the great Hindu kingdoms. It was in its origins a revivalist, strictly reactionary idea of the Indian nation on the part of a fraction of the provincial middle classes in opposition to the modernizing mission of the middle-class fractions that led the Indian National Congress, and this modernizing fraction included very prominently the Mahatma, all his chatter about Ram Rajya et cetera notwithstanding. No wonder that many of the great feudal landlords, the old ruling families of some of the princely states, patronized the RSS and large sections of shopkeepers financed them. But the princely states represented a defeated class; their power was greatly curtailed by the Nehrus and the Patels, hence their hatred of the Nehruvian Congress. RSS remained a marginal force until the 1950s when it began to assimilate more and more of the Hindu Right into itself and started gaining the confidence of the disgruntled capitalists after the failure of things like the Swatantra Party. Sections of the Indian right wing and of the capitalist class itself gravitated towards the RSS until a much larger coalition of such forces could be formed. That coalition then launched an extra-constitutional movement for regime change and right-wing takeover with hysterical slogans like 'Total Revolution'. That bid for regime change was led nominally by Jayaprakash Narayan but propelled methodically by the RSS cadres, which forced Indira Gandhi to declare the Emergency. She managed to interrupt the movement for immediate regime change, but the damage had been done and the RSS soon walked into Parliament with ninety-four members, capturing some key ministries. The closer they came to state power the more many sections of the capitalist class began shifting towards them, until, after the 2002 pogrom, virtually the whole of the upper crust of that class came to underwrite Modi's rise. Even so, RSS and its fronts are not the creation of that capital; capitalists united behind them only after their political opponents collapsed and they became the preeminent contenders for power. As Engels understood very well, there is always a certain distinction, a structural gap, between the ruling class and the governing caste. In post-colonial societies this governing caste is drawn overwhelmingly from the middle classes. We know more about the objective class character of the RSS but much less about its subjective class composition.

VP: It's so interesting to recognize that the language that you are using has disappeared. These are terms—intermediate classes, class analysis—that emerge from your essays in the 1980s, but this language has been so eroded in the general intellectual discourse. It is quite painful. We don't have a good analysis before us because we don't have a conceptual landscape for it. It is almost as if somebody has decided that this analytical framework has become anachronistic, and that you have to use a framework dominated by terms such as identity or religion, that you need to study the complexity of society through the framework of religious identity rather than through the question of political economy, class analysis, intermediate classes, imperialism and so on. That language has disappeared.

AA: Yes. But you know, there's something else. India has a very powerful Marxist tradition—one of the most distinguished in the world. Unlike much of the world, this tradition still continues. But there are certain problems I see that we need to address. One is the question of the nationalism that created the Indian nation. We rarely have the kind of theoretical attitude and deep scepticism towards our own nationalist past that Gramsci, for instance, has towards the Risorgimento. We often speak of this or that weakness or even error of Gandhi or Nehru or whoever, but we have no extensive critique of the structure as a whole. The short assessment of Gandhi that EMS published was a long time ago. Has any Indian Marxist of my generation—or of yours, for that matter—undertaken a bold, fearless critique of the Mahatma and the kind of nationalist movement he led? Gramsci quite correctly traces the defeat of Italian communism to the kind of nation the Risorgimento had bequeathed. We have no such thoughtful scepticism about the foundational moments of the nation as such. The second problem is that while we have produced great economists and historians we don't pay enough close attention to the political writings of Marx and we tend to read Marx's philosophical writings very un-philosophically. Theoretically, I have hardly ever seen any influence of Marxist writings such as *The Eighteenth Brumaire*. How does the dialectical method really work when you deploy this method not on the abstract theoretical level of the mode of production, for example, or in analysing long historical periods of the past, such as the transition from feudalism to capitalism, but when you try to analyse a determinate conjuncture in your time with the class content often occluded by the daily practices of political parties, bureaucratic institutions, ideological state apparatuses, and mass politics in the streets? Which is, of course, the crux of what Marx and Engels had written about the German revolution and counter-revolution, and what they had written about class struggles in France. They had done so much work on how classes actually functioned between 1848 and 1852—which Marx theoretically and conceptually condenses in *The Eighteenth Brumaire*. I have never seen any serious writings on the RSS in India that draw upon this politically nuanced side of Marx.

VP: What about outside India in the last twenty years?

AA: Outside India things are very different in different places, and I am not competent to speak of many of those places. If I had time, what I would like to do is to republish each of Marx's important political and philosophical texts with introductions that would place the texts in their context and also provide some sort of commentary that facilitates reading of the texts. *Economic and Philosophic Manuscripts* (1844), with perhaps a fifty-page introduction, *The Gotha Programme*, the 1857 and 1859 prefaces—and so on. The intention would be to introduce a new generation to the breadth and political acuity of Marx, not just the economics. If you separate Marx's economics from the rest of his writings, you will be closer to Left Keynesianism.

VP: Ignoring the breath of the Marxist method, you could devolve—as Warren did—into a developmentalism, with the Asian Tigers' economic data somehow suggesting that there is no imperialism. They don't take these societies or their context seriously.

AA: If these Asian Tigers were not small frontline states against

China, the Americans would have never given them what they gave them on the basis of which they became what they became. South Korea and Taiwan benefited from proximity to China. Americans told them to undertake radical land reforms or fall to the communism of their Chinese neighbours. They allowed a level of state control of the economy in both South Korea and Taiwan of a kind they never allowed the Latin American Left. And Americans gave them, or got for them from Japan, not only investment money but also cutting-edge technology. These countries gained a lot from the Chinese Revolution because Americans made sure that their level of capitalist development was so high that the revolutionary movements in both Taiwan and South Korea would be suppressed. That's not the logic of capitalism *per se*. That's the logic of American imperialism in a very particular historical situation.

POSTCOLONIALISM

VP: We are coming towards your most important book—*In Theory*, which comes out in 1992. In the 1980s, *Subaltern Studies* begins to appear, initially fairly straightforward narrative histories with certain pronouncements from Ranajit Guha that presage what comes next. You see texts that understand imperialism to be merely metaphorical. Postmodernism has its impact. Out of all this comes postcolonialism.

AA: *Subaltern Studies* and postcolonialism are neither identical nor reducible to each other. That is a category error Vivek Chibber makes in his book on the subject. Convergence between them was contrived later by the academic market, particularly in the United States. Subalternism arose in areas of history and social sciences, specifically in relation to India. Ranajit Guha had once been a communist militant; Partha Chatterjee used to write for *Frontier* in its heyday; Sumit Sarkar, who was in the original collective and left later, certainly had a very powerful Marxist grounding (I am not sure if he ever was or was not member of a communist party); even the first books of Gyan Prakash and Dipesh Chakrabarty's are not innocent of Marxist and communist categories of analysis. There were others like David Hardiman who did good empirical work. For Sumit Sarkar in that phase of his work the main inspiration was E.P. Thompson, 'History from Below', and social history as distinct from political history *per se*. But then the project of *Subaltern Studies* began to change perceptibly after the first four or five volumes and traffic between subalternists and postcolonialists begins at that point, becoming more brisk in later years. In this regard, a major moment for the Western academic market was the appearance of *Selected Subaltern Studies* (eds. Ranajit Guha and Gayatri Spivak) in 1988. Spivak wrote an Introduction that formed the bridge between postcolonialism and subalternism, and Edward Said contributed a Foreword. It was Said who squarely identified Guha as a post-structuralist and later said that subalternists were the ones who will carry on his legacy.

The subalternist project was also a decade older than the very term 'postcolonial'. The first volume of *Subaltern Studies* appears in 1982. Robert Young—who later appeared as a major theorist of postcolonialism—published *White Mythologies* in 1990.* Half of the book consists of the three essays on Edward Said, Gayatri Spivak, and Homi Bhabha. The word 'postcolonialism' does not appear in the index. Half of the book written by a future master of postcolonialism about the first three masters of postcolonialism does not mention the word. Postcolonialism is that new! A good deal of what came to be covered by this term was of course published earlier but the term *postcolonialism* itself starts gaining momentum and significant marketability around 1992, mainly in areas of literary and cultural theory.

How would I look at all this now, historically and structurally? I

---

* Robert C. Young, *White Mythologies: Writing History and the West*, London: Routledge, 1990.

would place such phenomena largely in the context of a world-historic crisis that begins in mid-1970s that I have described at some length in *In Theory*. That is when the retreat of Third World nationalism and the communist state system in fact begins, leading to the dismantling of communism first in China and then, some years later, in the Soviet Union and the Comecon [the Council for Mutual Economic Assistance] countries generally. One way of putting it is that while we were celebrating the liberation of Vietnam, the central event of that time—looking back—was actually the 1973 coup in Chile against Salvador Allende. This is the time when many projects begin to sprout within the broad Left that openly advocate conscious repudiation of classical Marxist categories. Guha's programmatic statement in the very first volume draws away from the established frames of Marxist class analysis and recommends terms like 'elite' and 'subaltern' as alternatives but with flexibilities of their own. Some social force may be elite in relation to another social force but at the same time subaltern to some other one. This repudiation is often done in the name of Gramsci, with the use of the word 'subaltern' and so on.

VP: We used to joke in this period that the Marxist you can take home to meet your parents is Gramsci. Between *Subaltern Studies* (1981) and *Hegemony and Socialist Strategy* (1985) by Chantal Mouffe and Ernesto Laclau, you had the construction of Gramsci an anti-Marxist.

AA: And an anti-communist in particular. Gramsci becomes a great father figure in what the world of Western theory calls the Cultural Turn. The culturalism that broadly underwrites the Cultural Turn proposes that culture is not only *an* instance of humanity's social experience but the *determining* instance. Classical Marxist theory assigns very great importance to the social and the cultural but political economy is what is assigned the power of ultimate determination. We can argue over what the word 'determination' means in Marxist thought. But this power to determine, or to set limits and define possibilities of historical change, is never given over to culture as such. That is what gets done in so many varieties of post-Marxism.

VP: What is so interesting to me is that from *Subaltern Studies* to Laclau and Mouffe to Stuart Hall, a range of people from different places, you find Gramsci as the person used to validate the cultural turn. Even Edward Said's *Orientalism* (1978) uses Gramsci in this way. What is there in Gramsci that is available to them?

AA: I do think that the kind of question that Gramsci raises can always be read or misread that way, particularly in the period when communism has been so much on the retreat. He is a great Marxist philosopher of defeat, unlike Lenin. By the time Luxemburg was defeated, she was also killed; when we read her we can only see her tremendous revolutionary elan and faith in revolutionary change. Mao is the theorist of innovations in revolutionary strategy that eventually led to a great victory. Gramsci is the theorist of defeat. He's trying to theorize this defeat. He asks: what is it in our society in Italy that all our work of so many years just gets wiped out in a matter of six or seven years as Mussolini's fascists take over the country? A structural explanation of a historical nature was needed to explain that reality. I mean, Gramsci was Marxist enough to say that there must be an actual material basis in our society, in our history, the kind of people we are, that enables this capture. That is exactly the question I ask about the rise and broad acceptance of the RSS in India. What is it about our country, about our society, about our history that makes it possible? That is a question that only a historical materialist would ask. Gramsci turns all the way back to the entire history and development of Italian culture, society, and looks at the typical kinds of classes, the typical kinds of intelligentsia that came out of that history. He is doing all this to read the present moment of defeat as a communist, as a Leninist in fact. That is not the kind of question subalternists or Laclau are asking.

Instead, they hold on to his studies of intellectuals, Church, religion, etc., and turn it all into a culturalism. They strip away the politics and take the insights episodically. Stuart Hall did a short piece on Gramsci.* None of these others have ever done a systematic analysis of Gramsci, nor any close reading of the sort Perry Anderson once did.

I wrote the essay on Gramsci—'Reading Gramsci in the Days of Hindutva'—soon after the demolition of the Babri Masjid had been televised and I had viewed that viscerally as a fascist spectacle. I actually read or re-read virtually everything of Gramsci that was available in English. I was just at the very beginning of collecting my thoughts not just about that event but about the Hindutva project, its social roots. I no longer subscribe to the kind of parallel I tried to establish between Italy and India in that essay but I did cull quotation after quotation from a very comprehensive reading of the texts to create a different kind of trajectory of Gramsci's thought, even on the question of culture, from what these people have ever done.† *Subaltern Studies* was always much too cursory and much too certain about the word 'subaltern' as it appears in Gramsci. What did Gramsci mean by 'subaltern'? Read just a few pages of Anderson's essay on Gramsci and you get to understand how many different ways the word 'subaltern' is used in the prison notebooks.‡ Subaltern here is the word for the working class, there it is the word for the intellectuals of the ruling class. He was trying to pass his text by the censors, and he was developing his categories of analysis at the same time, from one notebook to the next.

VP: Neither did Laclau and Mouffe do a full text on Gramsci. You

* Stuart Hall, 'Gramsci and Us', in *The Hard Road to Renewal: Thatcherism and the Crisis of the Left*, London: Verso, 1988.
† Aijaz Ahmad, 'Fascism and National Culture: Reading Gramsci in the Days of Hindutva', *Social Scientist*, vol. 21, nos. 3–4 (March–April 1993), pp. 32–68; republished in *Lineages of the Present*.
‡ Perry Anderson, 'The Antinomies of Antonio Gramsci', *New Left Review*, no. 100 (November–December 1976).

know, there's a straight line between, say, the incoherent literature on populism today and the abandonment of that language that you were working through in the early 1980s. Laclau writes a book of essays that tries to come to terms with Peronism, and then Mouffe now writes a lot about populism. When *Hegemony and Socialist Strategy* comes out, they move away from the language of class completely, in fact, they deride it; you then have a straight line from that book to much of the contemporary literature on populism, including the political programmes of several European Left parties. Is it even worth reflecting on that descent into a category like populism which means nothing, really?

AA: Yes, Laclau's very first book in English actually had a very long chapter on populism. Very early in *Hegemony and Socialist Strategy*, which is supposed to be influenced by Gramsci, I came upon a sentence that said something like—'The space of power is an empty space.' I shut the book and I thought: *this* in the name of Gramsci, who formulated all his pioneering thought as a prisoner of fascism; could it ever have occurred to Gramsci to claim that the space of power is an empty space?

In many cases, the bad faith is connected to radical repudiation of their own Marxist past without giving up the claim to a radicalism that is more radical than Marxism. Or you have a case like that of Derrida who writes that he was opposed to *everything* connected with communist parties but also claimed that his Deconstruction was nothing more than a 'radicalization' of Marxism. Now, much of the leftist Western intelligentsia is making that transition to, really, anti-Marxism. But they have to also cope with the fact that their only readership is on the Left; a lot of that Left comes out of some allegiance to Marxism.

VP: Your work in this period is at a remove from this sort of thing. There was a certain conceptual clarity, a structural whole around the concept of imperialism. We require an understanding of the internal class dynamics of societies weakened by colonialism or semi-colonialism; we need to understand which classes attain a certain political dominance even if they don't control the economy and so on, so then the intermediate strata is important, etc. That was a certain conceptual universe that helped provide an explanation for the rise of a kind of right wing that's not necessarily a dictatorship from above but which has a mass character. Now, the journey of Laclau and Mouffe and the post-Marxists goes to this term 'populism', which can be used to describe Donald Trump on the one hand, you know, Narendra Modi on the other, Erdoğan, Jeremy Corbyn; it's incoherent.

AA: The post-Marxists are located in the Western academic university milieu. All the modes of thought in the university press on them, and they accommodate a whole lot of all that, at the same time as they are trying to hold on to some niche which they can call 'Left'. I was never an academic in that sense. I have never published a single article in a refereed journal. Never submitted one, never want to. My location is very different. I lived in the US during periods of military dictatorship in Pakistan but always kept trying to go back to Pakistan. I have worked in Western universities because I needed to and because I really love teaching. In Pakistan, my home was in a very particular branch of the Pakistani communist movement. When all of that collapsed and the Zia dictatorship arose, I retreated to the US and waited. Very soon after that I decided to try and come back to India, because it was the country where I was born and where I grew up but primarily because it was a country where I could find a new political home. Much of my thinking is tied up with actual problems in our part of the world, and in the tricontinent more generally. So, it's a very different location. At the same time, though, I am a kind of Marxist who does believe that Marxism is an unfinished science, we have to take into account all the new developments, but from a Marxist position; from within the absolute iron frame of Marxist thought.

Therefore, I also read very widely, think and write about a great variety of things and try very hard not to reduce Marxism to a jargon. In short, I do take my role as an intellectual very seriously. But it's all, at the end of the day, connected with an active engagement with a very particular political home and identifiable political projects. I don't think the generality of leftist academics in the West have that kind of sense of their place in the world. With many honourable exceptions, of course.

RETURN TO INDIA

VP: You returned to India in 1985. What was the immediate reason to do so?

AA: Oh, there was no immediate reason. This was something I had been thinking about for many years. I grew up in India and came to Pakistan only after my high school, so there was a sense of belonging to India. When I came to Pakistan and went to college in Lahore, I always felt as an outsider. Then there was this nationality question in Pakistan much of which kept deteriorating into ethnic narrow-mindedness and xenophobia, so I started feeling even more alienated in that developing political culture. I belonged to a political party which started fragmenting towards the end of the 1970s and finally collapsed after the revolution in Afghanistan in 1978 and the Soviet intervention there two years later. I was looking for a political home because I no longer had one. I could not go back to Pakistan where I no longer had a firm political home and it was also quite risky for me after Zia-ul-Haq's coup. So, all these things were percolating in my mind. I decided that I didn't want to live in the United States; it was a very alienating experience for me, although by then I had lived in New York almost as long as I had lived in India or Pakistan. The communist movement in India was attractive as a possible political home. And a memory of the India of my childhood had always felt like an unfinished business of my life.

When I first went to explore the possibility of moving back I was still travelling on a Pakistani passport. People I spoke to told me that living in India was possible but not on a Pakistani passport. I had to have a Western passport. I returned to New York and acquired an American passport, which is also a story in itself. In any case, my reason for acquiring an American passport was very ironic—I got it to live in India, which was my birthplace. After I returned with this new passport, I soon became a Fellow at the Nehru Memorial Museum and Library.

VP: You had familiarity with the Indian intellectual world, but now being back in Delhi you had a deeper link, and you quickly got involved with politics. What were the new themes that were beginning to enter your thought, your work, your imagination?

AA: The first thing that I experienced was that the intellectual culture in Pakistan was so incomparably backward compared to India, and that I had to catch up with those higher standards of intellectual calibre. The other was that I realized within a few weeks of being in India that it would take me two, three, four years to actually understand where I am—that I really didn't know India except in this sentimental way of thinking, you know, that this is my home. I never believed that just being born someplace gives you any understanding of that place; the whole litany of identity politics. I actually went into another learning mode. I had spent the late 1970s and the first half of the 1980s reading an enormous amount; it was in those years that I think I became an intellectual. In India, I launched upon some three or four years of learning about India; again, a lot of reading, lots of meetings with intellectuals and activists, increasing involvement with party intellectuals. There was a learning curve, a very important learning curve.

VP: What were you reading in this time?

AA: Until then I had read about India very superficially here and there. A bit of Kosambi, part of Irfan Habib, part of Amiya Bagchi, Bipan Chandra from his early phase; things like that. Now I started reading more systematically, in two different directions. One, I read immense amounts on Indian history and society, more or less regardless of the political orientations of the author. That in fact included writings from the Right all the way from writings of the right-wing historians to files of the *Organiser*. At the same time, I launched upon reading the works of Indian Marxists. I read a lot of EMS. I read as much Ranadive as I could find. I remember acquiring all the three volumes of Ranadive on trade unions. I read CPI(M) [Communist Party of India (Marxist)] party literature very, very regularly and as much of it as I could. I read Sukomal Sen, the whole history of Indian communism. There were these many volumes of the Communist Party of India's history issued by the CPI; the CPI(M)'s volumes came later. I read all that stuff. By the end of four or five years of this I had several bookcases filled with books on India, and the bookcases kept multiplying subsequently.

VP: When did you start feeling that you need to understand the cultural side, namely caste. I do remember very well you talking about how the new literature on things like caste had made these quite superficial observations that caste and maybe even various forms of identity were socially constructed, that they had roots in colonialism and so on, and I remember you saying that there is a longer history. When did you start going back and reading the earlier histories and drawing some of those conclusions?

AA: Yes. I think you're referring to my own comments on things like *Subaltern Studies*, and the colonial construction both of communalism and caste—this is more or less the *Subaltern Studies* notion. I had difficulty with Gyanendra Pandey's book on communalism as a colonial construction. On a conceptual level, the idea of constructed identities is a turn towards the discursive, the cultural. It is a turn away from materialist explanations to discursive explanations. The linguistic turn and the culturalist turn in which it is discourse that determines history—in this case colonial discourse. Colonial administration, through census making for instance, is said to create or shape religious communities and caste communities into political subjects. This leaves open the question of what was the *real* that was constructed? There had to have been a material base—a historical, sociological, material base—which could then be represented in colonial discourse that way; but representation does not create the realities. There are some other realities which representation and administration may alter and shape, that is true. But what were the real relations? For example, when it is said that these were very *fuzzy* communities which were sharpened by colonial intervention, it begs the question: fuzzy communities? But caste was *never* a fuzzy community. These were very hard and fast communities. I mean, if you have a society in which if a Dalit's shadow falls ... or a Dalit is walking on one side of the street and the wind comes from this way and touches the Brahmin ...

VP: The fellow has to run and have a bath!

AA: The fellow has to run, yes. The Dalit is pollution personified and therefore his very presence pollutes the Brahmin; not only a touch, a shadow. I rather agree with Suvira Jaiswal, for instance, who argues that Brahminism is at heart not so much an orthodoxy as an orthopraxy. In other words, beliefs can be elastic so long as caste boundaries remain rigid. So there is nothing fuzzy about it but that is what Sudipta Kaviraj and people like that say endlessly*—communities were fuzzy, there were no sharp lines, it is the colonials who constructed these sharp lines and so on. This strikes me as a deep denial of what Brahminism has actually been, historically.

---

* Sudipta Kaviraj, 'The Imaginary Institution of India', *Subaltern Studies VII*, eds. Partha Chatterjee and Gyan Pandey, Delhi: Oxford University Press, 1993.

VP: It's completely different from Ambedkar, for instance, who always understood the hardness.

AA: That's right, yes. It's an absolutely Brahminical notion; it's a denial of the reality of what caste in India is. So, one of the things that happened is that I started reading people like Ambedkar, whatever was available of Periyar in English, whatever was available on caste. I read a great deal about caste, which had a cumulative effect on me over ten to fifteen years. It altered my sense of India. Caste was something that I became aware of in India very quickly. Having lived in Pakistan for a long time, and then coming to India with this notion that India had these great communist parties, and that it had Gandhi, Nehru, secularism and so on, I was so shocked by the subservience of the oppressed classes, which I immediately connected with caste. The way the upper caste, affluent types even *speak* to the poorer people; in Pakistan, they would get beaten up. In Pakistan, you embraced everybody from your own gender, you know, regardless of class, caste, and religion. Two men meet, they embrace. I come to Delhi and I find people born in upper caste families who no longer believe in caste divisions and who may even be on the left, politically, but who keep a certain physical distance even among friends, for whom an embrace is not a way of greeting each other. I connected that immediately with caste.

VP: That's very interesting. But it's also a class thing as well, because in different parts of India, you see different ways in which bodies function.

AA: Of course, sure, but I'm talking about the Delhi intelligentsia, left-wing Delhi intelligentsia among whom I was living; you say hello from a distance. But it is also true of many social conglomerates all over North India. So, for me, it was a very strange custom. I connected all of this with purity-pollution. The way people drink water; you pick up the bottle and keep it inches away from your mouth while you drink water from it—why can't you just put it in your mouth? I don't even know how to drink water like that! In the world that shaped me it was common for several people to drink water from the same glass. So just daily life, how bodies function, how manners function . . . simple daily things; what is no longer a belief but has become custom.

VP: And you know those are not rooted in some very modern period, these go back much longer.

AA: I connected all of this with caste almost immediately. Subservience of the oppressed classes of the kind that you find in India is [rooted in] caste; you don't find it in a country like Pakistan which has no or very little communist or socialist influence. The great majority of Muslims are converts. So, caste too has been carried into the life of South Asian Muslims. But not as purity-pollution, untouchability, who can enter the upper caste's kitchen and who cannot, who is allowed to eat with whom. It does manifest itself in choice of marriage alliances, things of that sort.

VP: But not in everyday life experiences and this consciousness of subservience, and so on, or superiority on the other side.

AA: Right, right. So, I became aware of caste in India on this level and increasingly began to understand that you really can't study either Indian society or politics without understanding caste. Soon enough, I also realized how caste was important in electoral politics, for example.

VP: You were reading all this Indian Marxist literature, but much of it doesn't absorb this lesson; the lesson of the pervasiveness of caste in society, the obstacles that it poses for praxis. So, what was your feeling about the literature you were reading at the same time as you were beginning to absorb this lesson from everyday life?

AA: Well, I came to understand very early the left-Ambedkarite thesis to be correct; that annihilation of caste is a precondition for class revolution in India. That, I think, has to be absorbed in communist practice and it has been absorbed rather spottily, unevenly and not deeply enough.

VP: I just watched a short video of Ambedkar being interviewed by the BBC, where he is sitting in a chair, the BBC reporter is sitting next to him and they're sort of looking into the distance and talking to each other; it's quite a charming little video. And the reporter talks about democracy in India and that the leaders are committed to ending caste and Ambedkar says, all nonsense; he says you need action. And then at one point, Ambedkar says, you don't just need a vote; democracy is a strange thing because people need to eat, they need a house, they need to live with dignity. And then the reporter says, well you sound like a communist and Ambedkar says, well yes, you know, this might very well be the way forward and that's in the 1940s.

AA: Oh, yes. Ambedkar's own ambivalences fascinate me. By education, conviction and temperament, he is a very recognizable kind of Anglo-American constitutionalist. Such people tend to be socially and politically quite conservative. But as a man of Dalit origin and fighter for annihilation of caste, he can be neither socially nor politically a conservative in the Indian context. Hence his sense of unease with mere constitutionalism and merely formal arrangements of representative democracy. Meanwhile, his understanding of caste is very acute. He knows that caste justice is a matter neither of juridic equality which is what liberalism proposes nor a question of class tokenism of reservations in educational institutions or government. He understands caste as a matter of dignified social existence as well as acute deprivation in all aspects of human life, including of course the economic. To the extent that communism is a doctrine of radical and substantive equality, not merely formal equality, Ambedkar would be time and again attracted to it. But, for the most part, he was infuriated by the relative indifference to caste in the theory and practice of Indian communism of that time—just as he was repulsed by Gandhi's duplicities on the question of caste. I have often wondered what Ambedkar's attitude would have been if CPI had acknowledged the primacy of caste, the absolutely fundamental link between caste and class, in Indian society, and if it had consistently adopted a real programme of action in that light. In that case, Ambedkar might have faced a crisis in his liberal constitutionalism.

VP: You had mentioned earlier that you had read EMS and BTR; at this time, do you recall reading those writings from the seventies on caste, class, and property relations, the review of Gail Omvedt, and essays on the Non-Brahmin movement.* Do you remember engaging with these texts?

AA: Yes, I read quite a few of those writings. Caste was of course a very punctual feature in the thinking of EMS from virtually the very beginning. Less so for Ranadive, I think, but what he said on the subject was very acute. But I felt there was very little reflection of it in the party programmes, in party functioning, as far as I could see in, for example, the party's programmatic documents of that period. I'm not that aware of any groundwork, but I think that this is an area in which the united CPI could have done a lot more. In a later period, from latter '70s let us say, a very different kind of caste politics started gathering great momentum—what I would even describe as casteism of the upwardly mobile sections of the middle and even lower castes. I mean the Mulayams and the Lalus and the Paswans and the Mayawatis and many a lesser light. Their ideological grounding was very slippery and became very adept at playing the games of opportunism and corruption that parties of the upper castes were playing. As leaders

---

* B.T. Ranadive, 'Caste, Class and Property Relations', *Economic & Political Weekly*, vol. 14, no. 7–8 (1979), pp. 337–48, and E.M.S. Namboodiripad, 'Caste Conflicts vs Growing Unity of Popular Democratic Forces', *Economic & Political Weekly*, vol. 14, no. 7–8 (1979), pp. 329–36.

and parties of that sort came to dominate the field of caste politics the Left found it very difficult to make much of a headway on the issue of caste. Wherever and whenever the Left did make progress in this arena it was never given credit for it outside the circles of the Left itself. And particularly not by the generally recognized leaders and spokespersons of caste politics because any success by the communists in that field— in mobilizing the oppressed castes and classes, the *bahujan*—impinges upon the interests of those same leaders.

Now, if you work amongst the oppressed classes, from the rural proletariat to the urban proletariat, then you are by that very action working among the oppressed castes. So, in that sense, the parties are in practice working among the oppressed castes on questions of oppression, inequality and so on. This is one of those many areas where communist practice has never been properly theorized. There are some areas in which communist practice is actually superior to communist theorization in India and this is one of the areas that has not been theorized extensively and it is not built into the programmatic statements on how you mobilize workers, peasants, the landless of the oppressed castes *with a consciousness of the caste question*, although the communist parties have worked very much amongst these castes and members of these castes have very considerable presence in the two communist parties. It is of course very difficult to insist on the question of caste as something very fundamental without conceding ground to the casteism of the caste-based parties. In recent years, though, communists have made very considerable practical advances in this arena.

VP: That's a very good point, I think it's an important point, but— coming back to you—it says something about how you read and how you begin to develop a theory. For you, the question of praxis is not far. In other words, you're reading all this material on contemporary India, Marxist material, you're reading party literature, you're grasping

everyday life in India with all its potential and limits, and that's
entering into your theorization of Indian society, Indian culture; praxis
is a necessary and important component of the theorizing—that's the
way you read and the way you think. Now at the same time, there is
this tsunami of literature within India and outside India. We have
mentioned *Subaltern Studies* a number of times but it's not fair to say
it is only *Subaltern Studies*. This deterioration happened around the
world. There was a germination of what becomes postcolonial studies,
discourse theory, and so on. You, of course, began to engage with this
literature.

AA: I read a lot of things. I read a lot of people whose work I deeply
dislike, whose politics I deeply dislike, the politics that generates that
work I deeply dislike. But I nonetheless read them very systematically.
Not all that they are saying is wrong. And even if you are going to
oppose someone you need to know in some detail what they think and
why they think what they think. I also believe that there has been much
in *Subaltern Studies* and postcolonial theory that is of much value. I
could name any number of their articles from which I have learned.
My disagreement with them is not on this or that piece of writing but
on the fundamentals. If I reject any of their writings it will always be on
the fundamental standpoint that governs that piece of writing.

IN THEORY

VP: This conversation was eventually going to get to *In Theory*; in
fact, it has found its way there. At the start of *In Theory*, you say that
this is not a chronological book, but it is a theoretical book; the book is
held together theoretically. It seems to me that there is a debate inside
the book between the post-structuralist, postcolonial disavowal of the
very dialectics of history, and then this other world, other approach
towards social relations and material conditions. I'm very interested

in the period of preparation for this book, the essays that you wrote which were later reshaped for the book and the kind of reading you were doing as you wrote these essays, and then the book. There seem to be two sides to the preparation—on the one side, reading the Marxists and the historians, the sociologists and the literary texts to catch up with Indian studies; on the other side, the post-structuralists and *Subaltern Studies* and Edward Said. Is this a fair characterization?

AA: Yes, by and large. But I would not call it 'preparation' for this particular book. That, and much else, is what I was reading and some of my own thinking arising from all that got distilled into that book.

VP: When did you first read Edward Said's *Orientalism* and what did you think of it?

AA: I read it immediately after it was published in 1978. I was bewildered by the fact that there was an undercurrent of extreme and possibly un-thought anti-Westernism in an author whom I knew to be a very urbane, cosmopolitan, even Europeanized intellectual (if I may put it that way). Said himself had written about the anti-Arab racism he had encountered in the US, which must have been very painful I'm sure. Could it not be the case, though, that the book that came out of the answering anger was itself tinged with a shade of reverse racism? Soon enough, the book came to be showered with such immense praise from all the quarters that I respected and got treated with such vitriol from the Zionist and Zionist-inspired press that a judicious appraisal of the book's achievement as well as its weaknesses became very difficult. Then Sadiq Jalal al-Azm, who was a lifelong friend of Edward Said published an article in *Khamsin*, a short-lived journal brought out by a group of Arab and Jewish leftists living in Europe. This article was called 'Orientalism and Orientalism in Reverse'. The main proposition was quite straightforward: if the West—from Greek Antiquity to Kissinger—had constructed an unchanging Orient that was everything that the West claimed itself not to be, as Said had argued in his book, al-Azm countered with the charge that Said himself had conjured up an equally unchanging West characterized by trans-historical malice, hubris and ethnocentric aggression. It becomes very difficult, then, to examine the actual historical roots of Eurocentrism or to find a material basis for Euro-American racism. For instance, if Marx finds something negative about Indian society—say, the caste system—we can no longer entertain the possibility that there might be some truth to what he is saying. It becomes easy to quote a line or two from him and dismiss him as yet another Orientalist. So, whether or not Said approved of identity politics, the kind of argument that is central to *Orientalism*, the book, has often been used to promote identitarianism. I liked the basic thrust of al-Azm's argument. I have always thought that a critique of ourselves is the first duty of any materialist nationalism.

VP: After all, our societies and our histories were also autocratic and brutal and had their own contradictions and so on.

AA: That's right. Whether it is *Subaltern Studies* or *Orientalism*, fuzzy communities and so on—colonialism is blamed not only for all of its depredations, which are numerous, but for all the evils of our own society as well. So, that's one aspect of it. The other aspect of it, I found, was that this scholar—who is a great scholar of Western literature, not only English literature but the whole of European literature—is writing a book whose scholarship is in some key respects superficial. I knew my Dante very well, so when I came to his section on Dante's representation of Muhammad, I was struck by how Said was textually just wrong.

VP: People have said that Said drew from Erich Auerbach's *Mimesis*, with Europe collapsing into terrible wars and this longing to return to the past. There's also the shadow of Horkheimer and Adorno's *Dialectic of Enlightenment*, with the ruins of Europe after the Second World War and the Holocaust, a very bleak journey that goes from the Greeks to the present.* There is this mournful journey through a Europe that is supposedly always present, not one created in the Reformation.

AA: Auerbach was a philologist, comparatist, classicist, medievalist—and an assimilated European Jew of the old stamp. But I don't think there is any great longing for return to the past as a response to the tragedy of his own time. The account of the European tradition of literary representation in *Mimesis* begins with Homer and comes down to Virginia Woolf, right into his own time. Much mythology has been created, not the least by Said himself, about a very lonely Auerbach in Istanbul, bereft of books, mournful for the passing away of his beloved European civilization, etc. In reality, he was there in the company of other European comparatists of his milieu and stature, surrounded by magnificent collection of books and engaged in a fruitful academic career, happy in his personal life thanks to the presence of his wife as well as his lover who had both come with him from Germany. After the War, he chose not to return to Europe but came to the US instead. So much for his love of Europe! By contrast, Adorno who was also Jewish and much more overtly engaged with analysis of anti-Semitism and Nazism, went back to West Germany as soon as he could. Said cites Auerbach and *Mimesis* many times in his work, with much poignant praise, but the strange thing is that *Orientalism* debunks the moral claims to social and human truth of precisely the Greece-to-Modernism tradition that Auerbach celebrates.

As for the *Dialectics of Enlightenment*, I have not read *Orientalism* in a long time, but I don't recall any perceptible influence of Adorno and Horkheimer in that book. There are many, many things in Adorno that I admire; less so in the case of Horkheimer but I have learned some

* Erich Auerbach, *Mimesis: The Representation of Reality in Western Literature*, 1946; repr., Princeton: Princeton University Press, 1953; Max Horkheimer and Theodor Adorno, *Dialectic of Enlightenment*,1947; repr., New York: Herder and Herder, 1972.

things from him too. So, I don't want to be misunderstood. Even so, I do want to say that many things that Frankfurt theorists said about the Enlightenment, instrumental Reason, etc., converge rather strikingly with some ideas of thinkers of the German Right in their own time—people like Spengler, Heidegger and, more ambiguously, Carl Schmitt. This is clearer about Walter Benjamin and the early years of Marcuse. Adorno's instrumental reason is not really all that distant from the 'technics' of Spengler and Heidegger, and it is not clear to me just how distinct instrumental reason is from any other kind of Reason. Adorno often seems to suggest that instrumental reason is all that is left of Enlightenment Reason in our time. I don't think that ideas of that kind were ever attractive for Edward Said who was a profound humanist. His criticism of Europe was argued on very different grounds.

VP: About a decade after *Orientalism*, Martin Bernal published three volumes—*Black Athena*—with a very different approach to Europe and history.* What did you think of these projects?

AA: I felt that there was something very important and historically accurate about such a project. This is a project that takes as a premise the unity of the Mediterranean world, which is not Europe, which is not Africa, which is not Asia, none of these hard geographical boundaries that have little to do with civilizations of Antiquity, even late Antiquity. So, there is something fundamental to recognize about this geography. Throughout Antiquity, Greece was closely tied to Egypt; Constantinople was in its time as central to Eastern Christianity as Rome was to be for the Western branch. Europe was invented around the Elizabethan times, during the Renaissance, at the onset of capitalism. Europe was *invented*—Bernal is absolutely right about that. There is no direct historical continuity between Greek Antiquity and

---

* Martin Bernal, *Black Athena: The Afroasiatic Roots of Classical Civilization*, 3 vols., Rutland: Rutland Local History and Record Society, 1987, 1991, and 2006.

modern Europe. There were some very fundamental propositions in Bernal's book which I found admirable. It is excessive, however; it is very interesting that you referred to that because what it shares with Said's book is that in order to make an argument against the prevailing academic wisdom both authors deploy much exaggeration.

There is undoubtedly a very powerful core argument in Said's book about the bulk of modern Western scholarship which is really correct and which is why it had a very good and positive effect on Middle East Studies in the United States and in England; I believe that is where the really positive impact resides. It became a very important text for people to argue against the way the Arab world had been constructed by the entire Middle East Studies establishment. There was a very important rational kernel to those books, to both books, *Orientalism* and *Black Athena*. But in both cases, there is also a great exaggeration. I'm not competent enough to really judge all parts of Bernal's scholarship, but I have a greater competence in judging the range of the scholarship that went into the making of *Orientalism*.

VP: You published *In Theory* in 1992, but you were obviously putting it together in Delhi before that. The book is—I think wrongly— understood largely through Chapter Five, which is on Edward Said, and then partly Chapter Six, where you critique Said's understanding of Marx. Nonetheless, this is a very important part of the book. Could you tell us when you began to put down the observations on these chapters?

AA: The chapter on Fredric Jameson was written towards the end of my stay in the United States, soon after Jameson published his essay on 'national allegory.' The rest of the book was written in Delhi but I

---

* Aijaz Ahmad, 'Jameson's Rhetoric of Otherness and the "National Allegory"', *Social Text*, no. 17 (Autumn 1987), pp. 3–25, which was a response to Fredric Jameson, 'Third-World Literature in an Era of Multinational Capitalism', *Social Text*, no. 15 (Autumn 1986), pp. 65–88.

am not sure just when it started becoming a book. In the beginning, I was just addressing various issues in the essay form. The writing of the chapter on Edward Said started with a group of history students doing their MA or MPhil at Delhi University. They came to talk to me at Teen Murti and mentioned that *Orientalism* was very much a central text in their course on Methodology. I told them that there are many wonderful things in the book, but methodology was actually one of its weak points. We talked about that for a bit and then they asked me to give a lecture on this issue. So, the chapter begins as a written lecture on the question of methodology in *Orientalism*. Many people came to that lecture, other than the students, and some said that it would be very good to have it developed into an article that could be used by students in the future. So, then I wrote it up as an article for *Economic & Political Weekly*, where it was eventually published.*

The chapter on Salman Rushdie's *Shame* was also written for *EPW*. It was for the *Review of Women's Studies*. Alice Thorner, who had come to India from the US initially as a result of McCarthyism, was visiting India. She and I were chatting about something or the other and the question of Rushdie came up. I told her of my discomfort with *Shame*, about the misogyny in the book, which is very disturbing. She said, 'Why don't you write it up for the issue I am editing of *EPW*?' Well, by the time I actually sent it to *EPW*, the issue was in press, so I was late for the inclusion in that but then they published it in the next issue.† That essay went verbatim into the book without any modification, so far as I can recall.

VP: Three of the eight chapters are based on one work of one

---

* Aijaz Ahmad, '*Orientalism* and After: Ambivalence and Cosmopolitan Location in the Work', *Economic & Political Weekly*, vol. 27, no. 30 (25 July 1992).

† Aijaz Ahmad, 'Rushdie's *Shame*, Postmodernism, Migrancy and Representation of Women', *Economic & Political Weekly*, vol. 26, no. 15 (15 June 1991).

person: Edward Said's *Orientalism*, Jameson's essay on national allegory in Third World literature, and Rushdie's *Shame*. But there are five other chapters on very many different things that detained you at that time. There's a chapter on Indian literature, there are two chapters— including the introduction—on literary theory and the historicization of literary theory, there's a chapter on the language of class, which is on immigration, and so on. As I said earlier, you note that this is a thematic and theoretical book. Could you tell us a little about when you started to think of these essays and the themes as a book?

AA: Alright, that's a very interesting question. You're quite right, the chapter on Marx's writings on India is of course related to the chapter on Said. When I was sending the Said essay to *EPW*, it was already too long for a proper treatment of Marx's writings. But I did want to spell out my view on the question of Marx's writings on India, on the particular quotations that Said had picked up which are the very quotations that get picked up by everyone else who wants to portray Marx as a Eurocentric defender of colonialism. Warren had invoked that same representation of Marx, not to debunk him as Eurocentric but to praise him for approving of the so-called progressive side of colonialism. That sort of superficial reading is actually quite common in Western academic circles and in all such readings Marx comes out as a defender of colonialism. So, I actually wanted to address a configuration much larger than Said *per se*. I did worry, though, that when Said lends his stature and authority to that very familiar kind of reading of those couple of quotations, that was bound to have a very great influence.

But then, in a different field of literary study, the idea of 'Third World Literature' had become very fashionable in American and even British departments of English. I had all kinds of concerns about it. I won't spell out all those concerns, but one problem is really quite obvious. Literatures in the tricontinent are written in scores of languages. What kind of competence would you need to have for just reading, let alone teaching, even a cross-section of that archive? Great comparatists who have worked on European literature tended to know half a dozen European languages well and then also have some competence in a few more. Do we have a single such scholar when it comes to this 'Third World Literature' where the scope and complexity is far greater? My chapter on Indian literature argues that there is no such thing as a unitary Indian literature, that we have distinct literatures in various languages that may have many things in common but are irreducible to a singularity. Hindi *and* Tamil *and* Oriya—all constituting *one* literature! So, in a sense that chapter was related to the Jameson essay. But I was also trying to come to terms with these aspects of the Indian cultural world in its own terms. I was in conversation with some Indian comparatists such as my late friends, Sujit and Meenakshi Mukherjee, and reading very widely in the whole field of Indian literary and cultural formations. The idea of a national literature was absolutely applicable in the European nation-states which were largely unilingual and each of them therefore had one literature, with a very tight fit between the nation, language and literature. This is true of England, for instance. The making of these unilingual countries was a very coercive process in much of Europe, in France for instance, but in some countries like Spain that process has not succeeded until now. The most extraordinary country in this respect is the United States where people have come speaking some two hundred different languages but within a generation these languages wither. Small children learn very early in life that they must forget the language of their ancestors and adopt English as exclusively as possible. Much of their success in later life gets bound up with how well they command this one language. There is a unilingual dictatorship of English in the United States, which is one of the most culturally and linguistically coercive countries in the world.

In India, we don't have a national language. I find this state of affairs quite satisfactory. There was once a serious effort to impose Hindi, but the state retreated in the face of insuperable resistance to the idea.

English and Hindi are not national languages in India; they are link languages. These are link languages that allow people with different mother languages to communicate with each other.

You cannot teach Indian literature as a national literature. You have to teach it as a comparative literature. For teaching it as a comparative literature, there is no archive because our universities do not teach the requisite languages. We don't as a rule teach languages of the South in the North. The three-language formula doesn't create ground for a comparative study of Indian literature, so that the result is that the archive for Indian literature is being constructed in English. Indian literature is an artefact created in the shape of English translations. These translations are very uneven. There are numerous individuals who have the competence and translate just for the love of it. In such cases, we get good translations, and many of them can be of very high quality indeed. But then you have a much more voluminous archive of translations that come out of the patronage networks of the Sahitya Akademi. Most of that tends to be lamentable.

So, this question of the relationship between English and the idea of Indian literature, and more generally the place of English in this multilingual world of India, was part of the subtext of the essay on Indian literature.

The contrast between the Indian situation as I encountered it in cities like Delhi and the post-Bangladesh Pakistan was quite striking. Urdu there was originally the mother tongue of the minority of Pakistanis who had migrated from Delhi, UP and Bihar. But Urdu was also the medium of instruction in schools not only in Punjab but also in the Balochistan and North-West Frontier Province where the state governments actually adopted Urdu as their medium of instruction because they felt that their languages were not really developed enough to become languages of instruction in school syllabi, and that was certainly true of Balochistan. So, some eighty per cent of the school-going population learned Urdu quite systematically as the language of literacy, knowledge acquisition and educated communication and discourse. Sindh was always different and I won't go into that complexity. Urdu was at any rate also the language of communication among people who had acquired any degree of urban experience. For example, if you went to the mountains in North-West Pakistan, and if there was a Chitrali and a Pashtun sitting there in the bus, they would speak to each other in Urdu. That was the situation when I was in Pakistan. Over time, other languages are bound to start making their own claims and Urdu may well retreat. One notable result was that no matter how well you knew English you avoided speaking it as much as possible. There was already a small fraction of people, particularly in Karachi upper classes, who spoke English as a matter of course but the rest of us did not. When I came to Delhi, I was so struck by the fact that the whole intelligentsia speaks English. I, too, had to adjust to that. Now I could immediately see that this is because it is a multilingual, multiregional intelligentsia. In Delhi, I'm sitting with somebody from Orissa, somebody from Bengal, somebody from Kerala. So yes, that makes sense. But the bulk of them in Delhi came from Hindi-speaking families—from UP, Bihar, or from cities like Lahore or Rawalpindi in the Pakistani part of Punjab? Why were *they* speaking in English? *That* struck me.

There is something that happened to me. I used to write in Urdu: poetry, fiction as well as on politics, economy, etc. I used to publish in journals from Allahabad, Bangalore, Hyderabad, Karachi, Lahore, and Mysore. All this while I lived in Pakistan, and while I lived in the United States. That dried up when I moved to India. Urdu, or what in India is called Hindi which is often very close to Urdu, was not the language in which I now communicated much with most people in my own milieu. In places like Delhi or Bombay or Hyderabad there was a class divide. One spoke in Hindi to the working class but in English to all the rest. For most of the rest of the country, it was exclusively English. I became effectively an English speaker and I started writing almost exclusively in English. I had actually not written that much in English when I was in the States. My writings in English suddenly increase from the second half of the 1980s, after I came to settle in Delhi.

In Pakistan, I did a lot of political writing in Urdu; never occurred to me to write in English. Our party had a weekly journal in which I used to write virtually every week. I published five books in Urdu in Pakistan. All political books. So, my political connection in Pakistan was an Urdu connection; my political connection in India became an English connection. As the party withered in Pakistan, as those connections began to fray, my link to that political Urdu world began to end. I became a part of the English-speaking, English-writing intelligentsia. The question of English in India was for me both a very personally charged question but also socially and politically a very significant question. So, it is there not only in the chapter on Indian literature but also in one of the opening chapters.

The question of English was related not only to intellectuals working inside India but also to intellectuals of Indian origin who were strategically located in Western, mostly American universities, exercising great influence in international circles and then, necessarily, in India as well. We spoke earlier about *Subaltern Studies* and postcolonial theory. Well, both these academic formations have points of intersection between Indian intellectuals living abroad and living in India. This is a class network. That much has to be acknowledged but then this fact has to be analysed objectively, in relation to material histories, not in light of indigenist moralism. I reflect on this much more in the second chapter but some more reflections come towards the end of the chapter on Indian literature where I insist that English *has* become one of the Indian languages and all this business of '*Why do you write in English?*' is bogus because, for those who write in it English *is* the language they are best at. It is also simply a fact that after a hundred and fifty years of presence in India, English has become one of the Indian languages and you have to understand its actual, material function, or rather the very many functions, some very contradictory functions, that English actually has in India.

VP: In 1983, Ashis Nandy had published *The Intimate Enemy*. It provoked a dilemma about authenticity, about speaking English, say, as an act of inauthenticity. It is a symptom of this exact thing that you are talking about, not an antidote to it.

AA: I did read that book of Nandy but about a decade after its initial publication. He does say some very trenchant things there, but I felt that the book did not engage adequately with the very complex role that English actually plays in India or with the role of the English-speaking intelligentsia, of whom he is one. Let me just give you a few random examples of the complexity. What does one make of the fact that English is spoken in today's India much more widely than was the case during the colonial period? Is this just a colonial hangover? Or does it have to do with specific features of post-Independence developments? Then there is the question of bi-linguality. Gandhi, said to be the apostle of tradition in India, was a London-trained barrister. Raghupati Sahay Firaq, one of the most eminent poets of the Urdu *ghazal* in the twentieth century, was a lifelong and much admired professor of English in Allahabad University—not to speak of his command of Farsi and Sanskrit. Faiz Ahmad Faiz did two MAs, in English and Arabic, wrote Urdu poetry, taught English in early years of his personal life, then served as Chief Editor of the English-language newspaper, *The Pakistan Times*, until the first of his many arrests in 1951. In colonial India intellectuals who wrote only in English were few. Most wrote in two languages. Those who write only in English became far more numerous and far more influential after Independence. The trend actually became more pronounced after about 1980. And, English in India has always been more punctually a language for academic production in the physical and social sciences than for literary production. Generally speaking, English is as much a language of class privilege as it is a language of market transaction and much more of an inter-regional link language than Hindi, for example, in elite discourse as much as in the marketplace. By contrast, there are very large regions of the country which would resist such a role for Hindi because that gives undue advantage to Hindi-speakers of the North. The problem with Nandy is that he often has some valuable insights but then slides into rigid one-sidedness and caricature. Much of *The Intimate Enemy* relies upon a kind of self-righteous native indigenism that I have always disliked. You have to deal with the contradictions of a situation and the complexities of a situation. It was that kind of indigenism which once led Ashis Nandy to argue against the women who started to write against *sati*. He calls these women deracinated, anglicized women who don't understand their spiritual traditions and the devotion that goes into the decision of a woman who decides to burn herself on the pyre. This was in 1987, only four years after *The Intimate Enemy*. I was just so shocked by that essay. This is where your indignation about anglicization leads you, where you say that all this communalism is a product of colonialism and modernity, and the answer to that is our tradition—for which then you end up inventing a fictive tradition that has little basis in actual historical past.

VP: This returns us to your first reaction to *Orientalism*, that it is—as al-Azm said—'orientalism in reverse'. The argument can go that secularism or rationalism are not of the soil of a place, which then says, 'return to the soil', meaning a return to irrationalism and social hierarchies.

AA: There is some bad faith in all this. You cannot take Marxism or secularism or rationalism because they all come from the West but, for some reason, there does not appear to be any problem with riding in cars or trains, flying in airplanes, drinking tea or eating sandwiches, or drinking whisky and wine, all of which were brought into India by the same British who brought the English language. There is actually a very famous social scientist who once wrote an essay advocating that Toleration is better suited for India because it is an indigenous virtue as compared to Secularism which comes from an alien intellectual tradition, which then led in the same article to the argument that instead of imposing a uniform secularism on all of society various Indian religious communities should be allowed to formulate their own rules, laws and ways of life. This entire outlook goes together with the edict that you must only criticize tradition from within that tradition. I tend to think that all traditionalism of this sort is strictly a neo-traditionalism, an invention very much of the present, which is then passed off as some everlasting, timeless tradition which is beyond history.

VP: Where does this argument come from, that a tradition should only be criticized from within? It's such a deeply parochial view of history. I mean, in what long historical sweep have traditions been so hermetically sealed that they haven't borrowed or been influenced by other forces and forms? Where does this argument come from?

AA: It comes largely from the reactionary ideas that arose in Europe in opposition to the Enlightenment and the French Revolution but some of it was already there in Catholic Counter-Reformation against Protestant Reformation. You only have to read de Maistre or Bonald to grasp the roots of this kind of thinking, or Fichte's *Addresses to the German Nation* or texts of right-wing Romanticism. And then such ideas also became very influential in the period of fascism in Europe, as you can see, for instance, in the texts of Heidegger's seminars from his Nazi period. The Hindu Right and Islamist Right are direct descendants of those reactionary lineages of European thought, whether they know it or not.

Colonial education popularized ideas that were congenial for colonial rulers, which mostly meant either liberalism or ideas further to the right. The problem with the subalternists is that they think that European colonialism brought Enlightenment to India. I wish it did, but colonialism was too retrograde to do any such thing. Let me give you just one example. You undoubtedly remember the first line of one of Marx's earliest texts, *A Contribution to the Critique of Hegel's Philosophy of Right*: 'For Germany, the *criticism of religion* has been essentially completed, and the criticism of religion is the prerequisite of all criticism.' That was in 1843. Marx is essentially saying that he need not undertake any criticism of religion because that has already been completed by others. The date is important: a very young man in 1843—almost two centuries ago—thinks that criticism of religion is complete and that such criticism is the *prerequisite* of *all criticism*. Marx has simply borrowed this thought from what I would call the left wing of Enlightenment philosophy. Did European colonialists ever bring into the colonial classroom any ideas of that kind, to methodically criticize religion and caste through scientific reasoning?

VP: There are many themes in your book. There is the critique of 'orientalism in reverse', this desire to affirm tradition against colonialism or colonial discourse, more precisely. The other theme is on nationalism and national aesthetics, asking the question whether there is a national literature, an Indian literature. Then there is the theme about Marxism being pushed off the table. Could you talk a little about the urgency of arguing not only from a Marxist standpoint but also *about* Marxism and its importance, in an intellectual terrain where these people were not only undermining but also, in some cases, just going around it; they were not even arguing against Marx?

AA: Yes, none of them ever argued against Marx in any systematic fashion. But what you're asking me refers actually to something that I addressed in the introduction to *In Theory*: the whole question of a certain decline in the prestige of Marxism, particularly in the West but not only in the West, in a particular historical juncture. I still hold to that rough periodization. Between 1970 and 1975, the world was faced with three different and overlapping crises. First, the great age of capitalist prosperity was over. By then Europe had completed its postwar reconstruction and economies were slowing down. The US was facing a very serious balance of payments crisis thanks mostly to the whole long war it had been waging in Korea, Indochina and elsewhere, which also involved paying for a huge number of military bases all over the world. The sweeping changes the US introduced into the global financial system in the early '70s was directly a response to that crisis. A corollary of that crisis of stagnation was the gradual dilution and retreat of social democracy in Western Europe. Second, and at the opposite end, the communist state system entered an even more profound crisis at about the same time. The so-called 'Deng reforms' of 1978–79, coming in the turbulent aftermath of the Cultural Revolution set the stage for slow but unmistakable dissolution of socialism in China. Communist state system in the Soviet-led Comecon countries unravelled more slowly but eventually even more completely than in China. Third, what I call 'the nationalism of the national bourgeoisie' faces various kinds of crises and defeat. This includes the 1965 coup in Indonesia, the crisis of Nasserism after 1967, the collapse of the Nehruvian agenda after 1975. The period of the nationalism of the national bourgeoisie was drawing to a close, though there were to be more manifestations of it in later years. By the late 1970s, the world was fully enveloped in those crises and historic ties between progressive forms of nationalism and communism were also very much in crisis. The declining affiliation of more and more Western intellectuals with Marxism was very much connected to that objective condition.

It is not possible to explain the itinerary of each particular intellectual, nor is that necessary. The widespread repudiation of Marxism is a structural fact. Intellectuals begin then to turn to various forms of thought that have been percolating at different times in great many places. Most post-Marxism tends to be pre-Marxism. For instance, a whole repertoire of indigenist positions is available from histories of the European Right. In this period of crisis, though, we witness a new kind of identitarianism or indigenism in many circles of the post-Marxist Left which draws upon many of the themes developed by the European Right without acknowledging it—or even knowing where these ideas come from.

I must add, though, that in India we have not only the Blood-and-Soil nationalism of Savarkar, Hindutva, etc., but tendencies of religious conservatism and identitarianism in what I call India's canonical nationalism. Syama Prasad Mukherjee could be accommodated as a minister in Nehru's cabinet—a very late expression of a tendency that had once made it possible for Hindu Mahasabha to function from inside the Indian National Congress. This is not a minor tendency in India's canonical nationalism. Sardar Patel approved of the Partition Plan on the ground that it was best to surgically remove a 'diseased limb'—a formulation that seems to suggest that he might have preferred a state comprised exclusively of Hindus. Even Gandhi found it much easier to deal with religiously conservative Muslims like Azad and the Deobandi *ulema* than with a modern, bourgeois Muslim like Jinnah.

VP: Too many monocles, too few *topis*.

AA: It was Jinnah, after all, who said 'Khilafat is an exploded bogey' while Gandhi was supporting, most opportunistically, the Khilafat Movement along with a whole gang of *mullahs* and traditionalist Muslims. So, this Janus-faced religiosity was always available within the high Gandhian tradition of Indian nationalism: you keep the Hindu Mahasabha on this side, the *mullahs*—the Deobandis—on the other side. This attitude, this tone was available to the intellectuals decades later. Gandhi says politics without religion is a sin and that is available to Ashis Nandy as a great truth of Indian 'tradition'.

VP: These are a rich set of themes for a book. There is one more chapter we haven't talked about, the chapter on the three worlds.

AA: The three chapters in the middle of the book—on single texts by Said, Jameson and Rushdie—were in my mind essentially illustrative, clarifying through textual reference arguments I had made in other, thematically broader chapters. Then there were other questions; how the category of 'Indian literature' was to be understood, for example. That closing chapter on the Third World was related to some other considerations. I had felt, for example, that the question of imperialism was getting detached from capital and class and was being posed now in terms of opposition between colonization and nation, nationalism, Third World and so on. I also felt that most people were just using the term 'Third World' to mean 'formerly colonized countries' with little sense of why the term arose in the first place or histories of the movement of Non-Alignment. Few people understood that different meanings were attached to this term by the Soviets, the Chinese, the middle-of-the-road non-aligned countries like India, and by journalists. I wanted to clarify all that, well beyond what had been said about the Third World in my response to Jameson's essay on the national allegory. And a large part of the reason for writing was self-clarification—to understand my own thoughts more clearly.

Once most of those essays were there, I began to see the shape of a basic argument that was spelled out in many parts. I decided to turn all that into a book. I had a visceral sense of the thematic logic which led to that particular arrangement of chapters but it was some years later, when I was invited to give a seminar on the book at the University of São Paulo, that I re-read the book, reflected on it, discussed it and finally grasped fully the logic of exposition at work in the book.

I might add that the Soviet system had begun to unravel as I was drafting the latter chapters and the terminal collapse of the USSR was approaching as I was doing my final revisions before sending away the manuscript. All of that was a novel turn in history and also an ongoing process. No one knew what the final shape of things would be or what long-term consequences might ensue. So, I did not want to write about all that directly. But this whole issue—the nature of the crisis, neoliberalism in place, the postwar periods, the national liberation movements now gone—all of this was related to the times I was living through, the collapse of the Soviet Union on the one hand and the chequered but unmistakable rise of the Right in many shapes and places across the world.

REACTIONS TO *IN THEORY*

VP: *In Theory* comes out in 1992. The USSR has just collapsed. India, which is an important part of the book, has gone through two related traumas—precipitous liberalization in July 1991, and then a year and six months later, in December 1992, the destruction of the Babri Masjid in Ayodhya. This is the context of the book's arrival. The reaction to the book is quite interesting. Were you surprised by it?

AA: I just explained to you why I did not address the collapse of the Soviet Union in the book. I also said earlier in our conversation that after I returned to live in India I felt that I need to learn a lot more, observe a lot more before I could write about any aspect of Indian society, politics or economy. So, until the publication of *In Theory*, I wrote rather little that had to do with India. Liberalization of the Indian economy had already begun and I had been watching the Mandir agitations, *rath yatra* and so on. But it is only after the Babri Masjid demolition—some months after *In Theory* had been published—that I felt compelled to start writing about India. *In Theory* was for me largely a matter of settling some accounts with my erstwhile literary-critical conscience, so virtually all the references to India in the book have that dimension. Did the reception surprise me? Yes, indeed! My first surprise was that it was taken so very seriously by so many people. In the UK, for instance, it was reviewed quite widely and for the most part positively—in *The Guardian*, even *The Financial Times*. In the US, by contrast, teaching of it became very widespread very quickly but there were no reviews and the vitriol was astounding, percolating first through academic grapevines and then taking a programmatic shape in, for instance, the special issue that *Public Culture* did on the book. When my article on Jameson was first published in *Social Text*, the only chapter here that had been published in the West as an essay, Jameson had responded in a later issue of the same journal with a friendly comment of two pages or so.* I don't think he actually read the essay carefully enough to grasp my argument. Even so his phrasing was courteous. But when the book appeared, Jameson and the Jamesonians reacted very sharply. So that surprised me.

Then there was the Said chapter. I was uncomfortable about that chapter. I respect Said enormously and had no wish to offend him. So, I showed it to a couple of his friends who were also my friends— Talal Asad, for example—and I said to them that I am anxious not to offend, so please advise me. They assured me that there was nothing in my essay that anyone could take amiss. Later, Talal Asad criticized the book in the pages of *Public Culture*—not the Said essay but other aspects of the book—and he did it methodically but very courteously. That did not surprise me at all because there have always been some very fundamental differences between him and me on the issue of Modernity, Secularity, Marxism and so on. There are of course other aspects of his work that I do admire. His short book, *On Suicide Bombing*, for instance, is very perceptive. In any case, the point I was making was that precisely because some of Said's own friends had approved of the essay so explicitly, the storm of abuse that came my way was indeed very surprising. Talal Asad had actually been downright enthusiastic.

* Fredric Jameson, 'A Brief Response', *Social Text*, no. 17 (Autumn 1987), pp. 26–28.

VP: ... the chapter begins with a great homage to his work.

AA: True. I might add that the extremity of that ill-tempered reaction was largely an American phenomenon even though what happens in America has great impact well beyond its geographical boundaries. The first edition actually had a blurb written by Terry Eagleton which was fairly typical of the reception in Britain.* That blurb got removed from later editions, and I wondered why. I was in any case no longer living or teaching in the US. But my poor friend Michael Sprinker, now deceased, took the brunt of it because he was the one who was officially the commissioning editor of the book at Verso. The denunciation came from such influential sources that only one person actually reviewed the book in the US. This was Neil Larsen, who reviewed the book two years later.† So, I was also very surprised by the fact that the book that has never been reviewed in the US was nevertheless taught across disciplines of the humanities and the social sciences so very widely, year in and year out.

The US academy is largely a private academy in which the most prestigious universities are private universities. The most famous of the public intellectuals are often caught up in a powerful star system, and that includes academic intellectuals of a Marxist persuasion. This kind of academic culture produces acolytes, factions, allegiances and patronage systems. Any attempt at debating the ideas of the iconic figures openly is treated as an act of disloyalty, which then leads to trivialization of thought as such. This form of intellectual life is now getting exported to much of the rest of the world, as part of the Americanization of the world.

Historically, Marxism is not simply an academic discipline for yet

---

* 'Some radical critics may have forgotten about Marxism. But Marxism, in the shape of Ahmad's devastating, courageously unfashionable critique, has not forgotten about them': Terry Eagleton.

† Neil Larsen, 'Postcolonialism's Unsaid', *Minnesota Review*, nos. 45–46 (Fall 1995 and Spring 1996), pp. 285–90.

another way of reading books. Rather, Marxism has thrived on debate, on commitment to ideas that are defended in fierce debate because ideas matter to those who are in any way committed to contributing directly to the making of powerful mass movements of the oppressed classes. At the same time, Marxism's intellectual life also demands intervention in the high culture of philosophy, political economy, the arts, the human sciences in general because without mastering that world of high culture you can neither become nor produce more of what Gramsci called the organic intellectuals of the working class. That is the legacy of Marx and Engels themselves: political commitment to revolutionary action combined with the ambition to produce the most advanced forms of theoretical knowledge. If you create an anti-intellectual world in which factions and patronage systems predominate and ideas begin to matter less and less, that leads directly to very degraded forms not only of academic life but of politics as well. One expression of this degradation of politics is that the Marxist Left is the only one that actually spells out its theoretical and programmatic positions. All other political parties no longer actually represent different positions on how a decent future is to be secured for the majority of the population.

VP: They don't have a programme, let alone a theory.

AA: Yes. That's what I meant, about programmes. Most politicians are professional entrepreneurs and any fundamental programmatic difference between political parties is becoming rare. For three decades now the Congress and the BJP [Bharatiya Janata Party] have competed in their loyalty to neoliberalism. The same could be said of Democrats and Republicans in the US. Chomsky is right. The two-party system looks more and more like competitions between two factions of the same party. The same is true of the overall academic situation in the US. The left and right ends of the academic spectrum are remarkably well adjusted to the basic structures of the system, and only a very small number refuse its basic demands. No wonder that one of the main contributors to that issue of *Public Culture* accused me of waging a *jihad* and diagnosed me as suffering from what Nietzsche called *ressentiment*. How else to characterize someone so disobedient?

VP: There is a straight line that runs from *In Theory* to your essay on Derrida and Marx, as well as your essay on Derrida, Badiou, and Žižek.*

AA: Yes. I wanted to write about them because they are leading European philosophers who are very popular among Western leftist intelligentsia and therefore have enormous influence in many other corners of the world as well. Derrida has written a whole book announcing affiliation with Marx. Žižek invokes Lenin quite often and Verso has published two selections from Lenin's writings that he has assembled with lengthy commentaries. Badiou has been a lifelong Maoist—a very *French* Maoist, I might add—and has published, among other things, a short book, *The Communist Hypothesis*, which does have a fascinating chapter on the Chinese Cultural Revolution. All these affiliations are very strange, however. Derrida writes in his book that he has 'always' been opposed to 'everything' that communist parties have ever done. I tried to show in my essay that the actual programmes of action that Derrida and Žižek propose are deeply rooted in pragmatism and liberalism. For Badiou, communism is an eternal *Idea* so much so that when he was doing his own very peculiar version of Plato's *Republic* he had wanted, he says, to translate the title of the book as *Communism*. None of this translates, though, into any affiliation with the Bolshevik tradition because in his view parties that capture state power necessarily degenerate. Now, I have argued in some places that the original Bolshevik model of revolution—frontal attack on the Winter Palace, the seat of power, by a revolutionary vanguard that has just emerged out of its underground existence—is no longer

* Aijaz Ahmad, 'Three "Returns" to Marx: Derrida, Zizek, Badiou', *Social Scientist*, vol. 40, nos. 7–8 (July–August 2012), pp. 43–59.

practicable in our time. That is *not* what Badiou is saying. In his view, the very act of seizing and retaining state power in the hands of the revolutionary party inevitably leads to degeneration.

VP: I just want to clarify something because I don't want anybody to misunderstand what you're saying. When you say that Bolshevism, in a sense, exhausted itself, you're not of course saying that the political party has exhausted itself as a form and now we need networks and so on. What you're saying is that the character of the state is a different kind now than it was a hundred years ago.

AA: Gramsci writes somewhere that the French Revolution created a particular form in which revolutions were to be made. That form was tried in France again in 1830 and 1848, and in many other places less prominently, but it was not possible to think, really, beyond that form until the arrival of a new revolutionary form, which only emerged as an embryo with the Paris Commune. Instead of repeating the revolutionary form of 1798 the Commune created a wholly new form in which a future form of the dictatorship of the proletariat could be glimpsed. Then, it took almost another half century for that form to mature and explode on the world in the form of the Bolshevik Revolution which then became the revolutionary form that many others tried to replicate subsequently in many other places. Gramsci was unquestionably a Leninist but, as I read him, he also seemed to believe that the Bolshevik form had to be modified very considerably in countries where the capitalist state was more developed and had taken deeper roots than was the case in Tsarist Russia. I think it is important to understand that we are talking of revolutionary *form*— *how* revolutions are made; the *method*—not of revolutionary theory, communist objectives or the party form. Mao and Hồ Chí Minh also led great communist revolutions, but their methods were not the methods of 1917. I think we are living in a period in which the strictly Bolshevik form of making revolutions is over but we don't yet know what the revolutionary form would be that is appropriate for our time. Gramsci's point was that frontal seizure of power was possible only in more backward states, the ones that had not developed a fully capitalist form. Today, the capitalist state is far more complex, reaching deep into the farthest corners of the polity, and it now commands a very different level of military power. On the other hand, what I would call bourgeois political subjectivity has now become very widespread: the questions of democracy, constitution, electoral representation, the question of developing organs of popular power and what Rousseau called the General Will. How will tomorrow's communism address the question of the Lockean Bill of Rights that has become so ingrained in popular consciousness in countries where liberal democracy has become part of political life? As for the use of violence, I am not preaching non-violence. I am actually saying something similar to what Engels said about street fighting by the 1870s and 1880s. He said that the time for the idea that fighting at the barricades could lead to a revolution is over because very different kind of weaponry is now available to the state; means and methods have to be different. The question is: how to be Bolsheviks not of 1917 but of a century later? On this Žižek poses the right question but gives the wrong answer.

VP: The reason I asked for clarification is that one of the things that's been frustrating in this long period from the collapse of the USSR is that—in history writing, for example—the organizer has disappeared as an important actor in history. People don't write about the organizer; they write about rebellion, as if it just appears. The period of preparation is not something that is documented; spontaneity is highlighted, movements just happen. This means parties can be disparaged.

GRAMSCI AND HINDUTVA

VP: After the destruction of the Babri Masjid in Ayodhya in 1992, you begin to turn your attention very seriously to the question of the rise of Hindutva, not just rise but the appearance to the surface of this force. You're reading Gramsci perhaps to orient yourself to understand these developments. You have several important lectures and essays in this period on Hindutva, on the RSS. There is no time for a book tour. You are enmeshed in this new crisis.

AA: I said a little earlier that when I first returned to live in India I realized very quickly that my knowledge of India was actually very shallow. I had to spend some time thinking, reading, observing, seeing as much as possible. Working at Teen Murti gave me a good base from where to undertake that education of myself. I didn't write seriously about India for a while. I wrote a little bit about Indian literature or teaching of literature in India. I also published a longish and very irreverent piece on Abul Kalam Azad which was my first attempt to question the ill-founded fame of one of the absolutely canonical figures of Indian nationalism.[*] It was the Babri Masjid demolition that forced me to renounce my inhibition about writing on India. In late December, just a few weeks after Ayodhya, I delivered the Amal Bhattacharji Memorial Lecture at the Centre for European Studies in Calcutta. The only thing on my mind was the RSS, but because it was the Centre for European Studies, I felt compelled to bring in a European thinker and Gramsci, the great intellectual of the period of fascism, seemed to be under the circumstances the right choice.

---

[*] Aijaz Ahmad, 'Disciplinary English: Third-Worldism and Literary Theory', in *Rethinking English: Essays in Literature, Language, History*, ed. Svati Joshi, New Delhi: Trianka Publishers, 1991; 'Azad's Careers: Roads Taken and Not Taken', in *Islam and Indian Nationalism: Reflections on Abul Kalam Azad*, ed. Mushirul Hasan, New Delhi: Manohar, 1992. The second essay is collected in *Lineages of the Present*.

Therefore, the lecture was 'Reading Gramsci in the Days of Hindutva.'* There are two big problems with that essay. One is that it is too analogical: this is how it was in Italy according to Gramsci, and this is how that has a resonance for us here in India. By the same token, I am not thinking in that lecture about India directly in my own terms, with Gramsci's thought incorporated into my own. Instead, I quote and cite Gramsci at great length to *apply* his thought, which is the wrong thing to do because political intellectuals of his kind think concretely, with reference to requirements of their time and their place. Then, I was invited to Hyderabad a year later to participate in a workshop on Culture, Community, and Nation organized by the Deccan Development Society. This was to commemorate the first anniversary of the destruction of the Ayodhya mosque. This second lecture—'On the Ruins of Ayodhya'—was a very long one; it took something like an hour and a half to deliver. I have of course changed and refined the argument a great deal since then but I still think that the basic premises of my thought on the RSS, on the question of fascism in India and related matters were spelled out in that essay.†

So, those are the two basic essays. Then there is an essay I did two years later for *Germinal*, the journal of the Department of Germanic and Romance Studies in Delhi University, which is on Italian fascism.‡ That was the fruit of my extensive study of Italian fascism and the way it rose to dominance in various parts of the country, including, most importantly, the countryside. Unlike the earlier Gramsci essay which is marred by strained analogies with the Indian situation, this one

---

* Aijaz Ahmad, 'Fascism and National Culture: Reading Gramsci in the Days of Hindutva'.

† Aijaz Ahmad, 'Culture, Community, Nation: On the Ruins of Ayodhya', *Social Scientist*, vol. 21, nos. 7–8 (July–August 1993), pp. 17–48; reprinted in *Lineages of the Present*.

‡ Aijaz Ahmad, 'Structure and Ideology in Italian Fascism', *Germinal: Journal of the Department of Germanic and Romance Studies*, vol. 1, ed. Shaswati Mazumdar, 1994; reprinted in *Lineages of the Present*.

reconstructs the specificity of Italian fascism and its class practices. Since then, I have always insisted that in practice every fascism takes a specifically national form and working too much with analogies is counterproductive. On a conceptual level, therefore, I have been trying to distinguish between what is specifically fascist about the RSS and, by contrast, what are its practices that are grounded in its understanding of the Indian polity and how it can make a revolution of the Right in this very concrete situation. One of the things that I've still not been able to think through in terms of India is the deep role of fascism in the agrarian world, which was very important in Italy. Only later I became aware of how important the agrarian question was in Germany and Spain, and generally wherever fascism grew. In India it is difficult to think about these things theoretically because the empirical base is not well developed. We don't really know much empirically about the role of the middle and rich peasantry in the generalization of the BJP's electoral power in so many parts of the country, not to speak of a far more generalized consent to the Hindutva view of the world. How does the UP peasantry view Adityanath and men of his ilk who lead the BJP in that state? I just don't have enough empirical facts at my disposal to make a reliable judgment.

VP: These essays after Ayodhya and on the RSS draw from your very considerable reading not only on India, but on developments in other parts of the Third World. You write in 'On the Ruins of Ayodhya' about the ruling class in our societies becoming 'unruly' and disparaging of 'democratic culture and public civility'. Their parties disregard political culture. It is the RSS and the Left, you say, that 'represent specific kinds of political culture', but that the RSS is the force that is able to draw from the worst elements of our culture. Can you say a little more about that?

AA: I started writing about communalism and political religiosity in India after some twenty years of engagement with such shifts in the Muslim majority countries. In one place after another, Islamism arose

125

to fill the vacuum created after the defeat of the Left or of secular Arab nationalism. Islamist organizations were major collaborators of Suharto's troops in bloodbaths of communists in Indonesia. One forgets now, in these times of Hezbollah and Amal, that Shia peasantry in Southern Lebanon had once been the social base for the Lebanese Communist Party. The ascendency of Saudi Arabia with its Wahhabism and what I call 'Desert Islam' was directly proportionate to the defeat of Nasser and Arab secular nationalism more generally. Same thing in Iran—in 1948, the British counsel in Tehran writes a secret memorandum to the foreign office, in which he says that the Tudeh, the Iranian communists, need make no revolution and can simply take power through the elections. That was in 1948. In 1953, the CIA overthrows the nationalists and starts training the SAVAK, the terrifying Irani secret service, which carries out the bloodbath of the communists, with the exception of those few who managed to go into exile and managed to survive in the underground. And who came eventually to fill the vacuum? The Islamists. A whole menagerie of Islamists and ethno-nationalists rose to prominence and power in Iraq as soon as the Americans had destroyed the secular Ba'athist state. The question of nationalism is an important terrain on which this conflict between the secular Left and the religious Rights gets fought out. The most retrograde kind of pan-Islamists arise after secular Arab nationalism is defeated. Nationalism is an objective necessity in recently independent societies, and in the age of imperialism. It is also an objective necessity for the transition to capitalism because that transition is a very painful process and there has to be a national cement to prevent the disintegration of society under the stresses of that process. If the secular Left fails to occupy that space, the religious Right will.

VP: The second point you make here, very chillingly, is about the culture of cruelty. You say that 'the political discourse of the Sangh has a ring of familiarity in a culture replete with authoritarian forms of religiosity and every failure to build the new in ways vigorous enough to allow large masses of people to take the risk of novelty must always push large sections of those people to seek refuge in what seems familiar; conservatism is born not only from privilege and the will to protect that privilege, but also and perhaps decisively from the experience of pain and the fear of future pain'.

AA: The plebeian mass base of fascism is very much tied up with not class privilege but with class and caste suffering. If you look at the images of the Babri Masjid being destroyed, you ask about those who climbed up to the domes, 'Who are these people? What class do they belong to?' They don't come from the upper classes or upper castes; these are people who are the ultimate victims of capitalism and caste society. This kind of gratuitous violence gives them a feeling of power—an illusory overcoming of their own powerlessness. There's no other way in which they have any sense of dignity, so this is the fiction of dignity for them. My thinking on this comes from thinking about the role of the lumpen-proletariat, their role over two hundred years in counter-revolutionary movements. How is it that the lumpen-proletariat, which is even poorer than the proletariat, becomes the fodder of all counter-revolutionary work? How is it that it is the *Adivasis* who participate quite prominently in the killings in Gujarat or the *Dalits* in the 1984 killing of Sikhs? All that is there in that passage you have quoted. The Sangh can call upon all this in the name of Hinduism, caste-less people being given the dignity of being called Hindus. This is a very violent version of Mahatma Gandhi's eccentric idea that replacing the word 'Dalit' with the word 'Harijan' would somehow enhance the dignity of the untouchables.

VP: But that person being given dignity by being named Hindu: the antidote is being given dignity as being part of a group of comrades to build something different, and yet, it's much harder. Because it's not in the taproot of culture.

AA: Right. But that is the Left's big disadvantage and contributes to its social isolation and defeat. You are swimming against the current and fighting for radical change. You can always be accused of following imported ideologies, not being authentic Indians. You cannot say that Marxism and communism are ancient Vedic virtues whereas even a judge of the Supreme Court can say, as one of them actually did, that Hindutva and Hinduism are the same thing. The Left grows against the odds; odds are always against the Left. In these religious societies, to create a communist—a mass-based communist—party is a very, very great achievement, regardless of how small that party is in the larger scheme of things. Mobilizing thousands upon thousands, and in the Indian case hundreds of thousands of people, actually millions— it's an incredible achievement. It is really quite impressive how well Brahminism has survived millennia of challenges to the caste system. Communism works in opposition to that very solid, very historically grounded power.

VP: In this sense, Ambedkar is genuinely the most profound critic, because his argument is that there is no reform within but only revolution against.

AA: Yes, exactly. When he burnt the *Manusmriti*, the message was that Hinduism is unreformable and that it must be destroyed. Suvira Jaiswal is quite correct: Hinduism is not an orthodoxy; it is an orthopraxy.* There is great flexibility in matters of belief but inflexibility in matters of practice. And what Jaiswal shows is that caste is central to this inflexibility of practice, a very central element in the order of *dharmic* conduct. In Islam and Christianity there is at least an abstract belief in social equality. The practice among Muslims or Christians may violate the principle but a way is always open for judging the practice in the light of that principle. In the Brahminic system, there is not even

* Suvira Jaiswal, *Caste: Origin, Function, and Dimensions of Change*, New Delhi: Manohar, 2000.

a principle of universal social equality; the hierarchical structure of the caste system negates any such principle.

VP: The claim is the opposite. The claim is to reaffirm social hierarchy; it's not challenging anything.

AA: Yes. And then you have someone like Gandhi telling you that *varnashrama* was really a very good thing, just got distorted over time and needs to be restored to the original spirit behind it. Gandhi was both a genuine reformer as well as a social conservative. Even for him, a total repudiation of the *varnashrama* was much too radical. You can see how deep the hierarchical culture goes. The Left is talking about radical equality that is the opposite of that kind of belief and practice. That is what I meant by swimming against the current.

VP: I'll give you an example, an ongoing political issue; we're talking about radical inequality, one of the ideological structuring features of this is pollution and purity. The Left Democratic Front government in Kerala realized around two years ago that there was a concern that, in schools, girls were missing a lot of days of school. The obvious answer was that during menstruation, they were not coming to school. The Chief Minister said, menstruation is not a penalty, it's a human thing and we will provide free sanitary napkins in schools. You come to school; it is a technological improvement; you take it, and study. Then there's the debate around the entry to Sabarimala, where between the age of ten and fifty—when women menstruate—you cannot enter the temple. That menstruation can be seen as a structuring principle of human behaviour; the ridiculousness of it . . . ! The Left was the only force to oppose this nonsense. Shashi Tharoor, who imagines himself to be a modern person, utterly defended this retrograde position. He even went about saying, 'I'm a proud Hindu', and that his mother and sisters were 'proud Nair women'.

AA: Exactly. And then in the Lok Sabha elections CPI(M) lost all the seats, for the first time since 1957. Many people believe that the Congress swept the elections in Kerala—the only state where it did—thanks to its stand on Sabarimala. That is why I have been saying since the late '90s that the programmatic isolation of the Left is such that there is no other political force in India with which, actually, the Left can have a durable and principled alliance. So, either you make completely opportunistic or tactical alliances, or the fundamental isolation is unbreakable. India no longer has even a properly liberal political party, let alone a social democratic one.

VP: In a number of your essays in the 1990s, you used the phrase 'culture of cruelty'. Could you reflect on that a little?

AA: I have actually published a full-length essay entitled 'Cultures of Cruelty'.* Thousands of women get killed in India every year, often by members of their own family, out of pure gender violence; other thousands get beaten up or get their faces disfigured for not having brought enough dowry or being disobedient to husbands or in-laws, and things of that sort. Thousands of Dalits get killed every year, countless Dalit women get raped, out of sheer class and caste hatred. In this sort of world, killing or raping out of communal motives comes easy. My view is that communal violence, specifically anti-Muslim violence is just one aspect of a much wider grid of daily cruelties. Many more Dalits have been killed in independent India than Muslims. Many more non-Muslim women have been killed or raped. There are all kinds of cruelties. I do believe that Nehru was right when he said that Hindu communalism needs to be opposed with particular force because it is the only organized tendency in India that can potentially turn into fascism. However, I think there is something deeply wrong with the way we are always talking about RSS and the like as if the rest

---

*   Aijaz Ahmad, 'Right Wing Politics, and the Cultures of Cruelty', in *On Communalism and Globalization: Offensives of the Far Right*, New Delhi: Three Essays Press, 2002.

of society was just very decent, liberal, very modern, and as if there is just this fringe that is carrying on with all this terrible cruelty against Muslims. Let us put this cruelty against Muslims into perspective. The RSS wants to occupy the souls of liberal Hindus by creating a hysteria around the Hindu-Muslim question. Because who defends the Muslims? It is the leftists and liberals of Hindu origin. Without that solidarity from leftists and liberals of Hindu origin, the RSS would find it much easier to kill a very large number of Muslims and relegate the rest to the margins of society as second-class citizens. RSS wants to create a mass hysteria against the Muslims so that they can designate as anti-nationals and even anti-Hindu those Hindu leftists and liberals who defend the equal rights of religious minorities. In all this, Zionism is the real model for the RSS, just as Nazism is the real model for the Zionist extremists in Israel for their treatment of the Palestinians. Even so, there is another side to this that should never be neglected, that this total concentration on the communal question tends to objectively suppress the question of violence against Dalits, against women, and so on. Whereas all those other cruelties are actually the structural feature of our society which you can't even connect with a certain regressive, fascistic politics—*it's just how our society is.* Caste violence is partly class, but partly just caste. There is the brutalization of Adivasis. That is the origin of the phrase the 'culture of cruelty'.

VP: And violence against Dalits is seen as a response to Dalit assertion, and not as part of a culture of cruelty that includes cruelty against Dalits.

AA: That is how it gets represented. But take a look at it historically. Indian propertied classes and upper castes find it so easy to molest and rape a Dalit woman. What difference does it make for them whether the woman they are raping is Dalit or Muslim? It is part of the same spectrum. An answering politics would not be just anti-communal but work for a genuinely united struggle for victims of communal, caste and gender violences; against that whole national condition that I have called a 'culture of cruelty'.

LACK OF A PROPER BOURGEOISIE

VP: The themes from the 1990s—on Hindutva, on Indian liberalism, on the culture of cruelty—these remain with you. You continue to write about them, and about what Tariq Ali calls the 'extreme centre', the harmony between liberalism and the Right.

AA: My own thinking has been changing as I think about all this, so there has been an evolution in my own thought between 1992 and 2014—when I wrote the *Socialist Register* essay on India. The argument keeps shifting a bit. It's not just that reality is shifting; it's actually that I am thinking more deeply about various issues. I no longer believe, for instance, that there is really any contradiction between liberal institutions and the rule of the far right. The far right can take over those institutions from within and rule through them, unlike the Nazis who abolished that institutional structure as soon as they took power.

Tariq Ali is quite right about the extreme centre. In the British context, that would mean the convergence between Thatcherite Tories and Blairite Labour. The same could be said about Republicans and Democrats in the US. Chomsky is right. The two-party system functions very much like a struggle between two factions of the party of capital. But I am thinking not only of the 'extreme centre' but also of the far right as it is represented, for example, by Orbán, Erdoğan, Trump and Modi in very different contexts. None of these far right people could be called fundamentally fascist; none of them have the discourse of abolishing the liberal state structures. They all come to power and then maintain power through liberal institutions. What they are most concentrated on is the long march through the institutions. They mean to dominate and transform all these institutions—universities, judiciary, press and television, the ideological apparatuses of the state, the legal and juridical apparatuses of the state, the bureaucratic apparatuses of the state, the military apparatuses of the state. They capture them, they transform them, they put their local personnel into them, they create the stability of their power through them; if at some point they need to concede power in the electoral arena, that is acceptable, since they have already taken hold of the state. The RSS, for instance, does have what Lenin called 'revolutionary patience': they have taken a hundred years to arrive at this point.

These forces understand that the frontal attack on the Winter Palace is no longer possible, that it cannot be done. You need to change the nature of the existing institutions. I don't know how deliberate it was, but the fact of the matter is that when Advani took over the Information and Broadcasting Ministry in the post-1977 Janata government, that is when the Indian media and everything else began to change. When Advani became home minister under Vajpayee in 1996 and then 1998, your entire system began changing rapidly. I went to the Foreigners' Registration Office and the personnel was RSS. I could see it. So, they were altering the key areas very rapidly. One of the reasons they want to be in power is to have the power of appointment; the other is the amount of money they can transfer to the base of the RSS from the state agencies. Hundreds of millions of dollars can just be distributed among their supporters through contracting and those sorts of things. You create a nation-wide patronage system. Also, so long as they are in power, the bourgeoisie will give them enormous amounts of money. So, parliamentary power is very important for them.

It struck me that if one is serious about the language one uses or the terms in which one thinks, one would have to reflect on the difficulty of using the word 'fascist' to characterize a political force that has never mounted a serious ideological attack on the institutional structure of the liberal state. The RSS has never threatened to suspend the constitution or abolish all other political parties, whereas the Nazis were very consciously and very openly against liberalism. The Nazi high brass—Alfred Rosenberg and others—said that they wanted to reverse the history that began with the storming of the Bastille and led straight to Bolshevism. RSS is of course anti-communist but even the most sophisticated of its leaders are too untutored to be interested in the tradition that runs from the storming of the Bastille to the storming of the Winter Palace. What they do understand is that they can take over the institutions of the Indian state one by one within the norms and procedures of liberal legality.

VP: You had said that your thinking has changed from the 1990s to the 2014 essay. Could you give us a few gestures towards those changes?

AA: Several changes. In the earlier work I used the word 'fascist' rather carelessly. Fascistic is fine. Time and again when the BJP comes to power or is about to come to power, the CPI(M) gets into this debate of 'fascism is coming' or 'fascism is not coming'. For that reason and because the question is being posed all over the world, I have been thinking and researching more deeply. We may dislike Orbán as deeply as we like but when he recommends 'illiberal democracy' we should pay attention. His phrase may actually be more apt for himself and his kind—Trump and Erdoğan, for instance—than 'fascism' *per se*. Today's far right is in very rare cases fascist in the sense of the fascist movements and governments of the interwar years. This raises the question of the relationship between liberal institutional structures and the forms of rule available within those structures. That returns us in a way to the oldest question, which goes back to 1914: can the Left take power through elections, and then bring socialism? The classic Social Democratic answer—in the guise of Bernstein—was to say, yes we can and we should. If Bernstein was wrong and if it is true that the Left cannot bring socialism simply by winning elections and taking hold of parliament—as Rosa Luxemburg argued—then can the far right achieve its objective through parliamentary means? Or is there a liberal force which will make it impossible for the far right to do it? Now, if it is true that the liberal state structure is predisposed towards capitalism and its entire *reason* for being is to give stability to capital, then you cannot destroy capital through this agency. That is why this agency, the liberal-democratic state apparatus, will never allow the communist Left to implement its programme. You can try it in Kerala, on the level of one state among many within a stable republic of the bourgeoisie, and you will be able to put through some very impressive reforms. That much the liberal bourgeoisie will allow. But on the level of the state? Chile? Venezuela? Bolivia? Not even communist, just very radical kind of anti-capitalist socialism with a heavy dose of economic nationalism. Even that cannot be allowed within the rulebook of liberal capitalism. But to the extent that the far right has no intention of destroying capitalism, in fact, they would try to further stabilize capitalism, there is no fundamental contradiction between the liberal state structure and the far right. The Nazis destroyed the liberal state structure because there was a real threat of communist revolution which could only be defeated through extreme means. Today's far right faces no such threat and will prefer to use the legitimacy that the liberal structure—elections and so on—gives them. They will prefer to rule through parliaments and pliant judiciaries. Brazil and India—not to speak of Trump's United States of America—are good examples. This is not fascism. We have to pay attention to the novelty of this political form as much as we need to be vary of its fascist potential.

VP: That means that the high bourgeoisie also is not worried about this; they are perfectly content.

AA: A very large part of the German big bourgeoisie was not disturbed by fascism. Hitler saved them from a possible communist revolution. Then he went to them and told them that his plan for German rearmament for world conquest was going to open up vast business opportunities for them, and he was going to impose labour discipline to make sure that capitalist industries could function without any trade union disturbance. They were ecstatic. They could use fascism just as they had used the liberal system. These are the two historical forms of the capitalist state.

It is said that creation of a bourgeois culture is part of the historic mission of the bourgeoisie. I have come to believe that the Indian capitalist class is culturally not bourgeois. It has no commitment to bourgeois culture; they are just money makers who are content with anachronistic social hierarchies of caste. The failure to abolish the caste system shows that the propertied classes have no intention of even reforming Brahminism, let alone abolishing the social and political order based on its values. Modern ideas have been grafted on top of deep anti-modern social conservatism. So, we don't have a bourgeoisie which is simultaneously a cultural entity as well as a force of accumulation, and which then makes a commitment to autocentric national development. This explains to me the whole phenomenon of the saffron yuppy which arose in India not so much in conjunction with the fascist project of the RSS as in the cultural domain of an upwardly mobile, Hinduized, upper-caste identity. By now, India too is caught up in the whirlwind of this new, post-Soviet form of capitalism—globalization through the agency of generalized-monopoly capitalism—which has led to an overall decline of bourgeois culture even in Europe, not that the United States ever had much. There is a general decline in what I am calling bourgeois culture.

This lack of a proper, stable bourgeois culture is one of the things that makes large sections of Indian urban educated middle classes even more prone to these right-wing, hysterical forms of politics. That is also why the affiliation of the middle class in India with the Left is very brittle; that kind of affiliation would be quite antithetical to what I'm calling their general intellectual culture. And they are very quick to accommodate with imperialism. They are extremely dependent on the West for their social ideals, lifestyles, and worldviews. It is quite astounding how quickly this American form of single-issue politics, from which have arisen these social movements and the NGOs, has permeated so much of the Indian educated urban middle class. There is a very peculiar combination of quite superficial Westernization and quite backward traditional culture.

Compare this with the Chinese bourgeoisie that has grown up under the tutelage of the Chinese Communist Party. It wishes to be not a subordinate ally of Western bourgeoisies but competes with them and is preparing to even dominate them. For this, it has accepted a state based on central planning and one that keeps the nation's finances and a large part of the nation's economic heights under its own direct control. It has accepted thus far, however reluctantly, that agricultural land will remain un-privatized. If the Indian bourgeoisie is complicit with the RSS in invoking traditional Hindu culture for superstition and irrationalist hysteria, the Chinese bourgeoisie has revived Confucianism as an ideological support for precisely the kind of patrimonial and authoritarian welfare capitalism that the Chinese state is in the process of shaping. As for its modern culture, just compare the respective educational expenditures of the Indian state and the Chinese state respectively, in absolute terms but also as proportion of the respective national budgets. While Chinese universities are joining the ranks of the world's most advanced universities, the Indian bourgeoisie has no interest in saving our universities from the offensives of the far right or even to fund them enough to do a competent job of producing a competent technocracy.

VP: Even our conceptual landscape is rejected by them, with a concept such as imperialism eroded from the imagination of people who might even consider themselves Left—not only liberal—intellectuals.

AA: Sure. They're on the side of growth, which has to do with capitalist prosperity. The fact of the matter is that neoliberalism has been very good for about 150, perhaps 200 million Indians; they have benefited a great deal. This is a substantial and decisive sector of society: the more affluent sections of the urban middle classes; their support for what in our view is imperialism is deeply connected to their material lives. If you think of percentages, my sense is that a larger part of the university going population is concerned about imperialism in a country like the United States than the university going population in India.

VP: That's a pretty damning indictment of the Indian college student and perhaps a reflection also of the teaching that they're receiving.

AA: Within just a period of fifteen or twenty years, the Left has become much more on the defensive in Indian educational institutions than it ever was since Independence. And certainly during the current Modi period this defensiveness has been growing. And in the midst of this sort of creation of purely consumerist middle classes which have either gained or aspire to gain from capitalism, the influence of the Left in very large sections of the middle classes has declined very substantially. Again, to remind ourselves, a majority of Americans between the age of 25 and 40 say that they would like to have socialism in America. I don't believe you would get that percentage in India.

VP: Maybe the United States of America is the new weakest link.

THE LEFT DECIDES

VP: In 1996, after the general election produced a fractured mandate for the Eleventh Lok Sabha, the BJP went into government for thirteen days, and then lost a vote in Parliament. The United Front approached Jyoti Basu,* CPI(M) leader and chief minister of West Bengal, to become the prime minister. There was a serious debate inside the CPI(M), and in the end the party's Central Committee decided not to take the helm of the new—very weak—government. You wrote an important essay in *EPW* in the midst of the debate.* Could you tell me a little bit about what provoked the essay and what you were thinking as you put it together?

AA: I wrote that essay in relation to several debates that had erupted inside the CPI(M), the Left in general and very notably in CPI, and among leftists and liberals outside such parties, not to speak of the media which used to have a far greater sense of responsibility and even integrity than it does now. BJP had emerged as the party with the largest number of seats but with no chance of proving a majority on the floor. Had the President done the right thing in inviting it to form government at all, just to be ousted in a matter of days? In my view, there was no such constitutional requirement and that the President should have asked Vajpayee for some proof that he commanded a majority in Parliament before inviting him to form the government. There was a view in left and liberal circles that all non-BJP parties should come together on a joint platform to form a government led by the Congress, the second largest party in Parliament. The Congress itself seems to have been opposed to that solution, possibly because the Gandhi family would not have liked Sitaram Kesri to become India's prime minister. As I recall, there was no such thing as the National Front until after a coalition had been cobbled together to form a government under Deva Gowda. The Left had nevertheless played a major role in bringing together a number of parties, other than the Congress and the BJP, into what it called the Third Force. What should be the role of this Third Force in the situation of the hung parliament? Should it try to form a government with Congress support in case the opportunity arose? This question was discussed very passionately

* Aijaz Ahmad, 'In the Eye of the Storm: The Left Chooses', *Economic & Political Weekly*, vol. 21, no. 22 (1 June 1996); reprinted in *Lineages of the Present* (Verso edition).

inside the Left and in the country more broadly before Vajpayee was invited to form the government, during the thirteen days of the short and unhappy life of that government, and after it fell. Since the Left had been the main force in assembling the Third Force, many people inside and outside the party felt that it should form government with Jyoti Basu as prime minister. Rumour has it that the General Secretary of the party [CPI(M)], Comrade Surjeet, was a chief proponent of that position. That was the general background. I want to emphasize that the debate was not only internal to the CPI(M) but it raged across the political spectrum. For instance, after the Central Committee of the CPI(M) refused to provide the prime minister or participate in the ensuing cabinet of the National Front, CPI did join that government and took up cabinet posts in it.

Inner conflicts within the CPI(M) on this issue were well known. But I was very much surprised when a rather impressive number of party members, including some very prominent ones, staged a demonstration on the premises of the CPI(M) office building in New Delhi and circulated a document arguing that the party should indeed form government—this, while the Central Committee was in session and the TV cameras that had come to report on the CC deliberations got an opportunity to cover this quite unprecedented event. The general norm in communist parties tends to be that debate and dissent be kept within the party and decisions be made through debate and voting in the appropriate party organs. The importance of this public and highly publicized show of dissent was threefold. First, it showed how divided the party was and that divisions were probably much deeper than the issue at hand. Second, there was a widespread perception, far beyond the party itself, that this unprecedented action could not have happened without support from a section of the top leadership itself. Third, as I just said, the debate was not at all confined to Left parties. It was much more generalized and there was a widespread view that Jyoti Basu should have been allowed to form a government.

I thought of that article as my contribution to that wider debate and I wanted to write about the historical moment in which, in my view, the decision of the party's Central Committee was correct. Given the intensity of the debate all around I too had a rather strong position, but I would never have discussed this in public had the debate not been made public already.

Part of my argument was simply a conjunctural one. I was not opposed to CPI(M) forming a minority government at the head of a coalition. But my view in that particular situation was that the party must have a large enough presence in Parliament—a quarter or a third of the seats, let us say—to have a credible chance to lead a coalition government long enough to put in place a couple of significant policies before its coalition partners oust it for being too radical. But with 32 seats out of 543, with a vote share of 6.1 per cent? It felt like electoral opportunism, with Jyoti Basu having to run to Sitaram Kesri for approval of every major or minor decision and the latter having the authority to make the government fall at a moment of his choosing.

That was the first time I wrote at length about how isolated the Left really was in Indian politics, notwithstanding its great moral prestige which itself far exceeded its actual material power. But material strength, measurable by number of seats in Parliament, was what eventually mattered when it came to the forming of governments. The Left was outside the absolute consensus in favour of neoliberal policies that included all the national and regional parties. This was itself a reflection of the structural changes in the nature of Indian capitalism. There was a time when the capitalist class needed a strong public sector, a protectionist state, a centrally planned capitalist economy to facilitate high rates of accumulation for itself. By the late '90s, they had reached a level of accumulation which needed none of those attributes of a strong state. Now they needed a state that would facilitate their cooperation with foreign finance capital and imperialism. India now has a powerful bourgeoisie that dominates regional capitalists and controls an integrated national market. This 'national' bourgeoisie cannot be understood in terms of any polarity of the national and the comprador because all sections of it want to be integrated into the imperialist structures of the world market as subordinate allies. At this juncture, they reject not only the communist but even the Nehruvian understanding of the nation state.

Many of the parties that were in opposition to the Congress as well as the BJP—and were the mainstay of the National Front—were largely caste-based parties, led by upwardly mobile sections of the middle castes, which in turn means that they had no material basis for opposing the neoliberal dispensation. They would align with the Left if and when that serves their interests.

VP: The essay has a first subheading on liberalization and saffronization, and it's around this time when you were using two phrases to describe, in one sense, the BJP camp and the other, the Congress camp. You began to talk about a *programmatic* commitment to communalism and *pragmatic* commitment. Could you talk a little about these categories?

AA: That also came up in relation to the isolation of the Left on all the substantive issues. On neoliberalism there was a broad consensus among political parties, backed by the bourgeoisie as a whole. Communalism was the other great issue and the truth of some of what I said at that time has become clearer in later years. That essay was written at a time when virtually all the political parties were refusing to join up with the BJP. That inhibition was getting dropped by 1998. By now, hardly any political party is left that has not cooperated at one time or another with BJP governments at the central and provincial levels. So, that is one meaning of the distinction between programmatic and pragmatic uses of communalism. RSS and all its fronts are founded on the principles and programmes of saffronization but all other parties decide pragmatically, from one day to the next, whether or not they will align with the Sangh *parivar* at any given time.

Congress is the main claimant to power against the BJP. So, it obviously doesn't join BJP-led governments and proclaims its commitment to secularism very loudly. But the actual record is ambiguous. Before Independence, the Mahatma's Congress not only included members of the Mahasabha but also a strong and permanent wing of Hindu communalists which included some great stalwarts of the party. At a later point, one of the things that Indira Gandhi learnt from the Emergency was the level of appeal of the RSS, and of Hindu communalism in general. She started to play a sort of cat-and-mouse game with the Akalis on the one hand and the Khalistanis on the other, but at the same time she made a straight-out bid for the Hindu vote in Jammu against the National Conference and started the practice of temple-hopping, which Rahul Gandhi was to then adopt so wholeheartedly. A Sikh pogrom after her death led to a short-lived consolidation of the Hindu nation behind her son which was broken only by the onset of the Mandir movement. Rajiv Gandhi then tried to play both sides of the fence: getting the Babri Masjid unlocked to appease the Hindus, then taking the side of Muslim fundamentalists in the Shah Bano case. Then came the icy, monumental inaction of Narasimha Rao as forces gathered for the demolition of the Masjid for days and weeks and then performed the ritual of demolition itself for hours, on camera. That the whole might of the Indian state could not prevent the demolition is implausible. Letting it happen was a deliberate decision. All that is part of what I mean by the pragmatic communalism of the Congress.

VP: There's a section in the essay called 'Barbarian at the Gates'. This section opens with a question—'Has fascism arrived?' Two questions arise from this. One, is India threatened by fascism, and two, if so, does one need a united front to confront it? These are unsettled questions. Everything about them remains with us.

AA: It is a very long article, written very rapidly. There must have been an overstatement here and there. I do believe that the RSS itself is fascist at its core. Its political front, the BJP, addresses that other question we were discussing earlier—that in order to capture power in a country where liberal democracy has become the stable form of rule, you have to go through the parliament, and you have to respect all the institutions of liberal democracy. At the same time, a revolution from the extreme right does need to exercise violence in order to terrorize its main antagonists and to release fantasies of power and virility among the paratroopers of Hindutva who are themselves drawn overwhelmingly from the plebeian mass of destitutes, mostly of the lower castes and even Adivasis. Hence the many fronts for the construction of that 'militarized Hinduism' that Savarkar had dreamt of. RSS is also the organization that has thought more deeply about the sheer heterogeneity of India and created dozens of fronts to work among very diverse social forces all over the country. In all this, the question of fascism needs to be posed with great care. I was writing in 1996 and I was trying to describe the situation at that time. RSS was and has always been a fascist organization. But to jump from that to the proposition that the formation of the Vajpayee government could somehow be construed as the coming of fascism struck me as erroneous. RSS was a much less effective force at that time and BJP's rise was eminently resistible. After all, even the more durable Vajpayee government was followed by ten years of very stable Congress rule. It is only since 2014 and especially after an overwhelming majority vote for the BJP more recently that the question of something resembling fascism has been posed in India. What has transpired since 2014 cannot be read back from 1996. That was a different historical moment.

VP: It is almost as if you have read this essay before speaking, or that you are reading from the essay. It says right here, 'Barbarians are at the gate. It is also true that the RSS is a fascist organization and the

BJP is, in the final analysis, its parliamentary front.' And then: 'But has fascism begun? No, it has not.'

AA: I haven't read the essay since 1996.

VP: But there's the logic.

AA: That's the logic and I will come to the roots of that logic in a moment. Let me first say that I hold the Congress to be the main culprit in not fighting hard enough to prevent the rise of the RSS, followed by all—and I mean *all*—the political parties that have collaborated with the BJP at one point or another. The Narasimha Raos and the Nitish Kumars and the Mayawatis and the Chandrababu Naidus have been deeply complicit and directly responsible for this rise and further rise of the RSS and its fronts. The Left suffers from the crimes of liberals.

Where does this logic come from, and where did I first learn this lesson? Well, from my study of the Nazis' rise to power, and the contrasting role of communists and social democrats during the 1920s. You have to keep in mind that until 1928, five years before they captured absolute power, Nazis were still a relatively small and ineffectual force. There is a great myth that an effective anti-Nazi alliance could not be formed because the communists did not want to form a united front with Social Democrats. That is, as I said, a mere myth. The career of Social Democrats in Germany after the First World War begins with the government headed by Friedrich Ebert. The Weimar government was the government of these Social Democrats, yes, the right wing of the Social Democrats but Social Democrats nonetheless. They killed communists; they used fascist troops—troops that soon went over to the Nazis—to kill Rosa Luxemburg, Karl Liebknecht, and others. And even then, after that, throughout the 1920s, the KPD—the German Communist Party—was under attack by the fascists; the police used to stand by, seeing communists being killed by the Nazis, remaining neutral under the orders of the Social Democrats. The Social Democratic state never intervened to protect the communists;

they were glad that the Nazis were weakening the communists. There was no active alliance but there was tolerance of the Nazis against the communists. So, when the Comintern took the position that the Social Democrats were 'social fascists', there was considerable truth in it. That was not the entire truth, but there was truth in it. A potential united front against the Nazis should have been more the responsibility of the Social Democrats, who were secure in their governmental power, than of the communists. I went to West Berlin after the unification, after the takeover of East Germany, and visited a museum for the struggle against fascism—the West German, Social Democratic version of that struggle. In the *whole* of that building, several stories of it, the communists do not appear as part of the resistance to fascism; they appear on the ground floor as opponents of the Weimar Republic.

That's where I first learned my lesson. Fascism comes to power where liberals and social democrats fail to fight against it, and the Left gets blamed for being dogmatic, sectarian, etc.

VP: The argument made is that the Left has the moral authority and should wield this to somehow right the tilted ship. The Left has moral authority, but little power.

AA: Where does that moral authority come from? From acting—and getting seen to be acting—on principle. If, in conditions of a hung parliament, you make a quick grab of governmental power while commanding mere six per cent of the national vote, and if you are then seen running every morning to get Sitaram Kesri's consent for everything you propose to do, while your cabinet is filled with rank right-wingers who represent your allies, what happens to that moral authority?

VP: And this debate is going to continue until we resolve it in a different way.

AA: Well, when this debate was being revisited in the [Communist]

Party, I actually wrote ten pages and then tore them up. I was going to send it for publication, and then decided not to. Part of the reason is that it became more a factional dispute than a real debate based on facts and principles. Moreover, the word 'fascism' is thrown around a lot but there is no real proper debate on what fascism is or is not. It has become—*Fascism was anti-Semitic; these people are communal; so, these people are fascists.* The discussion becomes just polemical because sides have been taken already.

VP: After this essay from 1996, you did not write more about communism as such, or even the communist movement in India.

AA: No, I didn't.

VP: And what was the reason for that?

AA: I have never thought about that. But now that you ask, I can think of two reasons. The primary one is that I am very much aware that my public criticism of anything that the party does can always be used by anti-communists and I don't want to be used that way. So, if I have any criticism, I would convey it to the party directly, through one channel or another. But the other reason is that thanks to that essay I got very badly caught in the factional disputes in the party. The assaults went on for years. I felt very bruised as a result and did not want to repeat the experience. Anyway, I would be curious to know what you think I might have written about.

VP: In 1996, you intervened with a sharp, precise essay in the middle of a public debate. In the period since there have been many debates on caste, communalism, fascism, and the role of the communist movement in fights against the hierarchies of society. In those areas, you hadn't intervened in public, in terms of a published text.

AA: That 1996 article was an intervention in a debate that was not allowed to stay inside the party and had spilled into the public sphere, precisely at a time when the issue was being discussed all over the country, far beyond the precincts of the party. So, a public intervention seemed appropriate. As for issues you just mentioned— caste, communalism, fascism, etc.—I have written on these issues a great deal, though not with reference to any specific inner party debates because those debates have really not spilled out into the public domain. As for the question of the role of the communist parties in fights against these issues, which you also mention, I'm very determined to not become one of those people who try to teach the communist parties what they should do. If I had anything to say about the actual role of communists in such struggles, I would say that to communists—the ones who care to talk to me—and not in journal articles. I actually wish that the CPI(M) had a tradition of its leaders and leading intellectuals debating issues of strategic importance in public forums, journals, etc., as the Italian party in its good days used to do—I mean the postwar period and particularly the decade before 1976, as the party came closer to actually form government. I don't mean party intellectuals writing about particular issues of importance, which is common in India. I mean, party leaders debating each other directly. That would happen in the Italian party in the '70s. By the way, do you remember the Italian elections of 1976 when the communists were expected to win and Berlinguer, the General Secretary, coined the slogan: '51 per cent won't be enough'?

POSTMODERNISM

VP: Sudhanva and I just travelled in South India, where many students involved in the Left movement said that there has been a revival of postmodern thought. From the 1990s onwards, you have been a very consistent critic of postmodernism, and indeed gave a party class on the subject in Hyderabad (which was published in *The*

Marxist).* Could you walk us through the world of postmodernism?

AA: The first problem with the word 'postmodernism' is that it carried too many meanings, claims and even disavowals. Lyotard, the philosopher most identified with the term, thanks to his very influential short book *The Postmodern Condition*, claimed some years after writing that book that postmodernism is simply the latest phase of modernism. Foucault, often identified as a master philosopher of postmodernism, disliked the word and once professed not to know what it means. Derrida, equally famous as a postmodern philosopher, had a distinctive philosophical method of his own, which he called Deconstruction, and hardly ever engaged in questions of postmodernism as Lyotard had defined them in his book. Lyotard's book was published in 1979. David Harvey published his book *The Condition of Postmodernity* the next year, 1980, which means that the two books were being written at roughly the same time but have hardly anything in common as they define postmodernism/postmodernity.

Then, there is also the problem of nomenclature. The word 'Modernism' refers to the field of the arts and aesthetic representation. One would imagine that the 'post' of 'Modernism' will then engage with what has happened to the fields of Art and Aesthetics since the end of Modernism—assuming that the age of Modernist art is really over. But Fredric Jameson is virtually the only major thinker who theorizes postmodernism mainly in relation to artistic production and aesthetic representation. Neither of the two seminal books I mentioned earlier, those of Lyotard and Harvey, have much to do with the arts except for some cursory comment here and there. I might add that both Foucault and Derrida were great enthusiasts of Modernist art. Most of what is designated as 'postmodernism' has to do with political, social, philosophical issues, not really with art and aesthetics as such, but of course these philosophical and political ideas have had great impact on

* Aijaz Ahmad, 'On Postmodernism', *The Marxist*, vol. 27, no. 1 (January–March 2011), pp. 5–38.

literary theory. That is why I make a basic distinction between what I call aesthetic postmodernity and philosophical postmodernity.

On the philosophical side, the essence of postmodernism resides in rejection of the Enlightenment, turn toward Nietzsche and Heidegger in philosophy and to Max Weber in the social sciences, and a largely negative view of Marx and Marxism. In their social and political thought, on the other hand, main influences were actually American. In his *The Affluent Society* (1958) Galbraith had argued that unlike the past when great industrialized societies were divided between fabulously wealthy minorities and a very poor majority, the US was in the process of creating a society in which even the working class was coming to own their homes, as well as cars and consumer durables. Around the same time, C. Wright Mills had spoken of a new postmodern society having arisen in postwar US that was increasingly detaching itself from the moral universe of the Enlightenment. These themes were greatly extended by Daniel Bell in his *The Coming of Post-Industrial Society* (1973).

Alongside those analyses of the changing economic and social structures of capitalism we also see Marshall McLuhan's work of the 1960s on the rise of a media-driven society and Alvin Toffler's diagnostic book of 1970, *Future Shock*, with its idea of 'information overload'. Such books were immensely influential in France at a time when an American-style capitalism was rising there very rapidly, thanks substantially to the Marshall Plan and its restructuring of French economy and society. All that American sociological thinking lies buried under the high Gallic theorizing of Debord, Baudrillard, Lyotard, etc.

This shift was very rapid. PCF (the French Communist Party) had played a tremendous role in the anti-Nazi Resistance and therefore emerged out of the Second World War as the largest party with 26 per cent of the vote. Being on the Left meant being either in the party or in some sort of positive relationship with it. Sartre was at that time the preeminent French philosopher, still wedded to his existentialism with its highly individualistic notion of freedom. However, as soon as the Americans offered the Marshall Plan to Europe, Sartre saw that the idea was to buy up the European bourgeoisie and decimate the Left. He got involved in mobilizations against the Marshall Plan and in the process drew closer to the PCF. He lost two of his closest friends during that period: Merleau-Ponty and Albert Camus. Closeness to the PCF did not last long but he stayed on the Left, worked as a militant opposed to French imperialism, and supported all anti-imperialist causes while moving closer and closer to theoretical Marxism. His *Critique of Dialectical Reason* (1960)—a magisterial, unfinished work—has in my opinion a status in postwar European Marxism similar to that of *History and Class Consciousness* of Lukács in European Marxism of the first half of the twentieth century.

Structuralism mounts an attack on Sartre and on the Dialectic (Hegel, Marx, Sartre) at a very early stage. Levi-Strauss himself used to claim that he was doing Marxism in the field of anthropology to study certain kinds of super-structures. The claim to affiliation with Marx has since then been a common feature among French philosophers who wanted to attack communists or wanted to propose a Heideggerianized Marx. The last chapter of Levi-Strauss's *The Savage Mind* (1962) is a direct attack at Sartre two years after the publication of the latter's *Critique*. Repudiation of Sartre, his particular Marxism and his fidelity to the dialectical method is a major element of French post-structuralist philosophy of the '60s and '70s.

This anti-Marxism is sometimes overt and sometimes more covert. Perry Anderson has unearthed the fact that the first time Lyotard used the term 'metanarrative' it was in the context of Marxism: the metanarrative that had lost its relevance was Marxism.* Not metanarratives in general; that comes later. By the time Lyotard writes *The Postmodern Condition*, he rejects what he called 'metanarratives

---

* Perry Anderson, *The Origins of Postmodernity*, London: Verso, 1998, p. 29.

of emancipation': not merely 'metanarrative' but 'metanarratives of *emancipation*'. What has lost credibility, Lyotard says, is Kant's idea of Humanity emancipating itself through Reason, Hegel's theorization of history itself in terms of Humanity's struggle for Freedom, and Marx's idea of universal emancipation through proletarian revolution. Kant, Hegel, and Marx: the guilty triumvirate in the eyes of postmodernism. Much of what they say about Reason and the Enlightenment is actually very familiar not only from the themes of the German Conservative Revolution during the first half of the twentieth century but also with much older discourses of the Counter-Enlightenment that go back to the time of the Enlightenment itself.

VP: Your essay on postmodernism—'Postcolonial Theory and the "Post-" Condition'—goes through the canonical texts, and then arrives via Francis Fukuyama at Homi Bhabha and Gayatri Spivak.* They are the two main figures in terms of postcolonialism and postmodernism.

AA: That was an extended version of a lecture I had given at York University in Toronto in 1996. Postcolonial theory had taken off as an academic discipline—call it fashion, if you will—only a few years earlier. In his 1994 essay, 'The Postcolonial Aura', Arif Dirlik had identified 1992 as roughly the time when 'postcolonialism' had first become something of a buzzword. It was *that new* when I tried to locate it historically. I did not really want to write a descriptive essay of what was published when and who said what. I was more interested in the very conditions of possibility for such a mode of argumentation to arise and become so very influential so quickly. As I began thinking about all this, I remembered Lutz Niethammer's magnificent little book, *Posthistoire*, which had dealt with an intellectual conjuncture around the years of the Second World War, before and after, when a good number of European intellectuals produced texts that exuded

* Aijaz Ahmad, 'Postcolonial Theory and the "Post-" Condition', *Socialist Register 1997*, vol. 33, pp. 353–81.

what Niethammer called 'posthistorical melancholy'. He dissected or referred to a large number of writers, from Schmitt and Jünger to Benjamin and Adorno, who did not share political or theoretical positions but did exude a shared feeling that history had somehow ended or, at least, failed to deliver what was expected of it. Neithammer himself speaks of Zeitgeist but we could also use the very useful concept of Raymond Williams: a structure of feeling.

I even borrowed the term 'the "post-" condition' from him, not to suggest that a similar conjuncture was at hand but that we were faced, from the 1970s onwards, with a whole plethora of words marked by the prefix 'post': post-Enlightenment, post-structuralism, post-Marxism, postmodern, post-feminism, postcolonialism, etc.—even 'post-contemporary' in Jameson's coinage. There were also: End of Ideology, hyperreality, End of metanarratives, End of History, and many such endings. So, I was asking two quite different questions: Is there something fundamentally common between Lyotard and Fukuyama, between 'End of the Metanarrative of Emancipation' and 'End of History' and between this variety of postmodernism and the anti-communist triumphalism of the post-Soviet era in the West? Secondly, could it possibly be the case that the view of contemporary history that is shared between Lyotard and Fukuyama is the very ground on which postcolonial theory flourishes?

These are structural questions about a general phenomena, not an inquiry into any particular person's specific views on this or that political matter. In other words, I am interested in the fact that at a particular historical moment a new generation of cultural theorists arises, led by some luminaries of Indian origin, for whom conceptual categories of post-structuralism serve as the metalanguage of discourse through which colonial histories are now to be re-conceived in opposition to the categories of thought that anti-colonial political leaders and intellectuals had deployed in their struggles against colonialism.

VP: To read history through post-structuralism can prevent analysis. Veena Das, who is cited by Bhabha, says that violence cannot be explained. There's a block. There is only silence. I remember reading this and thinking, so then what is the point of an intellectual or of intellectual activity?

AA: The claim of Veena Das is that we cannot understand violence but can only mourn for the suffering of its victims. That amounts to putting violence into the aesthetic category of the Sublime: unknowable and terrifying. This kind of claim is a part of the anti-rationalist revolt against the Enlightenment—the left wing of which was inherited by Marxism. There are immensely long histories of responsible scholarship that have sought to understand both the motives as well as effects of violence. For example, Freud was interested from the beginning in understanding the motivations for aggression and he became greatly occupied after the First World War with the *effects* of violence. I remember reading a long time ago Robert J. Lifton's work on the victims of the atom bomb in Hiroshima. There are thousands of such attempts to understand violence in all its aspects. Trying to understand what appears to be beyond rational understanding is precisely the undertaking of scientific inquiry. But then, you know, the Unknowable is the primary category of religious people and right-wing romantics. What they oppose is precisely this whole tradition which says history is intelligible, the unconscious is intelligible. You see, in that sense, Freud is also within the Enlightenment tradition, since he argued that unreason can be understood rationally. The idea that 'violence' is a category by itself is something I do not understand. There are all kinds of violences. We know the psychic and social structures that produce domestic violence of men against women. We know why imperialism has been making war on its victims for centuries. There are wars of national liberation and we know why those wars are fought. We know that most of what gets called communal violence is not spontaneous; it's organized and at the same time, once you have created this monster, it can then erupt spontaneously wherever some people can see advantage in it. If violence is just ineffable then you need do nothing about it.

VP: Which means, if you accept this view, then a communal riot is something you can't understand.

AA: That is it precisely; I think that is what her point is.

VP: Then there's nothing you can do about it.

AA: Sure, it's just human nature.

VP: And then you live with it.

AA: Yeah, violence is just part of human nature, which is unknowable.

VP: It's an extraordinarily cynical attitude.

AA: Well, for a scholar to say so is to abdicate the very basic responsibility of scholarship which is to persist in trying to understand what on the surface seems beyond reason.

VP: There's that.

AA: It's a very comfortable position. Yes, it is cynical, it is cynical in that sense.

VP: I mean, let's close the book on them because I think this is disturbing because it becomes influential but it's not intellectually interesting, is that correct?

AA: Yes, that's why I never actually wrote at length about any of them, you know? You see, Francis Fukuyama interests me partly because he is also misunderstood. I have written that the postmodernists, like Lyotard, are philosophically less interesting than Fukuyama. Fukuyama is more interesting intellectually. He knows his Hegel; he also knows his Nietzsche. He understands that the triumph of liberal capitalism has created a society of universal consumerism and idiocy, the ultimate decay of human society.

VP: Well, that's the two parts of the title of the essay: *The End of History*—Hegel—*and the Last Man*—Nietzsche.

AA: The intellectual as well as moral superiority of Fukuyama is that he does not celebrate the society that advanced capitalism has created, unlike Lyotard.

VP: The interesting part of 'Postcolonial Theory' is that the longest sections are the opening, where you deal with Fukuyama, and the end, where you deal with Gayatri Spivak. In the essay you reflect on *Can the Subaltern Speak?*, where Spivak has an interrogation of Foucault. You write, '[She] begins with a long and spirited criticism of Foucault and Deleuze on the ground that their delineations of the structures of Power are fatally flawed because they treat Europe as a self-enclosed and self-generating entity, by neglecting the central role of imperialism in the very making of Europe, hence of the very structures of Power which are the objects of analyses for such as Foucault and Deleuze.' There's something interesting in her project; could you reflect a little bit on your reading of Gayatri Spivak, and engagement with her work and how she's quite different from these others we just talked about.

AA: I think Gayatri Spivak is a serious intellectual, unlike Homi Bhabha. I may disagree with much that she writes but she's a real intellectual. For one thing, she is a very good reader of individual literary texts. The only reason that that section of the essay exists is that the essay—*Can the Subaltern Speak?*—is a part of the undergraduate syllabus for Delhi University. Mine is a commentary on an essay which Indian students at Delhi University are required to read, so essentially, my hope was that some Indian lecturers in Delhi University would read it. Otherwise, I am not that interested in these things. A basic point I make is that whereas it is supposed to be an essay on a Bengali woman's suicide, the main objective is to take a position in favour of Derrida against Foucault. Edward Said, among others, had said that Foucault is far more useful for political analysis than Derrida, who's essentially a reader of texts and thus far from the domain of politics or political theory. Spivak's essay is an attempt to refute that position without naming Said; it is an attempt to refute Said and to assert that Derridean kinds of reading can give you a more superior political analysis. In that dispute I am on the side of Said. But I had also found the essay very offensive because it keeps referring to an actual dead woman as 'the suicide text'. Moreover, the woman had left no suicide note explaining anything at all. Spivak picks up a number of facts from secondary sources about the general situation which she uses to ascribe to the dead woman all kinds of motivations including, for instance, that she had committed suicide while menstruating in order to prove that she was not pregnant. Offering this kind of speculative reading to prove that Derridean deconstructive methods yield greater insights was, I thought, bad scholarly procedure which was also rather arrogant towards the woman who could no longer speak not because she was subaltern but because she really was dead and Spivak was therefore free to make assertions on her behalf.

VP: To take this further, in the essay you note how postmodern thinking treats, as you write, 'all history as a contest between different kinds of narratives, so that imperialism itself gets describes not in relation to the universalization of the capitalist mode as such but in terms of the narrative of this mode'. This is a point you make here, and later in a Monthly Review book called *In Defense of History.** This seems a nice definition of postmodernist thought.

---

* See the two interviews with Aijaz Ahmad, 'Culture, Nationalism, and the Role of Intellectuals' and 'Issues of Class and Culture', in *In Defense of History: Marxism and the Postmodern Agenda*, ed. Ellen Meiksins Wood and John Bellamy Foster, New York: Monthly Review Press, 1997.

AA: Right, yes. This is what is variously called the 'linguistic turn' although, in my view, it is ultimately a very bookish kind of idealism, where there is really no history except the narrative of history. Again, the fetish of the Unknowable! There is no normative procedure whereby one narrative can be judged to be better than another because ultimately, if that is what it is, then all narratives are of equal value or equally valueless or interesting as fiction; just as you learn from fiction, you also learn from fictions of history, which again, goes back to the point that truth is essentially unknowable; it is a figment of the imagination, a construction among other constructions. This is an anti-scientific turn. Science is also said to be a sort of narrative, not only social sciences. The 'discursive turn', the 'linguistic' turn—it's a form of latter-day idealism.

VP: There's a question I wanted to end this section with, which would help us distinguish between, let's say, the structure of postmodern thinking and perhaps, you know, a rich Marxist approach; just to help us separate the two out. Foucault had the phrase, 'regime of truth'; some protocols that govern what is true and what is not true. Marx and Engels, in 1846, have, of course, the classical line, 'The ideas of the ruling class are in every epoch the ruling ideas', from *The German Ideology*. 'Regime of truth' suggests relativism. Marx and Engels are not relativist. They are talking about power.

AA: Marx and Engels actually talk about dominant ideas, not ideas as such. So, their point does not apply to ideas in general, but to dominant ideas—that's very important. Ideas that become dominant, ideas of the ruling class. And they may be false, but they become dominant through the force of the dominant classes, their systems of education, and other very elaborate ideological apparatuses. So that if you teach everybody neo-classical economics, that is what they think economy *is*. Marxism, for example, is not part of the dominant ideas; they are always oppositional ideas which may be based on much higher truth, unassailable truth, which you can reach dialectically and scientifically and prove that they are correct. That's all *Capital* is; it's trying to prove that what we claim about the capitalist mode is correct. There's a very strong belief in the possibility of obtaining correct ideas through exercise of reason and through accumulation of experience in actual social practices, historical agents. By the time you get to Lukács you have the theory of the proletariat as an agent of cognitive truth; the proletarian standpoint as the truth of cognitive practice. This is very different from Foucault's 'regimes of truth'. He says specifically: there is no Truth, only truth-effects, which are created by Power. For Foucault, there is no place outside this regime of truth-effects, because he refuses any suggestion that knowledge could possibly be simply objective, beyond its determination by Power. He says that there is no place outside Power. All that resists Power is another form of Power, so Power is this all-pervasive thing, almost mystical, godlike, everywhere but nowhere in particular. Foucault says that history cannot be told from the starting points of political economy or the state. You can only narrate history through micro-narratives of sexuality, of imprisonment, of medical practice. There is a multiplicity of discourses each of which constitutes its own Power-Knowledge complex. He relented from the extremity of such positions in the last years of his life. But what I have summarized here is found in the books that are the most influential.

VP: But *Discipline and Punish* is such an interesting text because the first footnote says, this structure I've got here, you can basically substitute for this x, y, z; it's not just the prison, it's the school, it's the this, it's the that. Seems to me a total view of history, not a micro-narrative.

AA: No, no, perhaps I used the wrong word, 'micro-narrative'. I meant delimited narrative of individual sites of the formation of Power. You know, different discourses, a multiplicity of discourse, the discourse of medicine as different from the discourse of incarceration or corporeal punishment. Each one of them has a history of its own. Medical practice has a history, madness has a history, the invention of madness has a history. But there is no point of unity in history. There are no agents of history and, therefore, history as such cannot be conceived as a history, as a totality. The category of Totality comes from Hegel into Marxism; it is rejected by the post-structuralists. For Foucault, representative bodies—political parties, trade unions, parliaments—are all coercive bodies. No one has the right to represent anyone else and all you can do in politics is to help people represent themselves. So, you can always go in this neighbourhood or that prison and help them form some sort of committee through which they can represent themselves: micro-politics of extreme localization.

You said that what Foucault says at the beginning of *Discipline and Punish* strikes you as a total view of history. Well, you cannot have a 'total view of history' if you eliminate political economy and the state as structuring structures—in Bourdieu's fine phrase—from your narrative of history. Also, when he says that you could substitute school for prison, that strikes me as intellectually highly irresponsible. The structural position of a school in society is very different than that of a prison. What is common between these two very different institutions is the idea of discipline. Foucault, the anarchist, can identify the two because he is opposed to discipline as such. Marxists would generally prefer a future history in which the need for incarceration is minimized and schooling is universal at all levels of education.

VP: What do you do against the RSS, from a postmodern standpoint?

AA: Once postmodernism becomes high fashion all sorts of people start speaking in its name. So, it is best to speak with reference to particular figures. That's why I keep referring to Lyotard, Derrida, Foucault, so that one knows which stream we are discussing. As regards your question about the RSS, there are two different things involved.

One is that people like Foucault and Derrida are no less opposed to fascism, the far right, religious bigotry, etc., than you or me. Foucault was also not just an armchair intellectual. He was a very familiar presence in left-wing demonstrations against right-wing policies in France. The problem arises when you ask the question that you just asked: what does one do, concretely? That is where the disagreements are. Communists believe in building a counterforce, on the same national scale as the RSS, in all the ways familiar from communist histories: the party, the mass fronts, the united front of anti-fascist parties, an underground armed resistance if and when necessary, build a counter-state in opposition to the existing state. That is where the disagreements would be: what is the alternative, and how to get there?

VP: Would their logic determine that you just let the RSS run riot?

AA: Their logic is micro-politics, from which what you get are NGOs, localized social movements, you cannot represent anyone else, etc. I think that is not just a very ordinary kind of individualism or anarchism but also a happy nihilism.

VP: In the lecture you gave on postmodernism, you say there are several parts of postmodernism. You say that 'postmodernism was comprehensively American before it became French'. The retreat of the state from social welfare, the backing of corporate houses for certain kinds of social programmes, all of this mandated by neoliberalism has meant an increasing role for the corporate funded NGO and social movements in areas where the state has abdicated its responsibility. 'All of this', you write, is 'legitimized by postmodern ideas'. This is the world of micro-politics.

AA: Yes. I don't think that masters of postmodernity would approve of neoliberalism. Both Foucault and Derrida have written extensively and scathingly against neoliberalism and even the rule of capital. On this, there is no fundamental disagreement between them and the

Marxists. The disagreement comes on what to do about it.

And it's very important to remember that the very term 'social movement' was meant to discard the idea of a political movement; the very idea of politics, the very idea that what you really want to do is change the nature of the state. Social movement is the opposite of political movement. The term 'social movement' is not an innocent term. It is a comprehensive rejection of politics and therefore political parties, trade unions, all the historic forms of political resistance.

This condition is not formed by the postmodern intellectuals. It is not as if Foucault went out to say that you should have NGOs. There is, however, a structural homology; it's not that one is directly created by the other, but it is a homology, it is part of a certain structural condition that we're living through, in which those ideas appear, those forms of political work appear. You know, back in the 1970s, I remember some Italian comrades had come to New York City. I asked them something about Italy and they said, you know we are facing a very difficult situation because American forms of local politics have emerged there, and everywhere basically this is the form of opposition that we don't know how to deal with because they *are* talking about very important issues that we also talk about, but their political form is consistently anti-communist. This we have seen in our part of the world as well. It started as the Second International against the Third or Communist International; funding used to come from Germany and Sweden, from the Social Democratic countries. Other sources of funding came later, and the Americans finally understood how important it was to fund these other forces and change the very mentality of people in the Third World. They found how successful this was politically. They competed with communists on the definition of radical action as such. They said: forget the state, what needs to be changed is society, many social norms, and what you needed for that was a decentralized network of networks. You therefore have what are called peoples' movements and then networks that coordinate these numerous movements. No party—that creates bureaucracy; just amorphous movements with no fixed structures, with localism as a virtue. This is the new form of radicalism in the postmodern age. If you think communists are the only ones who claim the ground of radical politics, you are wrong. So do the postmoderns.

VP: It's not my fantasy; I wish it were my fantasy. It's a fantasy, I agree. But the structure of this thought is so limited that it's extraordinary that it continues to attract people. And I think maybe that's something you could help us with a little bit—the attractiveness of this.

AA: You see, that is where I keep saying that all these things are in fact products of something very big, a long-term process, in which the defeat of the Left is the central moment. At what point the Left was defeated is a different matter. It did not happen suddenly in 1989. It happened in one place after another. Greece had a very large Communist Party, which was destroyed by the dictatorship, after which the Greek party—which remains—became much smaller. We all know of the enormous magnitude of the communist bloodbath in Indonesia. The ledger of such defeats is very long. The Left has been retreating and others have been trying to occupy that very space. At the same time, there have been contestations in the field of theory and ideology. Whole generations have been taught to cultivate what Lyotard called 'incredulity toward metanarratives of emancipation'—taught in other words to believe that communism is nothing but tyranny and the Gulag, and that postmodern kinds of pragmatism and liberalism are the real roads to freedom. The World Social Forum [WSF] was the alternative to the idea of the Communist International. It could never adopt even the narrowest of broad programmes that would be binding for all participating movements, because that would be coercive; all should be free to do whatever their particular parties decide to do. No wonder the World *Social* Forum was originally based on the idea that no political parties, certainly no communist parties, would be allowed to participate *as* parties. It was only in Bombay on our insistence that communist parties were allowed to hold a joint meeting within the framework of the WSF.

VP: I mean even the slogan was 'Another World is Possible', which is an empty slogan.

AA: Yes, 'Another World', you see, it's a very interesting slogan. Another world, a world other than neoliberalism but also other than communism.

VP: Yes, because 'Another World is Possible' means fascism is also possible.

AA: Well, not exactly. I don't think fascism would be acceptable to them. What they are talking about is a world that is an alternative both to neoliberalism and communism; so 'another world'. *Corporate globalization* was opposed but not globalization as such, as if there were globalizations that could be done by some entities other than transnational corporations and their transnational capital. Individuals in the WSF undoubtedly spoke against capitalism as such but that was not the platform of the Forum as such, and in any case, you could not propose an alternative to capitalism for which a common programme could be adopted.

IMPERIALISM

VP: After 2001, the US went into a series of wars, against Afghanistan and then Iraq. In this period, the term 'imperialism' had slipped out of the conversation. It was as if there was no purchase for the term and for the conceptual apparatus that would have allowed people to better understand these US wars. You wrote an essay in *Socialist Register 2004* with the powerful title, 'Imperialism of Our Time'. The title is borrowed from Michał Kalecki, who wrote an essay called 'The fascism of our times' (1964). Tell us a little about the context of that essay.

AA: There was just the sheer scale of what was happening in Iraq. This made people think of Iraq not as a structural result of the new forms of assertion of US power in the world, but as this event, this overreaction to 9/11. Moreover, there had been almost two decades of denunciation of Saddam Hussein with the word 'fascist' often used about him, so that even people on the Left such as Fred Halliday were saying, 'You have to remove fascists. We did it in 1945 with the Nazis, now it has to be these fascists.' The war on Iraq was being discussed in large sections of the Western Left in these terms, in terms of an overreaction and in terms of anti-fascism. The war was not seen in relation to imperialist triumphalism after the collapse of the communist state system. So, I wanted to put the war into a larger perspective. Unfortunately, the general discussion of imperialism was overshadowed—even curtailed—by too great an emphasis on the Iraq War. But that was of course the necessary result of the context in which the essay was conceived in the first place, to see that war in relation to the present moment in the history of imperialism.

My essay in that issue of *Socialist Register* was immediately followed by David Harvey's essay called 'The New Imperialism'. There were different kinds of discussions that were trying to displace Lenin's theory of imperialism; Harvey's was one of them. Some five or seven years later, Harvey would reject even the category of imperialism, arguing that Western domination was over, and more capital was going from the West to countries like China than was coming into the West. I could sense that people had either abandoned the category of imperialism or their understanding had gone far beyond any recognition of any continuity with the Marxist-Leninist understanding of imperialism.

I give great credit Leo Panitch and Colin Leys—the *Socialist Register* editors, who inherited it from Ralph Miliband—that they actually did four volumes on contemporary imperialism. My own brief discussion of Lenin was designed partly to differ with Panitch and partly to refute David Harvey, without any reference to either of them. What is still valid and what is not valid in Lenin's theory; what is now no longer valid but was valid in his time—you know, I was very keen on that kind of specification.

Periodization of imperialism, to me, was very important at that time. I have been trying to theorize my perception that the Second World War was fought between Germany and the United States primarily to decide which one of those two was going to inherit the colonies from the French and the British when their colonies become independent. Germany lost the war partly because it had a very antiquated notion of global domination; it wanted to have a colonial empire in the world. In that sense, the United States was much more advanced; it did not want a colonial empire, but what it wanted was an empire of global finance capital under its own dominion. The United States actually achieved what the Nazis had set out to achieve. That's something very important to understand, that the struggle between liberalism and fascism was certainly won by liberalism but essentially with the same object of obtaining a global empire.

The question whether there really is a basic contradiction between the liberal institutional structure and the rule of the far right has been with me for a long time. It has been with me theoretically and historically.

Now, what did the Americans do after the Second World War? The collapse of the national bourgeois states in our part of the world was not incidental; they were defeated and dismantled. The United States was as opposed to Third World economic nationalism as to communism. It perceived a certain commonality between communists and anti-imperialist nationalists: a common project of protecting their economies, resources and markets from imperialist penetration and domination. Whether it was Lumumba in the Congo or Nkrumah in Ghana or Nasser in Egypt, they were all enemies who had to be overthrown, just as imperialism tried to annihilate communists in Korea and Vietnam militarily. The Cold War was cold only against the Soviet Union because it was a nuclear power; war against Third World communists and nationalists was always very hot.

VP: As part of this struggle, imperialism also had to attain primacy over its team, as it were. To build the 'hub and spoke' system.

AA: I argue that one of the fundamental objectives of the United States after the Second World War was to fully, completely incorporate Europe into *its* project, and that unity of the imperialist block under US hegemony has always been fundamental for American imperialism's global domination. That integration has two sides. One is a structural one which has to do with the current, globalized phase of capitalism where national capitals even of the advanced countries have increasingly lost their autonomy, are increasingly amalgamated into or at least subordinated to a globally integrated capital under the leadership of the United States, symbolized by the fact that the dollar serves as the transnational measure of value and the US Federal Reserve commands primacy over all central banks in the capitalist world. This subordination of Europe and Japan to the United States can be witnessed in the fact that none of these other countries has ever substantively opposed any major political or economic decision made by the United States. What we sometimes hear about the possible emergence of the European Union as a rival of the United States is absurd. Even the creation of the European Union was primarily an American initiative even though many Europeans had expressed such aspirations. Similar hopes and fears have been attached from time to time to the idea of Japan rising as a rival power, and now we hear of the rise of China as a threat to the US. Such absurd ideas are sometimes propagated by the US establishment itself, to frighten its own people into a nightmare that diverse rivals and enemies are out to upstage

America. EU does not even have an independent defence structure of its own, and troops from many European countries go wherever the US tells them to go. Although the focus in most of the essay was on Iraq, I did briefly want to make the point that this imperialist integration—this total lack of any inter-imperialist rivalry—at a time when the Soviet alternative had also disappeared, created a very dire situation for countries of the tricontinent. American domination over EU and Japan, especially in military and political arenas, also meant that all rumours of the decline of US hegemony should be treated with great suspicion.

VP: The four essays in *Socialist Register* begin with 'Imperialism of our Time', which you lay out here. The other essays engage with the contradiction between liberalism and the far right. These two accommodate each other in different respects; it seems that these essays are a long attempt to theorize the intimacy between liberalism and the far right.

AA: Absolutely. Mussolini was a hero of the *New York Times*, right up to 1938 and 1939. Churchill saw him as a hero as well. These great liberals—Churchill and the *New York Times*—they loved Mussolini. Some of the most powerful German and American capitalists joined hands in rebuilding the German economy, including the armament industry right up to the onset of the Second World War. Throughout the 1930s there was always the possibility that the liberal West and the Nazis would jointly invade the Soviet Union. This is what led to the short-lived 1939 pact between the USSR and the Nazis, a pact sought by the USSR just to gain time against that very real possibility, to create uncertainties and contradictions among capitalist powers, and of course to gain time to prepare for a war that was coming in any case. There is that factual history of the very close intimacy between the two—the liberals and the Nazis—and the very great possibility in 1939 that they would invade the Soviet Union in an alliance. There is that whole history to consider. In reality of course there was no question of any enduring alliance between the Nazis and the USSR which gave twenty million lives to save not only itself but also Western Europe from Nazi occupation.

Liberalism and the far right are rival forms of the capitalist ideology and state, descended as they are from opposite traditions in the history of European modernity. So, we should not identify them with each other too glibly. However, precisely because both are forms of the capitalist state there is always an objective possibility that in some exceptional circumstances the two may unite. That is what I have been exploring lately, about the regimes and movements of the far right that have arisen in the recent past, in various corners of the world. Is this a return to fascism, as Samir Amin and so many others have argued? Or, are we dealing with a historically novel form of the capitalist state which combines features of the liberal institutional framework with some features of a fascist kind of authoritarian and arbitrary rule whereby liberal institutions are not abolished but dominated and put to authoritarian purposes? One reason you don't need fascism in the strict sense in India today is that fascism is the moment of crisis in a capitalist state system, used to restore the system back to its fundamental liberal form, and at this point Indian capitalism is not in crisis. Vast numbers of Indians are in crisis, but capitalism is not in crisis. Neither capital nor its state is in any crisis, so why do you need fascism if you're not in any sort of crisis, and the Left is backed to the wall in a defensive posture. And yet a very rabid regime of the far right is in place under the rising hegemony of the RSS. How does one understand this phenomenon?

VP: You know, at the time, reading it, I wasn't exactly clear of the implication of it, but now, going back and looking at it again, that was also a period when some Marxist tendencies had developed, two of them in particular. First, there was an approach that said that imperialism had basically dissolved—this is essentially the position of David Harvey. Second, there was the approach that said that the United States was in a terminal crisis, and that its hegemony was over—this is essentially the position of Immanuel Wallerstein and Giovanni Arrighi.

AA: Yes. I read all these people. That's what I believe is a very major duty of mine; to read the whole range of writings on the Left, and that also helps me define my own thought, by rubbing it against the thought of others, who are, in their own right, major intellectuals and knowledgeable people.

The idea that American hegemony is in decline goes back to the mid-1970s. There were then essays in *Monthly Review* about the decline of American hegemony, about which I have been sceptical. For one thing, how much decline are we talking about and in what forms of power. US share in the total world GDP has certainly declined but in my view seeing this as a definite decline of US hegemony *per se* is erroneous. Hegemony does not connote total domination. What it connotes is the power to coerce and the power to gain consent. From being little more than fifty per cent or so around 1950, US share of the global GDP has now declined to around twenty-five per cent. That is a relative decline but even in GDP terms the US is still the most powerful economy in the world. Even if China's GDP begins to match that of the US, per capita income in China is still a tenth of that of the US. I have believed that so long as the US currency functions as the preeminent world currency, and so long as the US military power is cumulatively greater than the next twenty countries—spread out in a hundred and forty of the two hundred countries in the world—it has a structural and global dominance that is quite unmatched and will remain so in the near future. Its financial institutions have such depth that it can destroy *anybody's* economy, as it has done so often; the mightiest countries like China and Japan are trying to stay out of its line of fire, because the US can do great damage, let's say to China, that China cannot do to the United States. They have that kind of overwhelming power.

VP: One more point before we conclude this section. Towards the end of the essay, you write, 'Postmodernization of the world is actually Americanization of the world, with considerable degree of local colour and imitative originality, no doubt. A good degree of this imitative originality can be seen in Europe, too.' Culture is not a trivial issue here.

AA: Not at all. Jameson's canonical work on postmodernism is entitled *Postmodernism, the Cultural Logic of Late Capitalism.* Let us not quibble over the term 'Late Capitalism' which has been used differently by different writers such as Adorno, Mandel, and Jameson. In all usages the term refers to the phase of capitalism that begins with the new technological revolutions after the Second World War. We could simply say 'the present stage of imperialism'. What the title of Jameson book implies is that postmodernism in the strict sense is neither a philosophy nor a social theory but a cultural practice that corresponds to the historical period in which we now live, specially as it pertains to the advanced capitalist world. Jameson concentrates on the arts and quite rightly singles out architecture as the domain in which the interrelations among art, culture, capital, and even ground rent is the clearest. All that is correct. But I want to look also at areas of social experience other than the arts that might be relevant to our discussion.

One of the things that the Americans did immediately after the Second World War was to create a university system for training of intelligentsias of the world on a scale and of a kind that humanity had never known in the past. They brought so many people from all parts of the world to be educated in the US, they created very advanced schools of diplomacy where diplomats from all around the world but particularly from the newly independent Asian and African countries could come and get training in etiquettes and presuppositions of diplomacy in the bourgeois world. They created magnificent social science departments and business management schools where the best and the brightest from the Third World were trained, as was also true of law schools, departments of physical and technical sciences, and so on. This whole design for the globalization of American forms of knowledge and culture was supported by an elaborate programme of scholarships, exchange programmes, specialized visa systems, etc. Most of the technocrats and higher echelons of bureaucracy in these newly decolonized countries had thus been trained in American systems of thought and sensibility, aided of course by others—a declining number—who were still going to British or French institutes of higher learning.

Then there is also the issue of popular culture. The US government actively promotes Hollywood cinema all over the world in all sorts of ways. Almost ninety per cent of releases in *Europe* are American. CNN and Fox News can be watched in every airport in the world. The only global music is American music. What I call 'imitative originality' is most visible in all the mass media. Jeans and fast food are now global forms of dressing and eating. Through these knowledge systems, cultural industries and just quotidian details of daily life (dress, food, music, etc.), America manufactures the forms of desire that become universal. Jameson has this wonderful phrase: 'colonizing of the Unconscious'. If there is one desire that can be found in all corners of the world, it is to become American or at least do things, and think and imagine in the American mould.

VP: It's from the military, to financial institutions . . .

AA: Absolutely. Everything.

VP: . . . to culture. And if you only look at share of GDP, you miss this.

AA: You miss *all* of this. Europe has no military apparatus of its own, it's incorporated into NATO and NATO goes where the Americans want it to go, and Europeans go with them. No state in the capitalist world has autonomous power. The enemy yesterday was the Soviet Union and today it is China, simply because the USSR in the past and China in the current phase have been states that sought to create and defend an autonomous space of their own, independent of US hegemony. USSR of course represented an alternative to the capitalist system; today's China, by contrast, is fully integrated into the system. But the will to encircle and strangle China is just as great because it refuses to be dominated.

ISLAMISM

VP: In your essay, 'Islam, Islamism and the West', you refer to those who attacked the US on 11 September 2001 as the 'monster of its own making'.* The general dyad is that Americanism is in one corner, and Islamism is in another. But you have a much more precise understanding, in fact there is much here that appears like your argument about the intimacy between liberalism and the far right.

AA: Immediately after the Second World War, as America expanded into various regions of the world that had been previously colonized by European powers—North Africa, West Asia, Southeast Asia—it confronted a growing Left. After the Second World War, communist parties were the largest parties in Iraq and Iran, and very large in Egypt and Sudan as well. The largest communist party outside of the USSR and China was in Indonesia, the most populous Muslim country. The so-called Muslim countries, where the majority of the population was Muslim, were extremely hospitable to communism. In India, a very large number of the early communists—including one of the founders of the party in Bengal—were Muslims.

Already in the 1950s, the Americans conceived of pietistic and

---

* Aijaz Ahmad, 'Islam, Islamisms and the West', *Socialist Register 2008*, vol. 44, New Delhi: LeftWord Books, 2009, pp. 1–37.

orthodox variants of Islam as the great barrier, the one force that could fight communism in all those countries. Building up right-wing Islamist forces was a major component of the Truman Doctrine. The Muslim Brotherhood was seen by the Eisenhower administration as the future saviour of the Arab world. Said Ramadan (the son-in-law of the founder of the Muslim Brotherhood, Hassan al-Banna) was extensively funded by the CIA and he led a delegation of Islamists who were invited to meet Eisenhower in the Oval Office in 1953, just as the Afghan *Mujahideen* met Reagan there in the 1980s, and then later just as the Taliban visited the US politicians in the 1990s. Robert Dreyfuss's *Devil's Game* lays out some of these very old relationships.[*]

On the other side, the Americans were doing as much as they could to stabilize the Gulf monarchies, partly because of oil but also because they were mortally afraid that Nasserism would defeat these monarchies, and the US associated Nasser with the Soviet Union. In Egypt, in Iraq, and in Libya, these middle-class revolutions were carried out by military officers and Arab secular nationalists—the key elements of Nasserism. The US funded and trained groups of extremist Islamists in a large number of those countries often in partnership with the Saudis and their networks. That is why when the question of Afghanistan came up, the CIA could easily bring people from roughly forty countries to fight for the *jihad* because they had been cultivating such groups for over thirty to forty years prior to that. There is an old tie between imperialism and Islamism, which then explodes into the war in Afghanistan. Osama bin Laden got involved when the head of the Pakistani ISI said to his CIA counterparts that it would be good if they could get a Saudi prince to lead the *Mujahideen* in Afghanistan. They looked around and found that no prince was going to run the risk of getting killed. They couldn't find a prince, but they found the son of a very, very wealthy family, connected with the House of Saud, who

---

[*] Robert Dreyfuss, *Devil's Game: How the United States Helped Unleash Fundamentalist Islam*, New York: Metropolitan Books, 2006.

was a bit of a playboy but who had also been indoctrinated at a Saudi university into the more apocalyptic versions of Wahhabi theology. They recruited this man and presented him to the ISI as a substitute for a Saudi prince. That was Osama bin Laden. So that's the sort of thing I was referring to when I wrote that *jihadi* Islamism was a monster that the US itself had created.

VP: The essay in *Socialist Register 2008* has a line that I wanted to raise with you. It says, 'Identity politics in the widest sense is now quite the norm.' This is an essay on Islamism, but you are raising a shift in the world towards culturalism, or—as you say—where 'the view that culture is primary and the determining instance of social existence'. Could you reflect on this a little, on this changed context?

AA: Yes, absolutely. One of the results of the defeat of the Left has been the rise of this identitarianism, and by the Left in this context I mean—to borrow that wonderful phrase of Eric Hobsbawm—the 'Enlightenment Left'. That phrase, 'the Enlightenment Left' refers to such forces as communism, social democracy, anti-colonial nationalisms, secular movements against religious obscurantism, anti-feudalism, and other analogous forces. In one way or another, all sections of the Enlightenment Left were either defeated or forced to retreat as the balance of forces shifted. This necessarily led to the rise of anti-Enlightenment irrationalisms. Nationalism was again defined in terms of race, religion or ethnicity—as the European Right, notably the Nazis, had always done. This repudiated the secular core of the progressive anti-imperialist nationalisms. This is an old European trope. Counter-revolutionary thinkers like Bonald and de Maistre argued vehemently that the French Revolution violated the true identity of France as a Catholic country and a monarchical realm. This identitarianism has been at the heart of right-wing nationalisms since at least the latter part of the eighteenth century.

Meanwhile, there is also a very strong and seemingly benign

multiculturalist discourse that arises particularly in the US but also in other Anglo-Saxon countries such as Britain and Canada. These are countries where ideas of national culture have been historically bound up with a deeply entrenched sense of white racial identity but have also received masses of Third World immigrants at various points since the Second World War who can never be assimilated into the 'true' (white) nation as immigrants from Europe can be. Multiculturalism is a liberal and, in some ways, even a postmodern discourse that encourages very communitarian forms of politics in this context of mass immigration and advocates what Freud called 'the narcissism of small differences'. According to this logic, various immigrant groups constitute distinct communities defined by race, religion, national origin or some other ethnic marker. Each of these communities is said to have a distinct culture as well as distinct interests of its own. How a community gets defined is a malleable process. There could be an Arab community or an Irani community or there could be a Muslim community that includes Yemeni shopkeepers, Turkish doctors, Pakistanis from peasant backgrounds or bankers but they are all presumed to have the same culture because they all believe in some variety of Islam. This sort of confusion between religion and culture is quite rampant but what this creation of communitarian identities does is, among other things, that it undermines solidarities of class. Vast majority of immigrants are working class but if they get divided into Mexican community, Yemeni community, etc., you undermine any possibility of their seeing themselves in terms of a class above and beyond the ethnic boundaries.

VP: In the essay, there is a section called 'The President, The Pope, and The Professor'. All three—President Bush, Cardinal Ratzinger, and Samuel Huntington—are united against these various migrants, who are hardly to blame for taking shelter in whatever is available to them.

AA: Well, the warmongering of Bush is well known. So, let us set that aside. But Cardinal Ratzinger who later became the Pope asserts this identity between European civilization and Christian religion, and by Christianity he implicitly means Catholicism. He has said time and again that Christianity and Islam are irreconcilable, that Turkey should not be allowed membership in the European Union because it is a Muslim majority country and therefore intrinsically non-European. This kind of preaching from the highest pulpits of Europe goes far to clarify the roots of all the Islamophobia you see all over Europe, not only on the Right but in circles much wider than just the Right. Huntington's canvass is equally narrow in the sense that he defines Western civilization strictly in terms of *Western* Christianity—in other words, Catholicism and Protestantism. All else is beyond the pale. So, no one should be surprised at what happens when Ilhan Omar, for example, enters the US Congress wearing a headgear that identifies her as a Somali Muslim woman and has to then face wild fires of white racist rage so intrinsic to US culture which the liberal veneer tries so hard to hide. Everywhere, from the President to the little carpenter, everyone is enraged by the fact that there are these two women, both Muslim women, flaunting who they are; one of them, Rashida Tlaib, is Palestinian.

VP: Right, she doesn't even have to wear a headscarf.

AA: She doesn't, and in fact she asserts her Palestinian origin much more than the incidental fact of being a Muslim.

VP: Her very existence is a headscarf.

AA: She strikes me as a very secular sort of Palestinian, not much of a Muslim except in a sociological sense.

VP: But it's irrelevant.

AA: Yes. The very fact that she is Palestinian *and* Muslim already damns her.

Ilhan Omar's rhetorical stance is very interesting. She constantly invokes the 'true' American values of freedom, religious tolerance, human rights, etc.; the figure 'we Americans' is a constant feature in her speeches. But she is so visibly a dark-skinned and *hijab*-wearing Muslim woman that she can never shed that identity even if she wanted to. So, in defiance of that racism, she is forced to take pride in her Somali origin and Islamic belief. These are the different ways in which identity politics of various sorts in the United States is already in place. And in this web of identities, religion is not a minor matter. Contrary to common belief, the US is a deeply religious society so that a very belligerent kind of right-wing, Evangelical Christianity is at once a very potent force in American politics and is also often interwoven with white racism. The book that I'm currently writing has a section on how not just Christianity, but a certain kind of Biblical millenarianism was foundational in the ideological formation of the United States at its very inception. Islamophobia therefore has many layers to it and reaches into the highest levels of the state. For the devout American, Muslims are the quintessential Outsiders, prone to violence by the very nature of their religion. Zionists and neoliberals have only fed into that pre-existing bigotry. And the culturalist idea of fixed and eternal identities of race and religion only confirms for them that there is some primordial essence of Muslimness which is by nature violent.

VP: Identitarianism, or more precisely culturalism, is what provides the link between liberalism and the far right.

AA: Sure, absolutely. You see, the liberal multicultural state, which has to deal with this ferment among the immigrants who have social grievances and economic grievances, wants to contain them both ideologically and institutionally. They talk to the leaders of mosques as representatives of the Muslim community. Most of these mosques, by the way, are funded by the Gulf countries, mostly Saudi Arabia. The most retrograde kind of *imams* become interlocutors on behalf of Muslims even though they are unchosen. Then these *imams* form a society or an association, and then they appoint themselves to become the voice of the Muslims and a hyper-Muslimness is constructed.

VP: In the same way as you say that the Left faces a penalty in this period, there is also a penalty faced by secularism. At the end of the essay, you write, 'The secular world has to be just twice over, in terms of what it has defined for itself and also to ward off the claim that god would have given them better justice. That is to say, the secular world has to have enough justice in it for one not to have to constantly invoke god's justice against the injustices of the profane; a politics of radical equality, so to speak.'

AA: Well, quite a bit of crafting went into the writing of that passage. The first sentence refers obliquely to Marx's reference to religion as the sigh of the oppressed, the soul of a soul-less world. I then go on to re-phrase his dictum that if you want people not to have illusions you must build a world that requires no illusion. Then comes that phrase 'a politics of radical equalities' which is obviously a euphemism for an anti-capitalist order, a communist sort of socialism. In other words, the alternative to right-wing religiosity, political Islam, etc., is not secularism as such, in the world of ideas, but to build a secular but also classless society. There is also a play on the word 'secular'. In early Christian thought the word secular simply meant 'worldly'—of this world—as distinguished from the godly, of divine origin, etc. In that sense, 'secular' refers to the material world, not to one kind of belief or another.

In places like India people who were moving to the left typically became atheists before becoming communists. Another way one could think about it is this: When Anwar Sadat was assassinated, many people were arrested and about twenty—just less than twenty—were put on trial—a very famous trial in Egypt! They confessed to the assassination. The interesting thing is that a majority of them had been Nasserists when they were in their teens. It was their disappointment with Nasserism, the failure of Nasserism to deliver on the promise to defeat Israel, that motivated their turn to what we might call Islamic millenarianism. The defeat of Nasserism in 1967, the defeat of secular nationalism, the trauma of that defeat is exorcized through creation of this hysterical form of belief in God—hysterical in the technical Freudian sense of the word. God will give us what these godless people could not win for us. It's a form of hysteria, it's a form of generalized social hysteria that arises out of the trauma of collective defeat, just as out of the *traumatic* experiences of poverty and social humiliation many from among the lumpen proletariat get gravitated towards various kinds of far right violence, including fascism, religious pogroms, ethnic cleansings, etc.

The basic argument here is that *all* of this rise of the far right in its various forms—jihadism, Trumpism, European neo-fascisms, Great Expansion of Hindutva—is ultimately a result of the defeat of the Left. The inability of the Left to create kinds of state systems that can deliver the forms of life that can pull people out of their collective trauma is the fundamental problem. A very large part of the social base for movements of this kind consists of traumatized people; traumatized by their own defeat and their inability to fight back the daily miseries and indignities they suffer under capitalism. Committing violence against others becomes an imaginary compensation for having been at the receiving end of so many daily violences committed by the truly powerful.

I may make a book out of these essays, on Imperialism, Islamism, etc.

VP: Yeah, they're incredible. Just reading them and going over them, you know, like 'Imperialism of Our Time', your essays are written in the moment. You describe what is happening; you explain things. But now, in our time, sixty per cent of our readers have never heard of any of that, because they were either too young or some of them not born.

AA: *The Eighteenth Brumaire* was also written in a conjuncture, Lenin's basic pamphlet on imperialism was also written in an urgent moment. Everything Lenin wrote is in the conjuncture, including his philosophical notebooks. After the February Revolution, he wasn't sure how to think about the situation, so he went and read Hegel's *Logic*, in order to be able to think about the Russian situation dialectically. That's the grandeur of those times and those people, that they thought, quite rightly, that reading Hegel would help understand and delineate revolutionary strategy, and he did it. Thinking through the logic of the conjuncture is at the heart of so much Marxist writing. It's an astonishing experience to actually go back to the moment in which each one of those texts of Marx and Lenin are actually written, this theory that lasts for hundred, two hundred, three hundred years.

That is the tradition I have inherited: writing in response to a political conjuncture in the real world.

EVERY COUNTRY GETS
THE FASCISM IT DESERVES

VP: You know, in your work, there are a series—for me, personally—a series of memorable lines and formulations. And perhaps the line that I have most quoted of yours is: 'Every country gets the fascism it deserves.' Could you talk just a little about that, as a preface to your writings directly on the BJP and RSS, and government in India?

AA: What might have struck you about that sentence is the use of the word 'deserve'. That, and the structure of the sentence as a whole, is actually a play on Clara Zetkin's famous statement that fascism is our just reward for not having made the revolution. It was the phrase 'just reward' that led me to use the word 'deserve'.

Beyond that there is the actual historical experience. When you think of German National Socialism and Italian Fascism in any depth, differences are on the whole more striking than similarities. Spain and Portugal are the other two countries which are counted among those where fascism succeeded. Poulantzas has made a fairly strong argument that those should be treated as dictatorships that lacked some of the fundamental characteristics of fascism. In other words, a *combination* of fascistic features and a military dictatorship. In our own time, I believe, we are witnessing various combinations of the liberal and the fascistic. History makes a country what it is, and politics therefore requires that political movements, whether of the Right or the Left, must correspond to the unique character of that country.

I have something of a dialectical view: a tendency towards fascism has been a generalized phenomenon in all capitalist states in the era of monopoly capitalism but fascism in the classical sense has been fully victorious only in a very few cases and no two fascisms have taken the same form. Why is that so? One of the reasons is that precisely because a far right version of nationalism is fundamental to fascism it necessarily takes the form that corresponds to the historical, social, political conditions of that nation and the kind of ideology and organizational form that have arisen out of those specific conditions. All the studies of Nazism will not teach you much about the RSS brand of fascism if you do not accord primacy to the political, religious, social, historical conditions specific to Hindu India. Strategically speaking, we need to pay less attention to what a fascism might share with the fascism of another country and more to the innovations it has made in accordance with the peculiar history and politics of the country where it takes organized form. The resemblance of RSS fascism with European fascisms is actually rather superficial. Marks of its originality are countless. We don't recognize those marks because we are more interested in condemning it than in understanding it. That is a moralistic stance, not a political one.

As you know, some of the roots of my thinking about fascism lie in my close reading of Gramsci. He posed to himself a rather large question: What is it in Italian society and history that paved the way for such an easy takeover by the fascists? What were the shortcomings in the nationalism of the Risorgimento, the social and political movement that had culminated in the emergence of an independent unified Italian state in 1871? Half a century later, that same state was engulfed by another kind of nationalism, the fascist one. Why? A powerful and unifying nationalism in the past, a massive socialist party in the present, legacies of the Workers' Councils Movement and the 1919 revolution in the immediate background—all of that was just swept away. Hence, the project of understanding and reinterpreting all of Italian history, society, popular fiction, etc., from the heights of the Vatican down to the novels that the Italian working-class was in the habit of reading. One has the grim duty to understand the real because, as Hegel famously put it, the Real *is* Rational. In other words, there are particular *reasons*, rooted in history and social structure, why reality takes, and must take, a particular form. Fascism succeeds only in particular conjunctures but only if it is rooted in some deep structures.

I have devoted a good part of the past twenty-five years to the study of Nazism in particular but also modern fascisms more generally as well as some two centuries of the counter-revolutionary Right in Europe. I have come to believe that the conjuncture in which Nazism and Fascism emerged will not be repeated. So, one really has to look at the kind of country we are and have been, the kind of social structures that are actually in place, the ideological densities, institutions through which those ideologies have functioned, which may be very old, some of them older than our encounter with Europe. And one of the things that happens is that things that are very much older than colonialism get re-articulated with what comes from Europe, by our exposure during the period of colonialism to the whole range of European thought including its irrationalisms. European forms of the far right get structured into our own religious, caste, communal conflagrations, and create what I call 'imitative originality'; imitation and originality. Something that is specifically Indian but bears heavy traces of elsewhere.

VP: If there is nothing there for the imitation to graft onto, then it cannot hold on. It's not a mirror; it has to have something, something in those historical densities. In the Verso edition of *Lineages of the Present* you have a few quite long essays that are under a section called 'The BJP in Government', when Vajpayee was the prime minister. Then in 2016, you have another essay in *Socialist Register* called 'India: Liberal Democracy and the Extreme Right'. These two ideas return— liberalism and the far right—two snakes intertwined with each other. This essay is a summation of a very long engagement with Indian liberalism and the BJP/RSS. Could you reflect on the 2016 essay and its precursors?

AA: The essay was actually written a year earlier, in mid-2015, and two things I want to say about it right away: that it summarizes my thinking until then and in that sense supersedes what I had been writing on this theme over the previous decade or so; and, it was written for a foreign audience and therefore simplifies some of the things specific to Indian politics and society. My very early essay of 1992, 'On the Ruins of Ayodhya', is the one which first formulated the larger analytic framework I was to use for the study of Indian communalism over the next many years. Writings between that essay of 1992 and the one that I drafted in 2015 were essentially elaborations of the same framework with new details getting added with the passage of time. There was a long essay I had written for *The Marxist* on communalism. And then the conjuncture shifted *enormously* with the formation of the Modi government. Elections of 2014 were a shock. Like most others on the Left I was unsure that the Modi-led BJP would win at all. So, the margin of victory forced me to re-think some assumptions. But I also perceived, as few others did at the time, that the defeat of Congress was no simple defeat; rather it was the terminal demise of a political party that had dominated Indian politics for a century or so. By that measure alone, the BJP under Modi had become largely unassailable and the rise of the RSS to a hegemonic position was at hand. This was very different than the Vajpayee moment. These forces had been penetrating the frame of the Indian state for a long time, since at least the late 1970s, but now a rapid takeover of the state from within was going to pick up speed, quite beyond the see-saw of electoral politics. The extent to which Modi had become the consensual candidate of the top corporate houses, with few exceptions, was very alarming to me. Not only did Indian monopoly capital as a whole give them an enormous amount of money, their political unity behind Modi also showed that they were anticipating the kind of collapse of the Congress that actually occurred and that their investment in Modi was for the long term. The conjuncture had changed drastically, and I had to make a fresh effort to grasp it conceptually. That is why you see in that *Socialist Register* essay some theoretical departures from my previous writings on the subject.

I had been thinking of the rise of Modi, and then also of Turkey and Erdoğan. Turkey, the most secular country not only in the Muslim world, but I would say aside from France, the country with the strongest frame of secular government anywhere in the world, was methodically Islamized. Not that Catholicism had gone away from France or Islam from Turkey, but these had the strongest frames for a secular state, guaranteed by the armed forces. Erdoğan used the liberal institutions of the state to destroy every rampart of secular society, right up to the military. Even after destroying the military, he does not stage a coup. In fact, some very shady sort of coup is staged against him, which he uses to further claim his loyalty to the liberal institutions and in the name of eradicating a competing Islamic movement—the Gülenists—gets rid of secular intellectuals from the university, bureaucrats, government servants, progressives in various areas of society. In France itself, the

National Front—or whatever these people call themselves now—this rise of the far right does not have in their programme the abolition of the secular state even though they are the descendants of the counter-revolutionary, anti-Republican Catholic Right. So why is it that these people—Modi, Erdoğan, Le Pen and many others of their stripe—do not feel threatened by the liberal and secular constitutional structures?

VP: It's a fundamental question.

AA: For two reasons. On the one hand, every liberal constitution in the world includes clauses which allow the government of the day to declare that the situation is exceptional and the constitution or part of the constitution has therefore to be suspended. Such a situation is called State of Emergency in the British conception, State of Siege in the French conception and State of Exception in German jurisprudence. In other words, existing governments can undertake many kinds of extra-constitutional measures while remaining within the liberal constitution. The liberal constitution can remain but you still have the Gujarat police, the UP police, the Bihar police, the scores of thousands of the RSS paratroopers trained in active combat, perpetual low-intensity communal violence against the minority, not to speak of a full-scale pogrom here and there—and all that exists regardless of which party is in power. That is one reason why they need not shift to full-scale fascism. The other reason is the lack of a Left strong enough to challenge their rule. They really have no reason to be afraid.

VP: You say in this essay itself that the only reason to move to fascism is if the socialist movement becomes stronger.

AA: Strong enough to possibly make a revolution.

VP: It's almost formulaic.

AA: A correct understanding of European fascism has been undermined by the successful Zionist and imperialist attempt to

reduce Nazism to Judeocide, the killing of six million Jews. They reduce
Nazism to one final, murderous orgy of anti-Semitism. The combined
strength of communists and social democrats even in 1932 was greater
than that of the Nazis. This alternative power was decimated by 1935,
well before the Judeocide really began. During the war, Hitler's war
machine killed twenty million Soviet citizens. All of that gets forgotten.
Only the killing of Jews seems to matter. That was a very great horror
but that too needs to be seen in perspective. The main reasons why the
German big bourgeoisie made Hitler the German Chancellor was that
they were afraid that the tottering Weimar government would not be
able to stem the possibility of a communist revolution, especially after
the Crash of 1929 had made the economic crisis much worse.

VP: And to put it very vulgarly, there are certain populations for
whom that suspension of the constitution is permanent.

AA: In India, the glorious republic, constitutional guarantees have
meant little for the vast majority of the people.

But there is also something else we should think about. India's far
right, centrist liberals and a very considerable part of the Left are all
agreed that the Emergency of 1975–77 was a time of pure evil. So,
when they have to denounce Modi's authoritarianism many liberals
and leftists say: oh, this is just like the Emergency. This strikes me as
bizarre. The anti-Indira agitation—for 'Total Revolution'—was a joint
enterprise of various shades of the Indian Right. The Akhil Bharatiya
Vidyarthi Parishad was the main player in the student agitations in
Gujarat as well as Patna; JP worked closely with RSS and Morarji Desai;
and JP himself was an old friend of the US since at least the days of
the Congress for Cultural Freedom. He was calling on civil servants to
stop working and rise in insurrection against the elected government
while Morarji was threatening to bring scores of thousands of people
to surround the Prime Minister's house and make it impossible to
perform her official duties. That 'exceptional' attempt from the Right,

including the extreme right, to bring about an unconstitutional 'regime change' became the constitutional basis for declaration of Emergency. When Indira Gandhi lifted the Emergency, called fresh elections and lost, RSS stalwarts walked into Parliament to occupy key posts, which was a main objective of the anti-Indira agitation in the first place. Today, when Modi has begun to implement the maximum programme of the RSS, comparing this with the Emergency of 1975–77 amounts to speaking metaphorically, not rationally.

VP: Actually, right through the Emergency, there was a kind of parliament.

AA: An elected parliament, I might add, with some clauses of the Constitution suspended. But the state of Emergency was lifted immediately as soon as she thought that the situation had been normalized sufficiently. Her belief that she would win the elections was a grave miscalculation. But the very fact that the basic constitutional commitments were in place meant that she could not extend that Emergency too long and took the risk of possibly losing the elections.

VP: Can you just finish that thought? Now there is the suggestion of an undeclared Emergency. You said such an idea was metaphorical.

AA: I have a rather different view of the historical meaning of the Emergency than most people, including many of my own comrades who suffered under the Emergency. I may think differently because I was not in India at that time and speak now, decades later, with the benefit of hindsight. As I said, I view the anti-Indira movement as an onslaught from the Right, even the extreme right, notwithstanding the fact that CPI(M) as well as ML [Communist Party of India (Marxist-Leninist)] also participated in that movement, for their own reasons. It was a movement against the progressive side of Indira's government and countless reforms ranging from the nationalization of banks and general insurance companies to abolition of privy purses. The objective was to bring to power, unconstitutionally, a coalition of right-wing forces—including very much the RSS as a central force. Once the Emergency was declared there were all kinds of excesses, against the Right as well as the sections of the Left that had been part of that agitation, and it was surely a period of arbitrary, authoritarian rule. A historical memory has been manufactured, however, which recalls only the excesses and the authoritarian rule and wilfully suppresses the memory of the right-wing nature of the coalition that had risen against progressive reforms. My use of the word 'metaphorical' was misleading. I meant that there are people who recall Indira's authoritarian interlude during the Emergency and witness Modi's authoritarian rule today and talk as if these two moments are identical, forgetting the political content of these two very different moments. The reforms Indira Gandhi introduced into the Indian economy—bank nationalizations for instance—were radically the opposite of what today's neoliberal rulers want. RSS was her enemy. Today, RSS is in power. Indira's excesses cannot be compared to the permanently neo-fascist character of its project. Nor can we forget the years of her rule preceding the Emergency. Conditions for the Emergency were created by JP, the RSS and the gang of former right-wing Congressmen like Morarji Desai, and those forces were the main objects of the excesses of the period. By contrast, those who suffer from the cruelties of the RSS during Modi's rule are mostly the most wretched of the Indian earth. The violence they suffer is not even a punishment for what they have done but unilateral violence on a widening scale which is the direct result of the RSS ideology and the strategy it has chosen in pursuit of its larger project. Indira Gandhi had no commitment to a religio-racist, right-wing project or to violence *per se*. The authoritarian conduct of the Emergency period was conjunctural in nature. On the other hand, commitment to violence begins with taking up a membership in an RSS *shakha*, putting on khaki shorts and entering into combat training. Comparisons between the Emergency and the coercions of Modi rule are outright facetious because the effect is to greatly understate the danger that the RSS poses.

FASCISM IN AMERICA

VP: I'd like to turn to your essay in *Socialist Register 2019* called 'Extreme Capitalism and "The National Question"'.* Here you quote from Kalecki once more, but this time from his 1964 essay on fascism. He's writing about the ascendancy of Goldwater to the Republican Party. He feels that given John F. Kennedy's assassination, the liberal government should have been able to deal a mortal blow to the far right. After Gandhi is killed in 1948, the Nehru government is not able to deliver a mortal blow to the RSS.

AA: Well, in the case of India, thanks to the Congress Right, led by Patel.

VP: Kalecki writes of Goldwaterism, which is not just Goldwater but the whole set of institutions, ideologies, including the John Birch Society. He writes, 'Goldwaterism is wanted by the ruling class as a pressure group against an excessive relaxation of international tensions and in order to restrain' what he calls the 'negro movement' or the civil rights struggle. Goldwater lost the election, of course, but Kalecki writes, 'Goldwater will be saved by those to whom he lost.' Having quoted Kalecki, you write, 'Trump has captured power and what the ruling class fears is not excessive relaxation of international tensions, for the context is different, but that he might not focus adequately on the military aspect of those tensions and create unnecessary ones in the economic sphere, even with allies and so on.' Your reflections on Trump draw from Kalecki, but of course in a different context.

* Aijaz Ahmad, 'Extreme Capitalism and "The National Question"', *Socialist Register 2019*, New Delhi: LeftWord, 2019.

AA: Okay, from what I recall, the argument there is that Trump is not *sui generis*, that you have to go all the way back to the postwar years. McCarthyism was designed to consolidate the anti-communist crusade and the unity of the American Right. Goldwater's candidacy represented that Right and he lost the election very badly only because of the way the Electoral College functions in the United States. But he got more than one third of the popular vote, close to forty per cent in fact. Which is very formidable. What Goldwater did was to coalesce very far flung far right constituencies into the very structure of the Republican Party. These new constituencies stood against the liberal wing of the Republican Party itself, led by Nelson Rockefeller, as much as it stood against the Democrats. The Republican Party was restructured into the party increasingly of the far right; this actually begins with Goldwater.

The next great moment in the organization of the Right comes in response to what is generally called the '60s. That is to say, the New Left and the anti-Vietnam War movement, the Black nationalist movement, the rising tide of feminism—these three forces in particular. After the defeat in Vietnam, the US imperial project was paralysed in terms of military interventions for the next fifteen to twenty years. The Left, the New Left, was held responsible for that. Hồ Chí Minh in his final testament, thanked the American anti-war movement for contributing to the victory of the Revolution. After that not only does Nixon come to power, but Nixon is the first president who takes seriously the religious vote as part of his calculations for elections. Erosion of many of the regulatory aspects of the New Deal begins in the Nixon era. Virtually all the think tanks of the Right were established in response to the '60s during this period. There are actual documents from various organizations of the top capitalist class that outline this strategy. By the early years of this century, the Republican Party had become increasingly a party of the far right, distinctly to the right of Goldwater himself. Some of the wealthiest of monopoly houses, such as the Koch brothers and the Mercers have intervened directly in pushing the Republican Party to the far right, a story that is told in books like Jane Mayer's *Dark Money*. Trump is a product of all that. The Tea Party movement seemed to arise out of nowhere, claimed to be unaffiliated to any party and even had a stance of being opposed to all party elites—a rhetoric very common these days among far right forces across the Western world. In actual fact, that movement converged with the Republican Right and moved it towards extremist positions, making it, in Chomsky's words, the world's most dangerous political organization. So, Trump is not *sui generis*. He is not this crazy, irrational person; he is an extremely shrewd politician, and he's a product of that long history. Kalecki connects directly the fascistic tendency and monopoly capital.

I think that fascism in the strict European sense of the 1930s in Europe has never been a significant current in the United States. But it is also important to remember Mussolini's own dictum that fascism is the system in which government and corporations become one. In that sense, capitalism in its monopoly phase and especially now in its neoliberal monopoly phase has a fascist core that is fairly global now. I think that Kalecki also had something of that kind in mind. In that article, I wanted to trace a certain genealogy of the far right in the US, because the tendency in the United States is to see Trump as some *sui generis* aberration in an otherwise liberal country. Everyone that I know was going to vote for Hillary Clinton. Now, yes, if you have a choice between Hillary Clinton and Trump, yes, you might want to vote for her. Outside the Marxist Left, however, there was hardly any discussion of who she was and what she had done. Suddenly, Trump becomes the ultimate horror, which suppresses all criticism of all forms of American liberalism.

VP: Same in India.

AA: Exactly.

VP: Modi is the horror; no need to talk about the Congress and its complicities and its limitations and so on. Same in Egypt. The Islamists are the horror; no need to talk about Sisi and the military and so on.

AA: Absolutely, that's right. So, you know, that's the problem: that once you create a monster out of a certain kind of historical outcome, no matter how much you despise that outcome, you have to understand it historically and it gives you no license to then develop some kind of nostalgia for the likes of Obama, for instance. Obama is now charging $400,000 for a speech. In the US, Bernie Sanders could have defeated Trump but the corporate Democrats who dominate the party preferred to lose to Trump than win with the nominally socialist Bernie. The same happened in Britain. The Blairite wing of the Labour Party prefers Tory rule to Corbyn. In France, the Socialist Party, the traditional social democratic party, did not have the vaguest chance of winning but refused to align with Mélenchon. Had they done so we would have had a leftist government there. In each, it is the liberal centre-left that prefers to have a rightist government to a leftist one.

VP: That's why I find these three essays to be very much kindred; the essay on Islamism, the essay on India, and this essay which is largely on the United States. When the socialist option has been set aside, when national liberation is no longer a robust movement, then you get this dance between liberalism and the far right, this intimacy between them.

AA: Absolute intimacy. You see, I believe that the Democratic Party is so sold out to corporate capital that it deliberately preferred Trump to Sanders; they would rather live with Trump than for Sanders to come in and implement something like what Roosevelt had once called the 'economic bill of rights'.

VP: In other words, even to have the whiff of socialism or social democracy is intolerable.

AA: Yes, well, the word itself; he identifies himself as socialist. The majority of Americans are ready to have him; they want him. The twitter following for Ocasio-Cortez, the young first-term Congresswoman who also identifies herself as democratic socialist, is astonishing. Within a month, it went from two million to four million. The mass of voters no longer has any problem with that phrase—'democratic socialism'. They listen to the progressive reforms Sanders is proposing and are glad to follow him.

VP: To be perfectly honest, some of this has to do with the fact that it's been a long time since you've seen an actual human being as a member of the United States Congress.

AA: That is true.

VP: I'm just talking about basic human being, not a robot.

AA: Yes, Ocasio-Cortez also has a sense of humour.

VP: Absolutely.

AA: For instance, she is quite capable of saying, oh, they all like me because I have a pretty face. A joke somewhat at her own expense.

VP: And even that is such a refreshingly honest thing.

CHINA

VP: In these four *Socialist Register* essays, China barely appears. It slips into the last of the essays in a section called 'Neo-Liberalism and Post-Communist Politics in the Ocean of Cheap Commodities'. You make some blunt statements about China. One of them is a factual statement: China is of course simply the largest economy occupying such a central role in the international division of labour, in the way commodities are moving. But what's interesting is that in this essay here, and in very much of your writing, unlike in the literature on the decline of America, there is no China as a major force in the analysis. How do you see the role of China in the world?

AA: Well, three of those essays are on 'the "post-" condition', Islamism and India. There was no logical reason to bring in China. In the latest of them, the 2019 essay on 'Extreme Capitalism' China gets discussed where it should be: the immense expansion in the global working class at the disposal of imperialism and the great fall in the global wage rate after the dismantling of the communist state system in China and the Comecon countries, but especially in China. Also, not just that China is now one of the world's two largest economies in aggregate GDP terms but also that it was now the principal locus for investment by global corporate capital for production of cheap commodities for the world market. Discussion of these aspects of post-1978 China first appeared in my writing not in one of the *Socialist Register* essays but in an essay published inside India, 'The Fallouts of 1989'.* Also, I have argued for some years and in many places that the dismantling of the communist state system began not in the Soviet Union in 1989, as is commonly supposed, but in 1978 in China. I have not seen much evidence but my hunch is that the transformations that began in China after Deng returned to become China's preeminent leader were discussed extensively among leaders of the Soviet Union and those discussions might have played a role in formulating the policies of *perestroika* under Gorbachev. I remember saying at great length in an interview on *Newsclick* that Chinese history since 1949 can be divided into two distinct phases, the revolutionary period that lasts roughly until 1978 and the counter-revolutionary period since

* Aijaz Ahmad, 'The Fallouts of 1989', in *Interpreting the World to Change It: Essays for Prabhat Patnaik*, eds. C.P. Chandrasekhar and Jayati Ghosh, New Delhi: Tulika, 2017.

then. I said then and I have said in many other lectures, interviews, etc., that regardless of what still remains of the old revolutionary system—notably the uncertain ownership structure of agricultural land—China is now fundamentally a capitalist country with a distinct sector of state capitalism. So, I have actually expressed many views that go to the very heart of the question of where China stands now and how we should view it in the global context.

As regards those essays, 'Imperialism of Our Time' might have been the one for a fuller discussion of China. We have discussed that essay earlier but let me clarify just what I had wanted to do in that essay. First, I wanted to respond to some of the ways in which the question of imperialism *per se* as well as Lenin's theory of imperialism were getting discussed in some circles of the Western Left. Second, I wanted to address the issue of periodization and proposed three different periods: that of inter-imperialist rivalry which Lenin had theorized; that of intra-systemic rivalry, between imperialism and the communist state system; and the post-Soviet phase of imperialist triumphalism that we were and are living through. My third objective was to locate the then newly launched Iraq War in the context of that imperialist triumphalism. As I told you when we discussed that essay a little earlier, my one regret about it is that the question of the Iraq War was so urgent that some other issues I wanted to address got neglected.

But China was not an issue that I wanted to discuss at any length in 2004, and in some ways, I am still rather reluctant to do so. The really dramatic take-off in the Chinese economy begins only in the early 1990s. When I wrote the imperialism essay in 2003/04 it was still very difficult to study the actual nature of the changes in the system or how the various sectors of the economy were functioning. I don't read Chinese. So, I have no access to primary materials. What primary materials do become available in English appear after a time lag. My capacity to understand what goes on there is therefore very limited.

And even the best of the secondary scholarship has to be treated with some scepticism because the question of China gets tied into very severe forms of partisanship, for or against.

I now know much more about China than I did fifteen years ago but I am still not terribly confident about many things. That is partly because trends in China are genuinely contradictory and many kinds of inner conflicts and compromises seem to be going on that are invisible to an outsider who does not even read Chinese. And there are many things that have remained unclear to me despite the passage of time. I still don't understand what actually happened in the 1970s.

It is quite clear that the eventual consequences of the Chinese Cultural Revolution were utterly disastrous for the material foundations of the Revolution. But what lessons did Mao really draw from those consequences of his policies? Why did Mao welcome Kissinger in Beijing precisely at that time and initiate a dramatic rapprochement with the US? Was the Chinese economy in such dire straits that Mao himself had started looking for an opening to the world capitalist market, a policy that Deng had proposed earlier and for which he had been purged as a 'capitalist roader'? What was the impact of that opening to the capitalist West on the inner thinking of the party leadership, and did that new thinking play a role in the fact that Deng, the 'capitalist roader' of yesteryear, became the preeminent leader of the party barely two years after Mao's death? I am sure there were those in the party who were opposed to Deng's policies, but that opposition seems not to have created any appreciable crisis.

Then there is the question of the present-day party and system in China. There are more billionaires and millionaires in the Chinese Communist Party today than in all the social democratic parties of Europe put together. The latest figures I have seen on income and wealth disparities in China—with 2016 as the base year—suggest greater inequality in China than in any European country and quite on the scale of the United States, the most unequal of all the advanced capitalist countries. Health and education provisions for the masses are not very different than elsewhere in a typical Third World country while the conditions of work and rates of exploitation for the working class are simply unspeakable.

In the writings of people like Harvey there is no mention of how much capital gained from the collapse of communism. This is part of their anti-communism; they don't want to say that this is the result of the collapse of communism because then they would have to say that what collapsed was an opposite pole of this capitalist world, and it was a bad thing that it collapsed. Now, after the collapse, rates of dispossession and exploitation amount really to a very primitive kind of accumulation.

VP: 2,458 per cent rate of exploitation of iPhone workers, twenty-five times more than the rate of exploitation of nineteenth-century textile labour!

AA: The availability of cheap consumer goods coming from China has played a major role in keeping social unrest in the United States under check, at a time when working-class wages have been stagnant since the early 1970s. They can still maintain some semblance of their standard of living by buying these cheap commodities. And the structure of Chinese capitalism means that all the Asian countries— Bangladesh, Malaysia, etc.—which are industrializing themselves have to compete with Chinese commodities and, therefore, cannot raise their wages. China comes in the discussion here, again, not so much in relation to itself in this case but in relation to the stability of global capitalism.

VP: Hence the ocean of commodities.

INTELLECTUALS

VP: Every generation of intellectuals has a discussion about what is the role of an intellectual, or at least it seems so. Somebody writes a book, or an essay, and there's a debate about this. I'm not going to enter into the general debate of what is an intellectual, but every intellectual has their own understanding of their own intellectual project, and their own understanding of themselves as an intellectual. So, it might be useful for us to hear first, from you, about how you see your work as a project.

AA: Yes, it is good not to enter into a general debate about what is an intellectual. Even so, it is important to clarify the sense in which we ourselves are using the term. I think there is a certain idea of the intellectual that goes back to the Enlightenment, especially the French Enlightenment, and to the French Revolution itself. An implied meaning here is that of someone who is not an academic specialist but a *general* thinker, one who thinks and writes about society, politics, history in general. Critical dissent is usually the heart of the matter. Diderot, Rousseau and Voltaire were among the paradigmatic intellectuals of their time, who wrote about the basic issues of ethical and political philosophy, religion as belief and as institution, foundations of the economic science, sources of inequality in society, and need for revolutionary change. Marxism inherits the revolutionary side of that tradition and gives it new directions. From Marx and Engels to Lenin, Trotsky, Luxemburg and Bukharin, all the great figures of classical Marxism and communist history were formidable intellectuals. One of the hallmarks of both these traditions, the left wing of the Enlightenment as well as Marxism, is that their intellectuals ignored today's sharp division between Humanities and the Social Sciences, traversing many areas of knowledge and aesthetics. Diderot and Rousseau wrote novels to propagate their ideas, and Voltaire was a legendary figure in the theatre of his time. Even Bukharin composed a novel in his solitary confinement. Marx, Lenin, and Trotsky made major contributions to literary theory and criticism.

I refer to all this because it is always good to recall the traditions that have been the shaping forces in one's own life. My own work has been comparatively very modest, and I am not quite sure that what I have done amounts to an identifiable project. As I told you earlier, I grew up and entered into my twenties wanting to be an Urdu writer of poetry, fiction and literary criticism with a preoccupation with the literary craft. A left-wing political orientation began early in life, got strengthened by the dislocations that the Partition imposed on my family and myself and survived into the radicalism of student politics. But I entered my twenties with very rudimentary knowledge of Marxism, having read some of the basic pamphlets: the *Manifesto*, Lenin's *Imperialism*, Engels' *Socialism, Utopian and Scientific*, Mao's *On Contradiction*, Liu Shaoqi's *How to Be a Good Communist*—a few texts of that kind. Any deeper engagement came later.

Like anyone else, my work has been shaped by the circumstances in which I lived at any given time. The cycle of migrations and exiles has been a determining factor. For instance, had I lived consistently in Pakistan I would have been an Urdu writer with occasional forays into English; it was life in America and then most particularly the return to India that made me an English writer. A more fundamental result of these multiple moves from one country to the other has been that I was unable to be part of a particular collectivity through much of my life—a political party, a consistent social milieu, a work collective of some stable nature—which also means that a consistent project has been hard to define. Even *In Theory* is the direct product of the fact that teaching of literature was the only paid profession available to me while I lived in the US during the 1970s and early years of the next decade. That book was an attempt to examine some of the dominant trends in that larger literary institution and to settle accounts with my erstwhile literary-critical conscience. Settling accounts does not mean leaving something behind—Marx and Engels did not renounce philosophical thought after writing *German Ideology*—but to find a different, materialist, more historically grounded method for pursuing those same interests. Interest in literature and culture, and in literary and cultural theories, has remained but as aspects of a much broader field of human practices. I have always been fascinated—almost haunted— by Marx's famous distinction between the economic conditions of production which can be determined with the precision of natural science, as he put it, and 'the ideological forms in which men become conscious of this conflict and fight it out'. In other words, ideology as a practical instance of the class struggle. Literature and Culture are in my view very significant areas of what Marxism understands as Ideology.

If I were to actually define my project, I would simply say it is an attempt to engage with the history of the present in different ways and at different levels. The university is in my view a very major institution in modern life, much more so since decolonization and the Second World War. Trends that become dominant in the human sciences have immense effects on thinking and practical life far beyond the university as such. Trying to engage with these trends as much as my own scholarly capacity allows has been a significant part of what might be called my project, if 'project' is the appropriate word. But I take it to be absolutely essential for an intellectual not to be confined to debates and confrontations in the scholarly field alone and to participate punctually in a much broader arena of intellectual and political culture. I have contributed well over a hundred essays of roughly five thousand words each on an extremely wide range of topics to *Frontline* magazine. I invested enormous amount of time and energy, research, thinking and the hard work of precise formulation in those essays, and I value them at least as much as *In Theory*, which has brought me so much fame and abuse (in roughly equal measure), and other more scholarly things such as the *Socialist Register* essays that we discussed earlier. That is what I have strived to do as a Marxist intellectual: work across many boundaries. I have tried to be not a narrow academic specialist but what Gramsci called a *general intellect*, reading and writing in many fields of human inquiry with no regard for the boundary between Humanities and the Social Sciences. I have thought it important to conduct ideological struggle in the upper reaches of High Culture, but I have also taken very seriously the more important task of helping sustain a broader culture of progressive ideas. I have also believed that the central issues of our time need sustained reflection and more or less permanent engagement with the intent of improving one's own understanding of those issues. Whether it is a complex text of Marx or the very complex projects of Hindutva, there is no such thing as a final understanding beyond which one need not go. One must always return to take another look, to think anew, reach a deeper understanding. Hence my repeated writings on the RSS over three decades or so, in a way that my more recent writing on the subject is bound to be very different from something I wrote a decade or two decades ago.

Since at least the time when I was in my early twenties, I would say, there has always been a connection between the kind of intellectual I was becoming and the world of Marxism and communism. I grew up on Progressive literature which you could describe as something of the cultural world of Marxism. In Pakistan during my college days the leftist current in student politics was very much connected with the communist underground. Communist intellectuals like Sibte Hassan were major influences on me. That connection remained alive even after I first arrived in the US. Once it became possible for me to return to Pakistan during the Bhutto era I became a punctual writer in party publications of the Mazdoor Party (of which the Mazdoor Kisan Party was a front) and also published several books in Urdu including translations of Lê Duẩn, Cabral and others from the world communist movement. Once it struck me that all these translations that have come from the Soviet Union are written in such atrocious Urdu that they're unusable. So, I sat down and rewrote, in Urdu, the whole of *What Is To Be Done?*

VP: Where is that manuscript now?

AA: Well, I actually published it. But all that got lost with my library when it was taken by the police in Lahore. God knows what they did with it. Anyway, I did things of that kind. Then, towards the end of the 1970s, the whole region entered into a crisis, with the Islamic Revolution in Iran, the Saur Revolution in Afghanistan, and the overthrow of Bhutto in Pakistan. With the onset of the Zia dictatorship I left Pakistan yet again.

Later, when I decided to try and settle back in India, I was struck by the sheer magnificence of India's Marxist intelligentsia but also with the intensity of their focus primarily on India itself. For instance, independent India has had an array of very distinguished Marxist historians but none who writes histories of other countries, not even of Pakistan or other South Asian countries.

VP: Could you give us a sense of why you think that is so?

AA: I don't really know. Once I was discussing this with Ravinder Kumar, himself a very notable historian, and he said something like: 'There was a time when we didn't have any history of any of the states; we only had a broad all-India history. Then came the phase of the states. Then will come the phase, undoubtedly, of local archives and of particular cities.' You find some serious histories of Bombay and Delhi but not with enough depth, and that's it. The colonial period produced very limited historical knowledge. There now are projects to produce detailed, cogent national history. India is a huge country, a world in itself.

VP: I take the point that India is continental. But there has always been an attempt to create an internationalist consciousness. In a way, I'm trying to reach into Nehru's ambition in the 1920s, when he establishes this group in Allahabad—the Foreign Department of the Congress, with Lohia in charge. They try to force the Indian nationalists to take an interest in Spain and China. This was not integral to Indian nationalism. Could you reflect on this very limited culture of internationalism?

AA: Sure, absolutely. You see, one way of putting it would be that Nehru was—within the world of Indian nationalism but particularly during those years which culminate in what are called his red years—always very much oriented towards the wider world, very much conscious of the importance of fascism, of the Bolshevik revolution, Spain as a testing ground for the struggle between these two great movements and so on. On the other hand were the Gandhis and the Patels and the whole lot, the Congress Right, for example, who wanted to look back towards Ancient India, glorifying village India, encouraging varieties of indigenism, ideas of our uniqueness, our Golden Age and so on. Nehru had some tendency towards that but on the whole he was secular and sort of left oriented. You look at those letters to Indira Gandhi when she was a child and he is instructing her from the prison, he explains the world to her, you know. The ambition of those letters is that this child of mine should know the world and also be a citizen of India. He and his close friends were the cosmopolitans within the Congress. This was a very minoritarian tendency.

VP: And it hasn't sustained itself deeply enough.

AA: Not in the Congress. The Left has never been strong enough to have that kind of internationalist impact on Indian culture. And for the Left itself, I think, internationalism means solidarity with the world communist movement but not an opening towards the world as such. Communist historians in India haven't thought of writing a new history even of a communist country—not even of the Soviet Union or China, let alone Hungary or GDR. I find this rather curious.

But I just thought again about my own project and how the changing circumstances of my life kept intervening in what I could or could not write. For instance, I wrote a great deal about the Hindutva project after Babri Masjid but once Vajpayee formed a stable government in 1998, I was advised increasingly not to write about India in journals that were much in the public eye. From then on, I always wrote about the rest of the world in *Frontline* but hardly ever about India. That is why my writing on India is so patchy. It is either those essays or once or twice in the *Marxist* or some other small publication of the Left. Having to leave India released me to actually write about it. Hence the *Socialist Register* essay on Modi.

VP: On the other hand, everything you've written from 'In the Ruins of Ayodhya' onwards is rooted in the densities of the place, the histories, but these essays are also deeply internationalist. For in your work, the international is present in almost everything. And I don't mean by analogy. I mean, you refer to theories from other places, you're looking at how to best understand something, you are looking at other experiences. When you had said earlier that as a young person you were translating things from French and so on into Urdu, that was an important thing for you, you retranslated *What Is To Be Done?*; there was never a parochial consciousness. It was about finding the best way to understand something. It's not always about the subject that you're looking at, I think there's an optic that's very wide.

AA: Yes, and it kept getting wider, I must say. But listen, I am a product of the period when nationalism itself was internationalist; it was an international of nationalisms. It was an anti-colonial project that encompassed continents and had a very dynamic relationship with the communist world, which was fundamentally internationalist. Internationalism was the outstanding characteristic with which I identified myself. That is where the real origins of this kind of thinking are for me.

VP: I mean, that's one very interesting way for me, at least, to think about your work, not just in the period after *In Theory* but I think in sum. The other interesting thing, and perhaps, an explanation for why, in certain places, you don't see this breadth, is that we have had—and this predates the neoliberal university—the tendency to create the expert rather than the intellectual.

AA: Oh, it's a very fundamental dichotomy. Intellectuals want depth of knowledge about everything that is pertinent for their thought-world but the expert, the highest product of the bourgeois university, wants expertise in as narrow a specialty as possible. And yes, that is true not just of the more recent neoliberal university but of the university more generally as it was reconstituted in the postwar period under US influence.

Sudhanva Deshpande (SD): I wanted to ask you about how you see yourself as a *communist intellectual*. As a communist, as somebody who's been an activist all his life, one sees intellectuals who are either embedded in the Communist Party as activists, whose main goal is as active union organizers, working on the *kisan* front and so on—and their job then is to produce material for that part of the movement; or there are say academics—only because they happen to be in the university at some level; college teachers or whatever it is—academics that are affiliated to the communist movement, and who generally tend to *analyse* what's happening, whether they're doing it in the field of history or current affairs, politics, international affairs, the economy and so on. When I read you, as an activist, I don't find either of these things to be the primary impulse. Which is not to say that there's no analysis in what you write, obviously not. Over these years, the sense that I get is that you are speaking to me in a manner of a teacher demonstrating a method; of showing me what the dialectical method is or can be, and how you look at the structures of the world—whether it is to do with communalism or whether it is to do with imperialism, or whatever might be the actual subject of what you're doing. But it seems to me that your project, in a sense, to use Vijay's term, has been different from almost every other communist intellectual that I've read through the Indian communist movement. Would this be a fair assessment?

AA: Well, I am very interested in your saying that what I seem to be doing is demonstrating a method, how to use the dialectical method in analysing the world. I am reminded of Lukács who said that method is the only thing that is truly orthodox in Marxism. That makes me an orthodox Marxist and an orthodox Marxist is by definition a communist.

Your observation has raised two different issues. One is related to my status in relation to the definition of a communist intellectual. You identify two types of communist intellectuals, those who serve in core class organizations of the party, such as trade unions, and those, such as school and college teachers, who serve the party in broader mass fronts. Each is to then produce knowledge useful and appropriate to the organization or front in which they serve, a knowledge determined presumably by party policy. That is clear enough and according to this classification I was a communist intellectual when I was in Pakistan and was a member of a party, and then ceased to be one after leaving Pakistan. This kind of classification actually also has a term for someone like me, and the term is 'fellow traveller'.

But it is the later part of your comment that I find surprising. What you have suggested is that my writings may offer some analysis here and there but when you read them you get the strong impression that I am writing like a teacher whose main purpose is to teach the dialectical method. This I find intriguing. I have hardly ever written anything on the Marxist method, and I have taught the dialectical method only in some of my graduate seminars. On the other hand, I mentioned earlier that I have published roughly a hundred 5,000-word pieces in *Frontline*. I thought that I was actually referring to a lot of facts in those essays and analysing them to the best of my capacity. Factual account and analysis—that's what I thought those essays were about. And yes, some historical or geopolitical context. So, I am taken aback that you think they were exercises in method.

For the rest, I am actually no exception to the rule that one makes choices about one's own life in circumstances given to one. When I was in Pakistan, there was a basic continuity in affiliations since my days in student politics. Choices were therefore simpler. One joined a party and over the years one saw that party collapsing under the double weight of extreme factionalism inside and a ferocious dictatorship outside. By the time I came to India, in the vain hope of retrieving my citizenship, things were very complicated. I was no longer young. I was wary of factionalism that is such a scourge inside communist parties and movements. People in communist parties did not know me, I did not know them. It took many years to develop some kind of mutual recognition. That is a very complicated story that need not be rehearsed. There was no direct discussion but, all things considered, it was silently and mutually agreed that it was best that I not join the party. Soon after my close cooperation with the party began, I got caught up, quite unwittingly, in the same kind of party factionalism I had feared. I did everything that the party ever asked me, but I was more glad than not that I never joined. But I have been very happy with that relationship with the party. I learned a lot and had a strong sense of having been useful.

As I understand the communist intellectual tradition that has come down to us from the great masters, there are at least two fundamental responsibilities. One is to write absolutely in the conjuncture, in the here and now, about the fundamental problems of the time from a strictly Marxist point of view. The other is to amass a body of writing that helps the growth of a kind of intellectual culture that would then be spontaneously receptive to communist ideas.

VP: Returning then to the role of the intellectual. These days we see intellectuals being arrested all over the place, from Turkey to India.

AA: When the Parisian police tried to arrest Sartre during the Algerian War, the permission had to be obtained from de Gaulle, President of the Republic, and de Gaulle said, 'You don't arrest Voltaire'.

VP: Wow. Imagine this is India, with the Central Bureau of Investigation going to ask Modi; extraordinary.

AA: Yes, and you know, India's post-Nehruvian ruling class is so blind to intellectuals that the bloody Indian state could not even see that giving back Indian citizenship to a globally known Pakistani intellectual who was born in India and now wants to renounce his Pakistani citizenship and return to India to reclaim his Indian-ness, would be a good thing for India's reputation as a secular, enlightened country. Indian law says that anyone who was born in India but then became a Pakistani citizen cannot regain Indian citizenship. Fine. But enlightened rulers should know when to relax some legal requirement and make an exception where it is not only helpful to an individual but is good for the larger interest of the country as a whole.

VP: I mean, those are the optimal reasons to give someone citizenship.

AA: Yes, I know. That's what I mean.

VP: Not to say intellectuals are so much more important than anybody else, that's a very interesting reflection.

AA: That is by and large true. But there is also something to be learned from the little anecdote I just recounted to you where de Gaulle compares Sartre to Voltaire and refuses to have him arrested even when Sartre breaks the law deliberately and repeatedly. The sort of indifference that I encountered in my attempts to regain Indian citizenship has also been a sign of the times. You have the very interesting case of Qurratulain Hyder, the Urdu novelist, who was also born in India before the family migrated to Pakistan. She was the daughter of Sajjad Hyder Yildirim, an Urdu writer, a friend of Nehru and, if I remember correctly, a senior civil servant in the closing years of the Empire. The story, as she told me decades ago, is that she had come to India for a visit at a time when an elder relative of hers was contesting for a Rajya Sabha seat about which he went to see Jawaharlal and told him that Yildirim's daughter was visiting. Jawaharlal said to him that he would like to see her. When she went to see him, Panditji apparently told her that he knew her novel *Aag ka Darya* (which she herself translated later as *River of Fire*) and asked her if she was ever going to settle this matter of divided loyalties (between Pakistan and India). Qurratulain told me that she felt tearful at the very thought that Jawaharlal knew her novel.

VP: After all, shops closed in Lahore Mall when he died.

AA: Nehru apparently played on her emotion, saying that if her father was alive, he too would have asked that question. It seems that he offered to have the evacuee properties of her family restored to her if she wanted to return to India. So far as I recall Qurratulain demurred but I don't really know what eventually happened. But I do know that she regained her citizenship.

VP: Which year was that exactly? '50s—
AA: ... probably '59.

VP: End of the '50s.
AA: Yes, *Aag ka Darya* was published in '57, so it must have been a couple of years after that.

VP: So about fifty years ago, you—
AA: This was Nehru!

VP: There's not even the consciousness to have that conversation.

AA: He did some other things like that. After Sajjad Zaheer was imprisoned in Pakistan, Nehru arranged for him to be released and sent back to India. Sajjad Zaheer had of course been a personal friend and Qurratulain was the daughter of a friend. So, one could say that Nehru did it out of a sense of personal obligation. But the story I have heard is that when Bade Ghulam Ali Khan was diagnosed with possibly a throat cancer while living in Pakistan it was Nehru who got him back to India for treatment.

VP: There was a different attitude towards intellectuals.

AA: Yes, absolutely; intellectuals, artists, etc. So that is what, you know, ... the story that I told you about de Gaulle and these stories about Nehru connect them into an Enlightenment project, which is international in character. Those who subscribe to that larger project have certain kinds of conviction that they share across national boundaries, and one of those shared convictions is a deep regard for those who contribute to the advancement of progressive ideas, art and culture.

VP: And it encourages thought, it is investment in making the world a better place; whether it's by expanding the imagination or by helping understand some procedures better—

AA: Sure. And that also means no deep commitment to national boundaries. There was a certain sense in Nehru and among Nehruvians in the Indian elite of that time that Partition was a reality and the creation of Pakistan was a reality but there was also a cultural unity beyond these new boundaries that needed to be kept as intact as possible. So anyway, I don't know how we got into this.

VP: No, this was interesting because it comes to that issue of what is an expert, what is an intellectual. I mean, the reduction of intellectual thought to the narrow kind of expertise is also one of the finest ways to decimate critical thinking.

AA: The sense that critical thinking is essential for cultural survival and advancement seems to be declining.

VP: And we are suffering for it.

AA: Yes, we produce fewer and fewer intellectuals. But, you know, I myself came to India in the mid-eighties quite largely in response to the question that Panditji had posed to Qurratulain: when are you going to settle your divided loyalties? Not that I had much loyalty to Pakistan as a national entity but that is where I had gone to college, had become a writer, had been involved in politics, had family connections, and so on. And, on the other hand, there was a great sense that India was the original home which had been left behind when I was a child and I should perhaps recover that sense of being rooted in a place. Looking back, of course, I can see that it was rather sentimental of me to imagine that I could, at a personal level, undo for myself what the Partition had done not just to me but also to millions of others.

VP: Well, but it's thirty years of your life that was spent in that. I mean, it wasn't that you went and six weeks later, you left; this was thirty years, some of your most productive years were spent in India.

AA: Oh, I was not expressing a regret. Those were not only very productive years, intellectually speaking, but years that were very fulfilling in my personal life and also in political life as much as my health allowed. But I was also very naïve. I had no idea that I would never be able to regain my citizenship regardless of who was in power, or that visas too will become increasingly more difficult to get or that a time would eventually come when I would have to leave, get uprooted again and look for yet another refuge. So, those very years, productive and fulfilling as they were, were also years of a very precarious existence.

Many things in my life were determined by that precariousness.

VP: In other words, your relationship to being an intellectual as well, because your understanding of an intellectual would have always obliged you to have that kind of relationship.

AA: Yes, if I had the security of citizenship, I would have led my life even as an intellectual very differently, taking very different kinds of initiative. I would have liked the option of having a different, more solid relationship. Even my relationship with the communist movement might have been different. At the same time, though, being a communist is for me a way of being in the world and an institutional affiliation may itself be an expression of that particular way of being in the world. So, in that sense, the precariousness I was talking about did not fundamentally alter my way of being in the world, my way of *knowing* the world or perceiving my own place in it.

VP: And that world welcomes that intellectual in different places as well.

AA: Oh, in different places surely but in India itself I had an enormous welcome, in virtually all sections of the Left, among the literary intelligentsia, universities and so on—no question. I mean, I wouldn't *at all* exchange that for anything else in the world. Rise of the RSS to such secure power made it impossible for me to go on living there, that's all.

VP: Yeah, but that movement still regards you as a part of it.

AA: Of course, yes. Quite rightly. I'm not surprised but it's a fact that gives me great pleasure.

VP: You're saying, as a *fact*.

AA: I meant that I know that to be true and I greatly value this fact. But what I was also saying was that, you know, all human situations involve vulnerabilities. These were among my vulnerabilities, that's all; you live in the conditions that are given to you in the world. You don't create the conditions of your own existence.

VP: But those vulnerabilities must have had an impact on your capacities and work as an intellectual, and for somebody observing your work, the vulnerabilities are not apparent at all. I mean, that's extraordinary, you know; the writing is of great sharpness, clarity. We don't get the sense of what was there in your own life. And maybe that's all very well.

AA: That's how it should be.

Selected Writings of Aijaz Ahmad

BOOKS

2004. *Iraq, Afghanistan and The Imperialism of Our Time.* New Delhi: LeftWord Books.

2004. *Reflections on Our Time: Seven Essays on the 20th Century.* Hyderabad: Prajasakthi Book House.

2002. *On Communalism and Globalization: Offensives of the Far Right.* New Delhi: Three Essays Press; 2nd ed. 2004.

2001. *Marx and Engels on the National and Colonial Questions. Selected Writings,* edited, with an introduction. New Delhi: LeftWord Books.

1996. *Lineages of the Present: Political Essays.* New Delhi: Tulika; *Lineages of the Present: Ideology and Politics in South Asia,* rev. ed. London: Verso, 2000.

1992. *In Theory: Classes, Nations, Literatures.* London: Verso.

1971. *Ghazals of Ghalib,* editor and co-translator. New York: Columbia University Press; repr., New Delhi: Oxford University Press, 1994.

ESSAYS

2017. 'The Fallouts of 1989'. In *Interpreting the World to Change It: Essays for Prabhat Patnaik,* edited by C.P. Chandrasekhar and Jayati Ghosh. New Delhi: Tulika Books.

2015. 'Thinking the Liberal in Liberal Democracy'. In *Democratic Governance and Politics of the Left in South Asia*, edited by Subhoranjan Dasgupta. New Delhi: Aakar Books.

2015. 'Karl Marx, "Global Theorist": Reflections on Kevin Anderson's Marx at the Margins'. *Dialectical Anthropology*, vol. 39, June.

2015. 'India: Liberal Democracy and the Extreme Right'. *Socialist Register 2016*, vol. 52.

2014. 'Alienation and Freedom: Marx's Ontology of Social Being'. In *Marxism: With and Beyond Marx*, edited by A. Bagchi and A. Chatterjee. New York: Routledge.

2014. 'Twelve Jottings on Liberalization of Democracy'. In *Marx, Gandhi and Modernity*, edited by Akeel Bilgrami. New Delhi: Tulika Books.

2012. 'Three "Returns" to Marx: Derrida, Zizek, Badiou'. *Social Scientist*, vol. 40, nos. 7–8 (July–August), pp. 43–59.

2012. 'Nation, Culture, Language'. *Beyond Borders*, vol. 7, no. 2.

2011. 'The Progressive Movement in Its International Setting'. *Social Scientist*, vol. 39, nos. 11–12 (November–December), pp. 26–32.

2010. 'Globalization and Agriculture: Some Propositions'. In *Punjab Peasantry in Turmoil*, edited by Birinder Pal Singh. New Delhi: Manohar.

2010. '"Show Me the Zulu Proust": Thoughts on World Literature'. *Revista Brasileira de Literatura Comparada*, no. 17, pp. 11–45.

2008. 'The Making of India'. In *India and Indology: Past, Present and Future*, edited by Sukumari Bhattacharji. Calcutta: National Book Agency.

2006. 'Debating the Current Conjuncture'. In *Contested Transformations: Changing Economies and Identities in Contemporary India*, edited by Mary E. John, Praveen Kumar Jha and Surinder S. Jodhka. New Delhi: Tulika.

2005. 'Terror, War, Culture'. *Bol*, no. 1 (Winter).

2005. 'The Making of India'. *Social Scientist*, vol. 33, nos. 11–12 (November–December), pp. 3–13.

2005. 'Frontier Gandhi: Reflections on Muslim Nationalism in India'. *Social Scientist*, vol. 33, nos. 1–2 (January–February), pp. 22–39.

2004. 'Indian Politics at the Crossroads: Towards Elections 2004'. In *Will Secular India Survive?*, edited by Mushirul Hasan. New Delhi: Imprint One.

2000. 'Postmodernism & History'. In *The Making of History: Essays Presented to Irfan Habib*, edited by K.N. Pannikar, Terence Byers and Utsa Patnaik. New Delhi: Tulika.

2000. 'The Communist Manifesto and "World Literature"'. *Social Scientist*, vol. 28, nos. 7–8 (July–August), pp. 3–30.

1999. 'Class and Colony in Mindanao'. In *Rebels, Warlords and Ulama: A Reader on Muslim Separatism and the War in Southern Philippines*, edited by Kristina Gaerlan and Mara Stankovitch. Manila: Institute of Popular Democracy/European Solidarity Centre.

1999. 'The War Against the Muslims'. In *Rebels, Warlords and Ulama: A Reader on Muslim Separatism and the War in Southern Philippines*.

1999. 'The Communist Manifesto: In Its Own Time, and in Ours'. In *A World to Win: Essays on* The Communist Manifesto, edited by Prakash Karat. New Delhi: LeftWord Books.

1999. 'The Politics of Culture'. *Social Scientist*, vol. 27, nos. 9–10 (September–October), pp. 65–69.

1999. 'Out of the Dust of Idols'. In 'A World to Win: Essays in Honour of A. Sivanandan', edited by Colin Prescod and Hazel Waters. Special issue, *Race and Class*, vol. 41, nos. 1–2.

1998. 'Right-Wing Politics, and the Culture of Cruelty'. *Social Scientist*, vol. 26, nos. 9–10 (September–October), pp. 3–25.

1998. 'Religio-Cultural Identities and the Nation-State'. *International Dialogue: A Philosophical Journal*, nos. 9–10, pp. 209–28.

1998. 'The Communist Manifesto and the Problem of Universality'.

Monthly Review, vol. 50, no. 2 (June).

1997. 'Postcolonial Theory and the "Post-" Condition'. *Socialist Register 1997*, vol. 33, pp. 353–81.

1996. 'Issues of Class and Culture: An interview with Aijaz Ahmad'. *Monthly Review*, vol. 48, no. 5 (October).

1996. 'In the Eye of the Storm: The Left Chooses'. *Economic & Political Weekly*, vol. 31, no. 22 (1 June).

1996. 'Globalization and the Nation-State'. *Seminar*, no. 437.

1995. 'Postcolonialism: What's In a Name?'. In *Late Imperial Culture*, edited by Michael Sprinker, Román de la Campa and E. Ann Kaplan. London: Verso.

1995. 'The Politics of Literary Postcoloniality'. *Race and Class*, vol. 36, no. 3, pp. 1–20.

1995. 'Culture, Nationalism, and the Role of Intellectuals: An interview with Aijaz Ahmad'. *Monthly Review*, vol. 47, no. 3 (July–August).

1994. 'Reconciling Derrida: "Spectres of Marx" and Deconstructive Politics'. *New Left Review*, no. 208, pp. 88–106. Reprinted in *Ghostly Demarcations: A Symposium on Jacques Derrida's Specters of Marx*, edited by Michael Sprinker. London: Verso, 1999.

1994. 'Nation, Community, Violence'. *South Asia Bulletin: Comparative Studies of South Asia, Africa, and the Middle East*, vol. 14, no. 1, pp. 24–32.

1993. 'Culture, Community, Nation: On the Ruins of Ayodhya'. *Social Scientist*, vol. 21, nos. 7–8 (July–August), pp. 17–48.

1993. 'Fascism and National Culture: Reading Gramsci in the Days of Hindutva'. *Social Scientist*, vol. 21, nos. 3–4 (March–April), pp. 32–68.

1992. 'Azad's Careers: Roads Taken and Not Taken'. In *Islam and Indian Nationalism: Reflections on Abul Kalam Azad*, edited by Mushirul Hasan. New Delhi: Manohar.

1991. 'Disciplinary English: Third-Worldism and Literary Theory'. In

Rethinking English: Essays in Literature, Language, History, edited by Svati Joshi. New Delhi: Trianka Publishers.

1991. 'Between Orientalism and Historicism: Anthropological Knowledge of India'. *Studies in History*, vol. 7, no. 1, pp. 135–63.

1989. 'The Counterpoint of Pakistan'. In *India: The Formative Years*, edited by Seema Sharma. Delhi: Vikas Publishing House.

1989. 'Some Reflections on Urdu'. *Seminar*, no. 359.

1989. '"Third World Literature" and the Nationalist Ideology'. *Journal of Arts and Ideas*, nos. 17–18, pp. 117–36.

1987. 'Jameson's Rhetoric of Otherness and the "National Allegory"'. *Social Text*, no. 17 (Autumn), pp. 3–25.

1986. 'After the Return of Benazir'. *Pakistan Progressive*, vol. 8, no. 1, pp. 1–25.

1985. 'Class, Nation, and State: Intermediate Classes in Peripheral Societies'. In *Middle Classes in Dependent Countries*, edited by Dale Johnson. Beverly Hills: Sage Publishers.

1985. 'Political Islam: A Critique (Part III)'. *Pakistan Progressive*, vol. 7, no. 2 (Fall), pp. 19–49.

1985. 'Zia's Second Coup'. *Pakistan Progressive*, vol. 7, no. 1, pp. 1–13.

1984. 'The Rebellion of 1983: A Balance Sheet'. *Pakistan Progressive*, vol. 6, no. 1, pp. 1–30.

1983. 'Imperialism and Progress'. In *Theories of Development: Mode of Production or Dependency?*, edited by Ronald H. Chilcote and Dale L. Johnson. Beverly Hills: Sage Publishers.

1983. 'Democracy and Dictatorship'. In *Pakistan: The Roots of Dictatorship: The Political Economy of a Praetorian State*, edited by Hassan Gardezi and Jamil Rashid. London: Zed Press.

1983. 'Political Islam: A Critique (Part II)'. *Pakistan Progressive*, vol. 5, no. 2 (Summer), pp. 3–33.

1982–83. 'Political Islam: A Critique (Part I)'. *Pakistan Progressive*, vol. 4, no. 4 (Winter), pp. 14–42.

1978. 'Democracy and Dictatorship in Pakistan'. *Journal of Contemporary Asia*, vol. 8, no. 4, pp. 477–512.

1975. 'The National Question in Baluchistan'. In *Focus on Baluchistan and the Pashtun Question*, edited by Feroz Ahmed. Lahore, Pakistan: People's Publishing House.

1975. 'Baluchistan's Agrarian Question'. In *Focus on Baluchistan and the Pashtun Question*.

1975. 'The Arab Stasis'. *Monthly Review*, vol. 27, no. 1 (May).

1975. 'Bangladesh: The Internationalization of Counter-Revolution; Supplemental Remarks'. *Monthly Review*, vol. 26, no. 8 (January).

1970. 'Erikson's Untruth'. *Human Inquiries: Review of Existential Psychology and Psychiatry*, vol. 10, nos. 1–3, pp. 1–21.

1969. 'Ghazal'. *Quarterly Review of Literature*, vol. 16, no. 1–2.

TRANSLATIONS

1979. Six poems translated with W.S. Merwin, in *Selected Translations: 1968–1978*, W.S. Merwin. New York: Athenaeum.

1972. Eight translations with Adrienne Rich, in *Asia: A Journal Published by the Asia Society*, no. 2, pp. 9–13.

1970. Four translations with Mark Strand, David Ray, William Hunt, and William Stafford, in *The Malahat Review*, no. 14.

1970. Eight translations, in *Poetry*, August–September.

1970. Six translations with Adrienne Rich, W.S. Merwin, William Stafford, and Thomas Fitzsimmons, in *Delos*, no. 5.

1969–70. Translations of twenty Urdu poems, with an Introduction, in *The Hudson Review*, vol. 23, no. 4.